BROKEN
SUMMER

OTHER TITLES BY J. M. LEE
(LEE JUNG-MYUNG)

The Boy Who Escaped Paradise

The Investigation

PRAISE FOR J. M. LEE

"Channeling timeless quests from *The Odyssey* on while highly reminiscent of Vikas Swarup's contemporary cult classic *Q & A* (the literary inspiration for celluloid sensation *Slumdog Millionaire*), Lee's latest should guarantee exponential growth among savvy Western audiences searching for a universal story with global connections. In a phrase, read this."

—*Library Journal* (starred review) on *The Boy Who Escaped Paradise*

"Another outstanding thriller from Lee (after *The Investigation*, 2015), whose novels have garnered massive acclaim in Korea."

—*Booklist* on *The Boy Who Escaped Paradise*

"Lee's novel touches on the literary need for character-driven stories that move beyond the strangeness and horror of life under the North Korean state. This, along with its thriller-like pace, make *The Boy Who Escaped Paradise* worth a read."

—*Paste*

"A smart, riveting read."

—*Publishers Weekly* on *The Boy Who Escaped Paradise*

"The language is mesmerizing. An exciting adventure added to rich characters, all multiplied by stunning language, equals an unforgettable novel."

—*Shelf Awareness* on *The Boy Who Escaped Paradise*

BROKEN SUMMER

A NOVEL

J. M. LEE

Translated by An Seon Jae

Text copyright © 2021 by Jung Myung Lee
Translation copyright © 2022 by An Seon Jae
All rights reserved.

Previously published as *Buseojin yeolum* by EunHaeng NaMu Publishing Co., Ltd in Korea in 2021. Translated from Korean by An Seon Jae. First published in English by Amazon Crossing in 2022.

Published by Amazon Crossing, Seattle

www.apub.com

Amazon, the Amazon logo, and Amazon Crossing are trademarks of Amazon.com, Inc., or its affiliates.

ISBN-13: 9781662505287 (hardcover)
ISBN-13: 9781662505041 (paperback)
ISBN-13: 9781662505058 (digital)

Cover design by Richard Ljoenes Design LLC

Cover photo © Miki Takahashi

Printed in the United States of America

First edition

BROKEN SUMMER

Hanjo

The people of the city knew him well. The old people who recognized him while out walking would acknowledge him with a passing glance. Young parents told their children in a low voice that they should try to become a great person like him. When the children asked who he was, the parents replied that he was a painter named Lee Hanjo, who was famous for his wedge paintings. Three of his works, they would proudly add, were hanging in the city hall lobby.

This was neither an exaggeration nor a falsehood. Hanjo was the pride of Isan City, which had a population of less than three hundred thousand. Hanjo himself ignored the whispering and the affectionate gazes directed toward him. He was content with living in the city. Those who said he was too trusting and those who said he was too demanding all agreed to love, respect, and envy him.

Hanjo's life was simple. Every day, from eight in the morning to three in the afternoon, he would paint in his studio, sometimes pausing to sit on the garden bench just outside to observe the street at the bottom of the hill. At sunset he would take a walk along the riverbank.

On his forty-third birthday, this routine, which was as slow and precise as the second hand of a clock, was disrupted. As with any other day, he woke up just before eight a.m. and ate the sandwich his wife had made for him. He then went to the studio, an annex off the house, and spent the morning observing the light shining through the window.

At two in the afternoon, he and his wife visited the food section in a downtown department store. They soon had a full shopping cart. In the evening, they were going to hold a small party for just the two of them to celebrate his birthday. They also planned to celebrate the high price his work had sold for at last week's Hong Kong auction.

On the way home, they climbed the hill, their faces flushed with moderate fatigue. At the top of the hillside road that stretched upward like a white belt, Howard House came into view. The mixed-style house, with its Korean tiled roof on Western-style redbrick walls, was harmonious, magnificent in its scale and simple formal beauty. Surrounding the house, which had a basement and two floors aboveground, stood three cedar trees, creating an idyllic atmosphere.

When they opened the forged-iron gate, the sunlight was silently sinking into the carefully manicured garden. A red rambler rose climbed the porch pillars, and the warmth of the heated stone steps formed a kind of haze. The sound of a sprinkler gushing and the scent of cut grass surged toward them. The solidity of the house, the bountifulness of the garden, and the comfortable space embraced them.

For the rest of the afternoon, Hanjo watched the subtly changing angles of light and shadow in the garden. The smell of food came drifting out through the French windows onto the terrace. As the sun went down, his wife laid a white tablecloth on the table beneath a leafy magnolia tree and brought out an oven-baked chicken. Dressed in a white sleeveless dress, she looked rather like a mannequin in a luxury store's display window, one that was deliberately designed with long, slender arms and legs to show off her dress.

They bumped glasses and ate the food. The sun sank lower, and the sound of insects' wings rubbing together filled the air. Little flying bugs and butterflies with unknown names went drifting up. In the cooling sunlight, Hanjo looked back at all the things that belonged to him, the position he had acquired, the achievements he had attained, the influence he had secured.

"What are you thinking about?" his wife asked.

"Now, I think this is the perfect moment and place. This moment belongs to us and we belong to this space. It's a perfect day."

Even before he finished speaking, he realized the error hidden in his words: the fact that a perfect moment is never perceptible and disappears as soon as it is noticed. Even so, the happiness that was right in front of him was his, and no one could take that away. As if confirming the obvious, he filled the glasses again.

Click. His wife turned around in her chair and took a selfie with the table and him in the background.

"It came out well. The sky looks lovely," she said.

His wife held out the iPhone to show him the picture she had just taken. He was sitting at the cluttered table, holding a half-filled glass and smiling. His wife in the picture looked more innocent than usual, maybe because of the wine she had drunk. The evening sky behind him shone like glistening dark-blue satin. When the gloomy winter came, he would gaze out of the window at the snow and remember this graceful evening.

"You look even lovelier," he told her.

It wasn't mere flattery. If it had not been for his wife's dedication to him, he would not have gotten where he was now. She was his mother, lover, manager, teacher, and watcher. She was neither lacking nor excessive; she neither changed nor disappeared. She was as quiet and steady as a turtle heading for shore with a shipwrecked sailor on its back.

The porch light came on. The air cooled quickly, heralding the night. His wife wrapped her arms around her bare shoulders. He hurriedly drank the remaining wine and stood up. His wife pulled the edge of the tablecloth up to cover the mess of empty bowls and leftovers, the half-eaten custard tarts from the department store, the wineglass marks on the cloth. Their gazes were directed toward each other with a warmth lit by lingering echoes of their own voices speaking softly to each other . . .

They walked hand in hand to the studio annex, which was warm and smelled of paint and turpentine. His wife sat on the sofa with slightly sleepy eyes. He went behind the sofa, to the cabinet, took out a bottle of whiskey, and filled a glass. She shook her head with an embarrassed expression, but she did not hold him back. Today was his birthday, and he deserved it.

He swallowed the cold liquid and his throat burned, as if on fire. His wife was studying him as if she were looking at an old painting. They were speaking about their love story, as they often did: when they met, how. His lips had hardened imperceptibly, he stuttered slightly, and red spots began spreading at the drooping corners of his eyes.

He drank from his glass repeatedly. The story of their love was like a gushing spring that never ran dry, no matter how much they drew from it. He was always interested in the memories, which changed little by little with each repetition. For example, they could not agree whether they had first met on July 8 or 13. Even after he agreed that her memory was correct, he remained doubtful.

"I must have drunk a lot. I suddenly feel tired."

He liked the idea of falling asleep in front of his wife at that very moment so that he could feel her gaze upon him while he slept. He imagined what she would see: a forty-three-year-old man who had suffered, hit rock bottom in life, and then risen back into the light. A pleasant sense of pride lingered around his mouth with its moderate wrinkles, the intelligence and confidence of a life-loving artist. He stretched out his legs on the sofa, and his wife got up and covered his knees with a rug. It felt cozy and warm. She put her hand on his forehead. It was like ice on flames. He closed his eyes with a sense of relief.

Now his wife would read his sleeping face as if reading a book, his sensitivity and talent, his intelligence and dignity, wit and desire, even his anxieties and fears. Then she would climb in next to him and fall asleep. This narrow sofa of theirs would be warm and safe. They would become watchmen guarding each other's dreams.

On the first morning of his forty-fourth year, light fell silently on Hanjo's eyelids. He raised himself, rolling a body that felt heavy and stiff. The blanket his wife had covered him with the previous evening lay rumpled on the floor. The chair she enjoyed sitting on was empty. It seemed that last night she had left him sleeping here and gone to their bedroom.

He walked slowly across the garden. The sunlight was sharp here, striking his pupils like the point of a needle. He entered the hall and found the house eerily silent. There was none of the usual noise from the television, no music, no wife's footsteps going in and out of the kitchen, no clatter of teacups. He had only crossed the garden, yet it seemed that he had entered a parallel world. Had his wife overslept? Or had she gone out in a hurry to buy eggs or milk?

"Honey! Honey, where are you?"

The house was neat and clean like a hotel room. He couldn't see the pair of socks he had taken off and dropped carelessly, nor the jumper he had thrown aside roughly. There was no spot on the bathroom mirror; a pile of light-blue towels lay folded neatly on the shelf. The kitchen sink was clean, without a trace of moisture. The dishes and oven trays used yesterday lay shiny in the dish rack. It seemed like a house someone had meticulously tidied before leaving on a long trip.

He opened the front door and ran into the garden. The dew on the lawn soaked his ankles above his slippers. The outdoor table was completely clean. There was no leftover food, no empty wine bottle, no dirty tablecloth.

"Honey! Where on earth have you gone? Damn it . . ."

On the landing, their three-year-old Labrador retriever, Rothko, looked at him with curious eyes. It was already 10:20 a.m., well past his breakfast time. Hanjo quickly prepared the bowl of dog food, which Rothko gobbled down.

"Rothko! Where's your mom? Huh? Where's your mom?"

Rothko emptied his bowl in a flash, then lolled out his tongue, gazing at Hanjo with languid eyes. Hanjo went into the living room and parlor on the first floor, the guest room, and the bathroom and the bedroom on the second floor, then knocked on the door of his wife's study and opened it slightly, in vain. There were no traces of his wife in the boiler room on the first floor, in the pantry next to the kitchen, or in the outdoor shed where garden tools were stored. In the garage there was no sign of her small car. There weren't even any wheel marks.

His wife had disappeared without a trace. She hadn't just popped out for a moment; she wouldn't be back soon. There was no knowing whether she had left him, abandoned him, or run away. Should he report it? Should he go to the places she frequented? But where did she often go?

He picked up the phone in the living room, but he couldn't remember his wife's cell phone number. She was always there for him when he needed her, when he wanted her. It was only now his wife had disappeared that he realized he knew nothing about her.

Hanjo finally remembered the speed-dial button for her number. A distant ring came, as if from underwater. After a while, a high-pitched mechanical voice rang out. "The person you are calling cannot take your call just now." He threw the handset onto the carpet. Fear of what might have happened to his wife and resentment at her leaving him unattended surged together. He thought what his wife would have done at times like this. She would have calmed him down and acted as if nothing had happened. She would have first looked around the house, then called people nearby. But he didn't know whom to call, let alone the phone numbers of his wife's close friends. There was no place left for him to look, nor did he have the energy to search.

His hangover made his head throb, and his throat was dry. His wife's absence was as painful as a stomachache. He had no idea why or to where she had disappeared, or why on the day after his birthday and the day he had made the highest auction price. Who knew where she was, if or when she would come back, or whether he should be furious or grateful if she did return?

In the afternoon, he attached Rothko's leash to his bicycle and pedaled along the path he always took when strolling with his wife. At least he was doing something familiar, he thought. On the way back, he passed by his wife's regular stores, one after another, starting with the bookstore and music store, then the bakery, the grocery store, the hardware store selling paint and tools . . .

The store owners all asked, "How come you're alone today?" and he realized he must look strange to them.

"We're not bad people, are we, Rothko?" he mumbled. "So nothing bad will ever happen to us. Right?"

When he reached home, he felt certain his wife would come out to greet him as if nothing had happened. Rothko lolled his tongue as he followed Hanjo, worn out. Contrary to his expectations, only silence and darkness greeted them. His shirt stuck to his sweaty back and he felt exhausted.

He went to his studio and fed Rothko. He himself had eaten nothing all day, but he didn't feel hungry. Instead, he felt intolerably thirsty. He opened the drawer of his workbench and found a whiskey bottle about one-third full. He filled a glass with whiskey and gulped it down. His throat burned, and a tingling energy spread through his body. Perhaps because of the alcohol, he suddenly remembered one last thing.

His wife always carried two phones: her own and his. She responded on his behalf while he was at work. Curators, critics, journalists, and producers, people saying that they enjoyed his work, others protesting and asking what on earth he thought that painting was about, spam calls offering loans, real estate agents offering a good investment, insurance salespeople, voice phishing . . . While he was confined to his studio, she took charge of all sorts of miscellaneous tasks, such as household chores, having the lawns mowed and trees pruned, moving furniture, coordinating meetings with galleries, responding to requests for interviews, planning exhibitions, checking sales and settling profits, making flight and restaurant reservations for overseas events. They were things he never did. He felt sure that nobody could act as a gardener, a housekeeper, a repairman, a secretary, a tax accountant, a spokesperson, and a fixer all at the same time. He was suddenly surprised at how many things his wife had done for him. Had her own life faded away because she was bearing his life on her back like a scraggy mule?

While the phone was ringing, he tickled Rothko's neck. At the second ring, Rothko raised his head and pricked up his ears. His dark eyes fixed on the stairs. Somewhere, Hanjo heard the faint sound of "Let It Be." It was the ringtone his wife had downloaded for his cell phone.

Rothko took the lead, his rear end swaying to and fro as if he had discovered something. Hanjo blankly pursued Rothko up the stairs. As soon as Rothko reached the landing, he ran to the door at the far right side of the hallway, panting. It was the room his wife had been using as a study for the past six months. Paul McCartney's voice was coming from inside.

Hanjo grabbed the doorknob, hesitated for a moment, then went in. The room was as usual. Books were neatly arranged on the bookshelf, and four of his paintings hung in a row on the wall. His phone was lying on top of a thick envelope on one corner of the large wooden desk. The music stopped when he answered the phone. No sound emerged from it.

He switched on the desk lamp, the light illuminating the package. Nothing was written on the envelope, and it was unsealed. He was about to open it, but paused. He had the impression that his wife was going to throw open the door and ask what he was doing there.

He opened it anyway. Blue letters were written on thick A4 paper: *Your Lies About Me*. It was her familiar handwriting. He remembered his wife once saying she was writing about him. At the time, it had sounded so natural. If someone was going to write a book about him, that person had to be his wife. No one else knew him as well as she did.

Suddenly, he wondered if this was all according to his wife's detailed plans. Before her departure, hadn't she cleaned every corner of the house, then lured him into the room where she had left the manuscript? The fact that she had left his cell phone behind suggested a wish to reject her subordinate role, a declaration of her intention to regain her own life for herself: *Now do things for yourself!*

He was frustrated by his inability to guess his wife's intentions. What was she planning? Why had she left the house without a word? What complaints did she have? And if she had any complaints, why hadn't she told him earlier?

A faint smell of his wife's perfume rose from the stacked manuscript. It was a bitter smell of hay and a sweet smell of flowers. She must have sprayed it on deliberately. Maybe his wife had left home for a while to give him time to read what she had written. If so, was this a gift from her?

The forty A4 sheets seemed to be an excerpt from a novel. It depicted a personal relationship between a nineteen-year-old high school girl and a famous painter who was nearly forty. It described the love of the precocious girl and her betrayal by the self-centered artist, told from the painter's wife's point of view.

The portrayal of the artist was nuanced. Although his behavior toward the young woman was clearly inappropriate, there was a side to him that made the reader want to understand him, maybe even excuse him.

However, no matter how much he was portrayed as a naive artist, that did not change the fact that a man close to forty was using a young woman. His seemingly plausible artistic sensibilities and uncontrollable emotions were nothing more than selfish acts that eventually ruined the lives of the women who loved him. In the end, he was a single-minded man who thought only about painting, a shameless man who habitually used women for artistic inspiration. The narrator was embarrassed by her husband's betrayal and felt a deep bond with the girl who had been abandoned by him. Both the wife and the girl shared a feeling of hostility toward him.

Of course, there was no resemblance between him and the novel's protagonist. Although someone might criticize him for his relentless desire for artistic recognition, something that he couldn't deny completely, he wasn't shameless enough to take a high school girl to bed like the character in the novel.

It didn't matter that in his view he and the protagonist were nothing alike. The outward similarities between him and his fictional counterpart were such that if this novel were published, everyone would believe it was really about him. But it was an absurd distortion and a lie.

Maybe he was being overly sensitive? His wife would be an unknown author who had never published a book under her own name. How many readers would be reminded of Lee Hanjo, who was a famous artist, by a character in a novel written by an author with an unfamiliar name?

Yet when it became known that this unknown author was *his* wife, the situation might change. Close art circles and bright readers would not miss the correlation between fiction and reality. Even if a work claims to be fiction, facts that correspond to reality will provoke vivid imaginations and make headlines.

No matter how much he thought about it, it was unfair. When the book was published, his life, which had been achieved at great cost, would inevitably be ruined. Curiosity would grow around him like poisonous fungus. Journalists would be bound to ask if it was based on a true story. He would answer that it was absurd, but rumors and speculation would not stop. His name, presumed to be shameful on the basis of the novel, would spread on the internet, and scammers claiming to be his victims might appear. People would gossip behind his back, and he would be stigmatized as an immoral human being, whether it was true or not. The price of his paintings would not stay the same, and the number of people who wanted to buy them would shrink and finally disappear.

He knew better than anyone the correlation between a painter's reputation and the value of his work. It was true that Picasso's passionate affairs and Modigliani's sorrowful love had made their myths more vivid, but he was neither Picasso nor Modigliani. Moreover, this was the twenty-first century. He stopped thinking about whether it would be more distressing to lose his reputation, to be financially ruined, or to have his marriage break up. In the end, he would lose everything.

If their marriage had been shaky, he could have understood the situation more easily. However, the two of them hardly ever raised their voices at each other, let alone argued. They went everywhere together, and there was always a sense of trust between them. Although there might have been slight misunderstandings, they were not serious enough to warrant portraying her husband as such a shameful villain.

But why had his wife written such nonsense? Did she really intend to publish this book? Did she not realize what would happen after? Or did she know how reckless she was being and still intend to do it?

The wife in the picture on the wall looked like a mass of light and joy. He stared into her eyes, which he had painted long ago, and asked, "What is the reason for this?" His wife didn't answer. He asked again. "What the hell do you want me to do?" Again, she did not answer. Fear struck him. It wasn't that he was afraid he would be disgraced over this false portrayal. It was that his wife knew the whole of his life, which had been hidden from others for so long. Not only his present, but his hidden past, his greatest glory as well as his worst moments, his respectable appearance as well as his disgusting side.

He thought back to the long-forgotten summer he'd turned eighteen. A dead body lying in the river that flowed through the city. The loud sound of gravel at the bottom of the river stirred by shallow dry-season currents. Water dripping from a wet hem. Plants on the corpse's cheeks, water droplets on its forehead . . . So different from everything that had happened up until that time, and different from everything else combined.

Now he knew. He had lacked the courage to face his shameful and immoral past; he had put it off until now. But he couldn't put it off any longer.

Jisoo

In the afternoon, a white car drove up the hill, swaying gently like a beetle. Two houses of different styles and sizes stood on the soft, grassy slope of the missionary compound. At the top of the hill was the magnificent Howard House, with its single-story annex. Below it was the smaller Malcolm House. The two three-story buildings of Hamil Middle and High Schools were at the foot of the hill. A long, narrow hillside road loosely linked the buildings like a white, unwinding ribbon, before reaching the summit and disappearing down the far slope.

The car stopped in front of Howard House. From the driver's seat, a tall man wearing a white suit and a white peaked cap jumped down and went round to open the other car door. A middle-aged woman in a white jacket and wide pants emerged from the front seat; then a high school girl in a white school uniform and another girl who looked to be six or seven years old got out from the back. The little girl was wearing a white dress decked with lace. Perhaps because of the clothes, which contrasted sharply with the grass, they looked like a flock of white birds that had flown across the sky to land, lightly, at the top of this hill.

The group looked at Howard House with awed expressions, like sailors arriving in the New World. This historic monument, which had guarded the hill for nearly a century, had been built by Stone Howard, a medical missionary sent to Korea from America by the Northern Presbyterians in the early 1900s. The Howards had lived in Howard House with their children, four sons and two daughters, and devoted themselves to medical missionary work. After the Korean War, they had continued educational projects and free medical treatment for war orphans and poor people.

The red tiles decorating the front of the house shone clearly in the afternoon light. From the house's antique windows and magnificent porch, you could see a sprawling garden. If you looked over the knee-high stone wall along the garden's edge, you could glimpse the red tiles of the shabby single-story annex. It was a medical office building, built by Dr. Howard early in his life. Once the Hamil Hospital had been built at the bottom of the hill about twenty years later, the annex had been converted into visitors' accommodations, before being used as a warehouse to store things.

About thirty yards lower down lay Malcolm House, named after a missionary who had come along twelve years after the Howards. This missionary arrived in Korea at the age of twenty-nine, stayed single, and lived in the simple house, which was a third of the size of the Howards' residence. After he returned to the United States, Malcolm House was used as lodgings for the teachers and administrators of Hamil Middle and High Schools who had been brought in from elsewhere. Later, it lodged the janitor and his family.

When Dr. Howard died in 1968, his second son, Dr. George Howard, took over from him. He doted on Hanjo, the son of the janitor, as if he were his own grandson. It was he who recognized the child's talent for painting early on and indulged it, pretending not to notice the eight-year-old's scribbles all across the terrace of Howard House.

After working at Hamil Hospital for forty-three years, the doctor returned to the United States at the age of eighty-two, his health having deteriorated and his chronic asthma worsened. Before leaving Howard House, the doctor gave Hanjo an armful of sketchbooks and drawing materials and allowed him to use the empty basement of the annex as a studio. For years, Hanjo waited for him to return, drawing Howard House again and again with the crayons, pencils, and watercolors the doctor had gifted him.

After the doctor died of pneumonia in Atlanta, Howard House was unable to find a new owner for four years. The house lay empty, mold growing on the wallpaper and lint forming on the old rugs. The floor, which used to make a pleasant sound every time you walked over it, began to creak and rot. Rust on the handles of window frames left a stain on your hands, and, on rainy days, the sound of rainwater was loud in the drainpipes.

One month before the new owner arrived, major repairs began. The exterior walls were cleaned, the roof repaired, the rotten floors and window frames replaced, and the bathroom replastered. The annex was left untouched, since the structure was sound and in good condition. But this space could no longer be Hanjo's studio. Easels and canvases had to be cleared out and the place returned to the new owners. As he gazed through the window at the two removal vans driving away, he felt regret at the loss of his studio and anticipation at having new neighbors.

The family dressed in white disappeared into Howard House. After a while, the window on the second floor opened, and the high school girl appeared. As she looked down the hill, her eyes met those of Hanjo, and she gave him a smile like a dagger. Panicked, he pulled back from the window and hid in a dark corner of the room. From downstairs, he heard his father's voice.

"Hey, you guys! The Howard House family has arrived. Why don't we go say hello and see if there's anything we can do to help?"

Hanjo followed his older brother, Suin, who took the lead up the hill, running about four or five yards ahead. The white car stood in the shade of an elm tree in the garden of Howard House. The shadow of the elm tree fluttered over the hood. A sweet fragrance wafted through the half-opened windows. It smelled like wealth and elegance.

A man in a silver-gray jacket opened the glass door leading to the terrace to welcome them. His greased black hair was neatly combed, and he smiled openly, like a boy. He introduced himself as Jang Heejae, the new owner of Howard House. The boys had heard from their father that he was a businessman who ran a car-rental company, with branches in major cities across the country and a headquarters in downtown Isan. He also owned a large maintenance plant in the western factory area.

"Hello," Suin said. "We're from Malcolm House. We were wondering if there was anything we could do to help."

The man held out his hand boldly. There was a sense of dependable power in his sturdy grasp, and a pleasant smell of lotion drifted from his shirt. Beneath his rolled-up sleeves, you could see the delicate muscles of his tanned forearms flexing.

At that moment, a woman came gliding from the dark living room onto the terrace. She was Kim Seonwoo, the new mistress of Howard House and Jang Heejae's wife. Although she was tall and slender, she did not look fragile. Her thick curly hair made her small face look more distinguished. She laughed without making a sound, her even teeth sparkling. When she smiled, it was warm and friendly.

Suin was transfixed. His mother couldn't smile like that. She rarely smiled, and even when she did, it was never bursting with joy and happiness, but always sad and weary.

"You must be the sons of the caretaker. You'll be Suin, and you must be Suin's younger brother?"

She pointed at Hanjo as she spoke Suin's name, and when she said "Suin's younger brother," she turned to Suin. The brothers were about the same height, but strangers often mistook Hanjo for his older brother, thanks to his wide chest and shoulders and Suin's slender build.

"No. I'm the younger brother, and that's Suin. My name is Hanjo."

Suin was the center of their family. His father was referred to as "Suin's father" instead of his name, and his mother was called "Suin's mother." Hanjo had been known as "Suin's younger brother" rather than by his name from the time he entered elementary school. It was as if without Suin, their family wouldn't exist.

"Right. Suin and Hanjo. We'll be good neighbors."

She swept back her bangs in the breeze using her long fingers as a comb. The high school girl, who had changed into a blue floral dress, appeared through the open terrace door. She had a round forehead and delicate eyes. Clear curves flowed from her neck to her shoulders, as if drawn by light. A faint smile lingered on her lips, and she held a blue-covered book with an invisible title.

"Say hello," Heejae instructed his daughter, and turned to the boys. "This is Jisoo, our eldest daughter. She's a first-year in high school, so she's the same age as Hanjo. We also have a younger daughter, Haeri."

At Heejae's words, Jisoo bobbed her head in greeting. A short silence ensued. Just then, they heard the wooden floor creak inside the house. The little girl came running out into the garden. Her cheeks were red like a peach, and the sunlight shone golden on her skin. She wore pants that reached her calves and a Donald Duck T-shirt already stained with tomato ketchup and some unknown food. The gaiety of this unpredictable child gave her old-fashioned home an intense vitality. It was obvious that she was loved by all her family.

The child tried to descend from the railing onto the lawn and stumbled. Jisoo immediately dropped her book and ran to her sister. Her movements were quick and smooth, as if she'd expected the child to fall.

Her little sister indeed fell, just before Jisoo could reach her, and lay on the lawn whimpering. When she saw her big sister rushing to help, Haeri burst into tears. The sunlight colored the inside of the child's mouth red. A blue vein running from her collarbone split in two as it reached her Adam's apple. The louder she cried, the thicker and clearer the vein swelled. Jisoo picked her up and soothed her with calm, skillful movements. A smile soon appeared on the child's face, even before her tears were dry.

After a while, the sisters held hands and began spinning. The hem of Jisoo's floral dress swelled like a balloon. The grass crushed by her bare feet gave off a deep fragrance. The girls' heels turned green. They looked like the woman and child in Bonnard's painting. Howard House, so familiar to Hanjo, quickly became unfamiliar as it expanded into a different time and space like a warped mirror. It was as if Jisoo could distort time and space at will; she was a black hole, bending light to change time.

Jisoo's foot narrowly avoided a sharp stone. Hanjo was worried her bare white feet might be cut; then he suddenly longed to see red blood on her scratched little toe.

Thanks to his father being head manager of Hamil Middle and High Schools, Hanjo's family lived rent-free in Malcolm House, which belonged to the school foundation. The two-story Malcolm House, with its Korean tiled roof on redbrick walls, had a living room, three bedrooms, a porch, and a terrace. *Head manager* sounded rather grand, almost like an administrative position, but it was just a convenient name for a general facility manager who was responsible for maintaining and repairing all the school's buildings and facilities. He was also responsible for cleaning the plumbing in Howard House, repairing the floors and stairs, fixing leaky roofs, painting rusted porch pillars, and taking care of the garden. Hanjo's mother, Miran, had worked as a housekeeper at Howard House when the doctor lived there, and she returned to this work after Heejae's family moved in.

Hanjo's father, Lee Jinman, was a skilled carpenter. He wore a leather belt with hammers, pliers, cutters, and small handsaws of different shapes, which was reminiscent of a cowboy's gun belt. At the touch of his fingers, collapsed areas were rebuilt, broken items were replaced with new ones, and empty spaces were filled; creaking doors, pillars consumed by termites, collapsed shafts, and clogged pipes were revived.

Once they entered middle school, the two boys naturally began to help their father with his work. Hanjo was captivated by the nobility of Howard House, opening the windows to check if the hinges were loose, sweeping the garden, checking to see if feral cats had been digging in the flower beds. He not only marveled at the house's stunning architecture but also felt secret joy at exploring the traces of time in the sturdy structure rooted in the past. Each time the brothers swept the floors, wiped down dirty counters, replaced old parts, or painted over stains, they felt they were protecting something that might easily disappear. Caring for a house that *needed* their care made them feel like members of a simple religion that believed in indestructible history.

The splendid Howard House and the lowly Malcolm House were peaceful neighbors. Nevertheless, a secret boundary existed between the two families. Once the relationship of close neighbors was taken away, there was the grimmer structure of employers and employees. Their relationship was defined by a heartless class system that reduced humanity to the rich and the poor, the smart and the shabby, those with opportunities and the marginalized, those who serve and those who are served. Even though the inhabitants of both houses spent time together every day like a family, they weren't a family. Howard House was a place that the Malcolm House inhabitants could dream of but not own, an area that they could see but could not reach.

Hidden power structures are more severe and lethal than visible hierarchies. Lee Jinman urged his children not to forget their status as caretakers and not to take for granted the favors of the people of Howard House, irrespective of how kind and friendly they were. As a result, both houses maintained an altruistic relationship based on consideration and favor, while being aware of boundaries. So long as they tried to accept each other, their relationship would not make them uncomfortable.

The composure and generosity of the people of Howard House, their dignified manner, inspired awe. They were like a different race that had retained its graceful qualities and pure virtues long lost to others. Hanjo's family didn't have these traits. They called each other's names loudly from a distance, shouting at each other to get some tool or to dig a pit deeper.

Seonwoo treated Hanjo and Suin with loving care and respect. One day, she waved a long, thin arm at Hanjo as he was passing. He thought that something must be broken, or there was a problem in the house. When he came running up the hill, she made an unexpected suggestion.

"I heard that you're good at drawing. Why don't you continue to use the basement of the annex as a studio? Then I hope I can see your drawings someday."

Hanjo was not sure whether to thank her for her kindness or to feel sad about her condescension, but he was relieved that he had not lost his studio.

Suin stayed away from Howard House, and made excuses to avoid working there. Jobs at Howard House became Hanjo's province. At the dinner table one Saturday evening, Hanjo complained that he had sweated all afternoon mowing the lawn by himself. His father continued chewing his food silently—he seemed to think Suin didn't help out because he was concentrating on his studies. Furious, Hanjo put down his spoon and went out onto the porch. There was a bittersweet scent of mown grass in the darkness.

"I'm sorry I made you work alone . . . ," said Suin, who had followed him out. "I have an assignment I need to do over the weekend. The exams are just round the corner."

Hanjo bit his lip, thinking of some way to contradict him. As far as studying was concerned, Suin was the golden child of the family. Since elementary school, he had never missed honors and had swept up awards and plaques in the various competitions he had participated in as the school's representative. The scholarships he received from different organizations helped finance both brothers' tuition and the living expenses of his family. Now Suin was using his status to hide the truth.

"It's the same for me," Hanjo said, after hesitating awhile. "My exams are also just around the corner. But still I've been mowing the lawn and cleaning the drains all afternoon alone. You're making excuses about studying, but you don't have the courage to go to Howard House, because you're ashamed of being the manager's son!"

Suin could not deny it. At Howard House, there was not a moment when he was not keenly aware of his identity. In school, he was the unchallenged leader. Everyone accepted his status without protest, and their silence enhanced his authority. When it came to solving difficult problems, even his math teacher looked at him nervously.

But things changed once he left the school gate. At Howard House, he was just the manager's son. His status was clearly divided between the time he spent in school and the time he spent at Howard House; he was like Cinderella, forced to return to harsh reality after the delight of the ball. He tried to persuade himself that the label *manager* fell on his father alone, and that he did not *have* to be his son, but his identity was as clear as his name and defined his existence.

The following weekend, the brothers went to Howard House together. They had to clear away the jacaranda stems that scaled the walls to the roof and clean out the leaves clogging the gutters. They skillfully climbed the porch pillars to the roof without a ladder. Thanks to their intense focus, they were able to get the job done before sunset. They loosened their shirts and lay on the roof to catch the evening sun.

From the roof, Malcolm House looked shabbier and smaller than they realized. Suin felt inferior, and recognized that it was a dangerous feeling. Hanjo did not care about Suin's mood and talked about the Howard House family. "I wish I had a cute little sister like Haeri," he said.

Suin ignored him, looking sour. Suin seldom smiled, and even when he did, he gave the impression of being cynical. He didn't care: he was his own man and did not bother about what people thought. He was determined to be unkind and rude to everyone in the world. Despite repeated requests and recommendations from his teachers, he stayed away from the student-council or club activities, and did not take on the role of class leader. He pretended not to notice when his peers were giggling over porn magazines.

It had been a long time since Hanjo was able to understand his brother, but Hanjo didn't care. He kept talking. "Jisoo," he said. "What do you think of her? Isn't she pretty?"

"Then you make out with her."

Suin leaned against the chimney railing and grinned at the setting sun. Hanjo was grateful for that smile, even if it was only a penny's worth of alms and even if his gratefulness wounded his pride.

The old city center was spread beneath the southwest slope of the hill where the missionary compound was situated. Beyond a church and hospital, commercial and residential areas were located in blocks on both sides of Main Street, which stretched straight through the city, from north to south. Less than a mile to the east, Borim Stream flowed through the town. Although it was really too small to be called a river, people referred to the "riverside road" and the "riverbanks." Upstream rose the Borim Dam, and downstream there was wide farmland with plastic-covered greenhouses. The road running across the hill with the missionary compound led directly to the riverside road that followed Borim Stream.

The beauty of Howard House, combined with the gentle hilltop and the well-tended garden, attracted amateur photographers and painters. On snowy mornings, the sound of camera shutters never stopped, and in the spring, when the cherry blossoms were blooming, art-club members settled on the slopes of the hill to paint.

On sunny days, Hanjo would set up his easel and spend the day observing the changing light, the contours and shading of Howard House, its sharp and smooth lines. In the afternoon, the light gave a distinct vitality to the terrace and porch, as well as to the window frames on the first and second floors and the brick patterns. When evening came, the sun would set to the west, scattering golden rays. The sharp light and shade created an intense contrast, bestowing Howard House with the solemnity of a veteran soldier.

Hanjo's skills in observing landscapes and capturing emotion on the faces of individuals were outstanding. He'd been drawing since he was four, sketching pictures of doves, a cat on a wall, and his father fixing a fence. When Hanjo sometimes nodded at an empty space, whether on a wall or on the ground, Jinman would look at his son with anxiety. It was clear to him that his son's easy dexterity, far from being a benefit to his life, would be a burden, but Jinman had no ability to suggest a different career. The fact that his son resembled him in his dexterity felt like a curse rather than a source of pride.

Jisoo would sit on the blue windowsill of her room all afternoon, reading a book. She ignored Hanjo, as if she weren't aware of him. In contrast, Hanjo's eyes seemed nailed to the second-floor window, and he could not tear his gaze away from her face. As he watched, Jisoo's face would transform, like a model's before a camera. No matter how hard he tried to concentrate on his painting, the secret joy of peeking at her wouldn't let him go.

One day in September, the sun's beams were slowly growing shorter, moving imperceptibly like an alley cat. Anxious to finish before sunset, Hanjo drew more swiftly. Suddenly, from somewhere in the garden, the scent of unfamiliar perfume—or was it a flower?—drifted to him on the breeze.

"I'm disappointed. I thought you were drawing me, but you were just drawing Howard House. I didn't realize that and didn't once leave the window . . ."

Jisoo's expression, as she looked at the picture, seemed admiring and patronizing at the same time. Hanjo stuttered slightly as he pointed with the tip of a pencil at the second-floor window. It was drawn larger than it really was.

"This . . . this is just a sketch now. First I'll draw the house; then I'm going to draw a figure in the empty window on the second floor."

Jisoo looked curious. "Who are you going to draw?"

"You . . . I'm going to draw you. If you let me . . ."

She gazed into his eyes for a while, as if deciding whether Hanjo's reply was true, but he'd meant what he said and she knew it. He turned back to the drawing and changed the topic.

"As I draw, the house's expression changes, and the roof sometimes makes a whistling sound. When that happens, I feel as if the house is alive. I'm not wrong. This house has been here since long before we were born."

Hanjo was finishing the delicate curves of the gutters with a newly sharpened pencil. Jisoo was still staring at the second-floor window that was to contain her own image.

"Does your brother love Howard House like you do?" she said, not taking her eyes off the square.

Hanjo frowned. He hated that she was treating him the same way others did—that she saw him the same way. People often thought of Hanjo as his brother's spokesman or messenger. If they met him, they would ask him how his brother was, talk about his brother's thoughts, or ask him to ask his brother to do something for them. He never got used to it, although it kept happening.

"Ask him yourself."

The next day and the day after, Hanjo set up his canvas on the hill. The essence of Howard House came into view only when he looked at it with the eyes of a painter, not the son of a manager, a worker, or a repairman. He painted the broken pillars of the porch, the ivy climbing over the bricks, and the blue of the roof tiles that subtly changed over time.

One day Jisoo came, and one day Haeri. One day the two came together to see the painting. As he peeped at their eyes full of curiosity, he felt like a king.

In autumn, the angle of the sunlight changed and the wind grew cooler. One Sunday morning, Hanjo oiled the chains of three bicycles parked in front of Howard House. The parents of the two families had allowed their children to go on a cycle trip. Their destination was Jisoo's family's villa, not far from the dam.

Hanjo positioned Haeri on his rear saddle and set off first. Jisoo followed, and Suin came last. They rode in a line, like brothers and sisters of a single family. The excited mongrel, November, ran ahead, and when the children lagged behind, he stopped and looked back. November accompanied them down the hill, then went home, having lost interest.

Their six silver wheels cycled past the electricity substation and the old warehouses, refracting rays of light. They entered the riverside road, and pedaled upstream like salmon swimming against the current. Once past the embankment path, they entered a forest road so narrow, two cars could barely pass. They cycled slowly under larch and oak trees.

After about five minutes, the red roof and white walls of Jisoo's family's cottage grew visible among the trees. The owners of Howard House often visited this elegant Mediterranean-style villa. During the vacations, it served as the place where Jisoo could do her homework assignments uninterrupted, and Haeri liked to play in its attic.

When the children arrived at the villa, they left their bicycles in the gravel yard. Haeri ran straight to the swing fixed to a zelkova tree. She stood on the seat, rocked it several times to get it moving, then jumped off as it picked up speed. She seemed to have mastered the law of inertia. Hanjo photographed Haeri showing off an insect she had caught with her bare hands. The silver Leica camera left behind by Dr. Howard was his father's prize possession.

They laid out mats in the garden and ate the sandwiches they'd brought. Then they went down to the lakeside, picked up warm pebbles, and sent them skimming over the water in a game of ducks and drakes. Whenever ripples appeared on the surface of the water, they all burst into laughter, as if they were being tickled.

Haeri led Hanjo into the house, asking him to play with her. On the first floor, there was a living room and two bedrooms; on the second floor, there was an attic and a hallway leading to an outdoor terrace. Haeri went bounding up the stairs to the attic. It had a low ceiling that slanted on one side, like a cabin. Light shone through a round gable window, and you could see water sparkling in the distance. Hanjo chased Haeri, running around the room with his back bent in fear of hitting his head against the low ceiling.

He enjoyed spending time with Haeri. She was very fond of his family, and had even taken to calling his parents "Uncle Malcolm" and "Aunt Malcolm," after their house. Compared to Jisoo, who was as quiet as a still-life painting, Haeri had inexhaustible energy. Her body never stayed still, and her gaze roamed curiously from place to place like a little bird. It seemed to him that the child was made up of movements, not skin and muscles. Then Haeri suddenly asked, "Hanjo. Do you like my sister?"

It was an unexpected question from the mouth of a seven-year-old child. Hanjo stopped himself from asking, *How did you know?* and instead answered, "Haeri. I like your sister and I like you."

Hanjo pinched Haeri's cheek lightly, so that it wouldn't hurt. In response, she stretched the corners of her mouth with her index fingers, sticking out her tongue. Even though it was a playful gesture, he could sense that the child would always be as self-centered as she was now.

"Then will you draw my face like you do hers?"

"OK. Once you're bigger, I'll make a pretty drawing."

When Hanjo came out carrying Haeri on his shoulders, Jisoo and Suin were sitting side by side, against the wall. Jisoo was squinting up at the birds flying through the canopy. Both were silent. It seemed they had fallen silent after a long conversation, or perhaps they had been silent all the time. Either way, it was not an empty silence, but full of tensions that were about to burst.

The road on the way back to Howard House was bathed in the sunset glow. Hanjo pedaled steadily, like a boatman rowing. Memories of the day and the landscapes glimpsed passed before his eyes. He imagined his own body as a container for memories and scenery. No matter how happy the moment, it always passes, but if you can store it in your memory, it remains yours forever. Hanjo vowed to remember this moment when he faced unbearable times in his life.

When they arrived at Howard House, the smell of food came wafting through the wide-open front door. Haeri dropped from the bike and ran inside, to her mother's arms. Kim Seonwoo looked at the children, and her smile seemed painted with a brush.

Dinner was served on a table on the terrace. Seonwoo offered the children food, and poured juice for them throughout the meal. As she watched the children eating, her eyes were patient and warm. Suin had the illusion that she was looking only at him. His mother never did that. Even when the brothers needed their mother most, she was always tired. When food was ready on the table at Malcolm House, each brother would eat silently on his own.

Darkness fell, and the wind turned cold. Crickets and grasshoppers trilled everywhere. The children laughed and chattered, flirty and tired, and stayed together until late in the October night, like brothers and sisters who had returned home after a long journey.

When Heejae offered the reception room on the first floor of Howard House as a place where Suin, Hanjo, and Jisoo could study together, Jinman accepted it happily. He was concerned about the tiny upstairs rooms where the boys lived, their beds divided only by thin plywood boards. Neither had a proper study room. Suin, who was preparing for the university entrance exam, usually stayed behind at school to study, while Hanjo had simply given up studying altogether. That evening, Jinman carefully mentioned Heejae's proposal at the dinner table.

"I don't need a study room," Suin said coldly. He put down his spoon and went to his room.

Jinman stared at his empty chair for a while, and then stood up. The scraping of his chair over the wooden floor sounded like a moan. He went out onto the terrace with slow steps, like a plant taking root. His wife, Miran, deliberately banged the bowls together as she did the dishes. It was her way of expressing her dissatisfaction with her husband, but it was also resentment at herself for not providing her children with even a small study room. Hanjo got up quietly and went to his brother's room.

"Howard House's drawing room sounds OK . . . It's spacious and quiet, so it's a good place to study, right?"

"Jisoo's father is thinking I should help Jisoo study," Suin replied with annoyance. "Can't you see that?"

"It would be nice if you could help her out."

"You don't know what kind of person Jisoo's father is. What do you think is the reason he and his family moved to Howard House?"

"I don't know. Do you?"

"That man is so ignorant and puffed up, and he's acting like he's someone great. He bought Howard House because he wanted to feel the superiority of an English lord in a magnificent mansion."

"But he's not just a rich man with a lot of money, as you say. He knows a lot and has a lot of culture. Have you seen all those books in the Howard House library?"

Of course. How could Suin forget the serenity and coziness he felt when he first visited the Howard House library? One weekend, he had entered the library—or, more accurately, Mr. Jang's study—carrying a toolbox. It was dim because there was no sunlight there even in the day. The walls were covered with books, and he could smell old paper and dust.

Suin had fallen into the illusion of being another person. The room was full of books he longed to read, books that were not in the school library. As he turned the pages of magazines from several years back, like *Discover* and *Science*, he grew absorbed in fascinating articles such as "The Function and Operation of Machines and Tools," "The Effect of the Steam Engine on the Evolution of Intelligence, Rather Than Aspects of Human Life," and "The Einstein–Niels Bohr Debates."

He had a strong feeling that this was where he should be. He dropped the toolbox and stroked the books one by one. He completely forgot his mother's direction to fix a drawer in the study desk that had warped and was squeaking. He quietly pulled out a copy of *The Sound and the Fury*. Just then, a voice came from behind him.

"I think Steinbeck would be better than Faulkner. You can borrow both books if you like."

Seonwoo was approaching him through the dim light in the library. She took a book from the shelves, glanced at the cover, then handed it to Suin: *East of Eden* by John Steinbeck. The moment her gaze rested on his shoulders, it seemed that Suin had become her long-lost only son.

"Can I?"

"Sure. Books should be read by those who need them, right? If there's a book you want to read, take it, read it, then put it back where it was. Actually, Jisoo's dad has little time to read."

Despite his intense satisfaction, Suin couldn't help but feel loss that this library wasn't simply his. Hostility toward Mr. Jang swept over him. He did not deserve to be the owner of such a room.

Now, in their small bedroom, he told Hanjo, "How many of the thousands of books in his study do you think Mr. Jang has read? All the books in the room are just ornaments to show to other people."

"You seem to see only the bad in Jisoo's father. Yet he donates to people in need and does a lot of good things. Some say he's going to run in the next mayoral election . . ."

Suin envied his younger brother's optimism, and his determination to believe the world was a good place. He didn't see it that way. To him, Heejae's unrelenting kindness made him uncomfortable, and goodwill toward the people of Howard House felt like a denial of his own existence.

Honestly, Hanjo was also reluctant to accept Heejae's proposal. It felt like a criminal act, stealing Suin's only assets, time and talent, so that Jisoo could perform better. However, he could not go against Heejae's will. From the next week onward, the children gathered at a long table meant for eight people and studied every day.

In the spring of the following year, Hanjo completed four paintings depicting the four seasons of Howard House and submitted them for the school's art exhibition. In all of the pictures, Howard House seemed to be struggling to keep from collapsing in a storm, and a girl in a white dress stood at the second-floor window. In *Spring*, she was looking away indifferently. In *Summer*, she had opened the dark shutters on a stormy night and was confronting the wind. In *Autumn*, she was almost invisible in the shade of a large zelkova tree, and in *Winter*, she was depicted as a yellow silhouette in the second-floor window on a snowy night.

In each of the paintings, she seemed a warrior looking out at the future from a high watchtower, not succumbing to time or fate. The award-winning *Summer* was praised for its composition, coloring, and detail, and for showing a different aspect of Howard House than what people were familiar with.

The boys in school whispered about who the mysterious girl in the paintings could be. It would have been an interesting scandal for children that age, but the rumors never had a chance to grow; they lost their power before the sheer impact of the paintings on the viewer. The emotions and gossip created by his paintings gave Hanjo an invisible authority. Whether the origin was Howard House, Jisoo, or the skill of the painter itself, his paintings had irresistible power and beauty.

The evening news had started, but Jisoo was still not home. On the screen, a weather report was followed by news on corporate restructuring and the fates of dismissed workers, as well as calls for measures to support the homeless after the IMF bailout. Heejae glanced at the wall clock. His daughter had never been late before.

As ten o'clock approached, his anxiety increased. He was feeling more upset with his wife, who had not yet returned, than with his daughter. He encouraged his wife to participate in charity events and alumni gatherings only because of the unwritten rule in political circles that "men run politics but women run elections." Even so, it seemed to him there was a problem when a wife and mother neglected the house like this. Was he wrong to believe that even if she participated in other activities, she should keep the household running smoothly?

When Seonwoo returned home, after ten o'clock, she was restless and did not bother to change her clothes. After reading a fairy tale to Haeri, who had not yet gone to sleep, she couldn't stand it any longer and, at eleven o'clock, called Malcolm House. The family from Malcolm House came running. The men mumbled a few words with stiff expressions and then scattered into the dark like dogs hunting pheasants. They came back one by one around dawn, their pants stained green with crushed grass. There was still no news of Jisoo.

Seonwoo clenched her fists until her fingers turned white. It wasn't a simple feeling of helplessness, but despair accompanied by a gut-wrenching pain. She hoped her daughter was spending the night at a friend's house and would come back safely in the morning, but she couldn't decide whether to be furious with her when she did return or to react as if nothing had happened.

When morning came and Jisoo still hadn't returned, Seonwoo dialed all the phone numbers she knew. The academy instructor who answered the phone said that Jisoo had not come to the academy yesterday. The schoolgirl who served as accompanist for the choir said she had last seen her at choir practice the previous Sunday. The phone call to the school was taken by Jisoo's homeroom teacher, who was already preparing for the start of classes.

"I was wondering why I hadn't seen Jisoo this morning," she said. "She started preparing for an English debate last week. Maybe . . . Is there some problem at home?"

The handset felt slippery in Seonwoo's sweaty palm. She was finding it hard to speak; her lips kept sticking together.

"Oh . . . yes . . . ," she said, softly. "It's not serious."

Heejae stared at his wife's lips, at their dry, dead skin cells, and muttered, "Not serious? What's serious if this isn't?"

He thought his wife was to blame for Jisoo's pliable and passive personality. It didn't matter to him whether it was hereditary or because of how she was raised at home. Jisoo's delicate appearance, resembling his wife's, gave the impression of weakness. Even her intellect, like his wife's, was expressed through weakness. He often urged Jisoo, "Don't make concessions; demand your rights." He also added, "You should cut off that long hair—it makes you look weak." But Jisoo, once she had cut her hair, didn't look like Jisoo; she just looked awkward, as if she were trying to be someone else but couldn't.

Haeri was different from Jisoo. She wasn't pretty; she resembled Heejae both in her appearance and in her frank personality and fondness for arguments. She made grown-ups feel tired as soon as she started to talk. She was constantly asking questions, and if they couldn't answer, she looked at them with pity. It was different from simply being smart;

she was like an impassioned adult who clearly knew how to monopolize love for herself.

The sunlight shining through the wide window cast a square block of light on the floor. Heejae silently picked up the phone. He could no longer postpone reporting her disappearance to the police.

At eleven thirty in the morning, gravel crunched in the front yard of Howard House. Two police officers got out of a car. A detective in his early forties introduced himself as Sergeant Yun San, from the investigation department at the Southern Police Station. He wasn't very tall, with short hair and tight skin at the nape of his neck.

Behind him stood a policewoman in full uniform. She was tall, strongly built, with acne scars on her face. She was strong willed and sincere, but seemed to lack flexibility. Yun San introduced her as Nam Bora, newly deployed the previous spring.

"More children than you might think leave home for more reasons than you might think," Yun San said. "Not all are problem kids; model students do it, too. Most of them come back on their own after two or three days, at the latest a week. So far, it hasn't been twenty-four hours, so we'd better wait."

Sergeant Yun San's attitude was relaxed, as if Jisoo's disappearance were nothing. It might have been intended to reassure her family, but Seonwoo felt humiliated rather than comforted. Did telling them to wait and see because it had been less than twenty-four hours mean their daughter would come back after twenty-five hours? Or thirty-six hours? Forty-eight hours? Yun San asked her for a detailed description of Jisoo.

"So . . . in the morning, she went out wearing her school uniform. Her hair is cut short and reaches the middle of her neck. What else? Oh . . . she's wearing white sneakers. You know, the kind that high school girls wear with their school uniforms."

Yun San was disappointed. School uniforms, bobbed hair, white sneakers were common to every high school girl. Nam Bora wrote down Seonwoo's answers in her notebook. Yun San asked again.

"Is that all? For example, any kind of physical characteristic, a striking way of walking . . . ?"

Seonwoo thought about Jisoo's gait, her speech habits, her facial expressions, and her attitude toward people. Nothing came to mind.

"I don't know. Her backpack was dark blue. Or was it dark brown?"

Seonwoo looked at her husband with an expression suggesting she was about to cry. Heejae explained that the backpack had been brown until a year ago, when Jisoo changed it for a dark-blue one. Nam Bora recorded both statements. Seonwoo went on.

"I got a phone call from her around one thirty p.m. She said that she and her friend would be preparing for an English debate that was to be held at school in a month. I didn't think much about it. In the past, Jisoo often went to school during vacations for club activities, such as preparing art exhibitions, or choir practice, or self-study."

"What's that friend's name?"

Seonwoo racked her brain. She felt stupid she couldn't remember the name of the friend from the same debate team as her daughter. For some reason, she thought of Jisoo as a baby, lying in her cradle. She had black eyes, and was immersed in her own world. Her limbs were struggling as if she were trying to grab something in the air.

"Please tell me if you remember it," Nam Bora said. "There are also ways we can find out . . . Could I see a picture of Jisoo? I'll need it to print flyers."

Heejae took out the family photo album from the cabinet drawer. Yun San looked at it and handed it to Nam Bora, who examined the photos. When selecting photographs for missing-person flyers, one always had to choose the most recent ones. This was especially true for teenagers, since their faces changed between morning and evening.

Another rule was to exclude photographs where the person showed too much emotion or was smiling.

In most of Jisoo's photographs, she was staring at the camera. She looked bright and tidy, but rather stiff. She seemed too cold and secretive to be expected to return after a few days, having run away from home for a simple reason. Nam Bora finally pointed at a picture of her.

"How about this one? I think it shows the missing person's personality more clearly than too stiff a picture."

In the photo, Jisoo was looking angry, with her head down and eyes slightly raised, but there was a slight smile around her mouth. Yun San removed the cellophane cover and took out the photo, then asked to see Jisoo's room. Heejae and Seonwoo accompanied them to the second floor.

The room was like a deep, dark well. There were none of the photos of singers, actors, or baseball players usually found in the rooms of children of her age. Instead, the wall was covered with honors and other prizes, and the shelves were filled with plaques. On the opposite wall, there was a poster of a painting by Georgia O'Keeffe, and the bed was neatly made. Nam Bora looked around and wrote down the location and peculiarities of the items in her notebook.

On the bookshelf, there were textbooks and reference books for each subject, the two volumes of *Crime and Punishment*, *A History of Western Art*, a volume of Renaissance paintings, and student magazines arranged by issue number. On the desk, a paperback edition of *Hamlet* lay open facedown; she seemed to have been reading it. It was the scene where Gertrude tells Laertes about Ophelia's death. Nam Bora replaced the book as it had been.

When they went downstairs, a woman in her midforties with a white apron came out of the kitchen; she was carrying a tray with cookies and coffee.

"This is a lady who helps with our housework," Heejae said. "She is the wife of Lee Jinman, the manager of Hamil Middle and High Schools. She lives in Malcolm House, down the hill."

The woman bowed, wiping her hands on her apron. Yun San offered no greeting but asked her about the time she usually went home.

"It's usually around eight thirty," Miran replied calmly, "after dinner here is over. If the boss is late from work or goes out with his wife, it's earlier."

"How about yesterday evening?"

"Since Jisoo and her mother were both late, I waited until almost ten p.m. and then went home. Around eleven o'clock, Madam called, saying that Jisoo had still not returned. I came straight back up to Howard House, and, with her mother, I searched Jisoo's room, the terrace, the basement, and the garden. My husband and two sons went with the boss, and searched from the bus stop at the foot of the hill to the ridge at the back."

Yun San nodded, put Jisoo's picture in his inner pocket, then grabbed a handful of cookies and put them in his jacket pocket.

"I hope that I won't need the picture," he said. "Once Jisoo returns, we'll give it back to you as soon as possible."

In the car on the way back, Nam Bora said to Yun San, "About what you said earlier."

"What do you mean?"

"Do you really think Jisoo ran away?"

"That's the point; I don't know."

"But why offer useless hope to the parents of a missing person? You don't have to say that."

Nam Bora sounded critical. Yun San ran his hand over his crew cut. This newcomer was tactless but practical. She couldn't stand unfair treatment, probably because she didn't know the world of crime yet, an absurd and ridiculous world where nonsensical and unacceptable things happened more often than could be understood with common sense and logic.

"Because I hope so, too," he said. "Like those people, I want the child to come back as if nothing had happened. It's good for everyone to think of it as a simple runaway until the kidnapper calls or the body is found. In any case, having hope is a good attitude."

Yun San took out a cookie from his pocket, crunched it, and then stepped on the accelerator, staring at the asphalt as it scorched in the dazzling sun.

Three days after Jisoo disappeared, the case was reclassified from a simple runaway to a violent crime. The possibility of kidnapping had been quickly ruled out. In kidnappings, an attempt at contact is usually made within forty-eight hours of the crime. The police did not rule out the possibility of murder, and continued to produce flyers for a missing person.

A police squad began a search that covered a triangular area connecting Howard House, the school, and the dam and irrigation pond. After two days of searching, there were no significant results and no obvious suspects. There was no sign at either the train or the bus station that Jisoo had left the city.

Detectives searched the forest villa more than three hundred yards away from the irrigation pond. There was nothing unusual about the living room furniture or the kitchen utensils. There were only instant-food products, canned food, and beverages in the refrigerator. In the yard, which seemed overgrown and neglected, the lawn was untended, and the trash bin had only leftover food and wrapping paper. They did find something, though. It was a bicycle abandoned in the bushes beside the path leading to the villa. It belonged to Jisoo, but it was not clear why it was near the road rather than in the villa's yard. Detectives didn't pursue this intensively, though. The priority was to find Jisoo herself.

Yun San visited the dam's management center. It was a building next to the dam, with four full-time employees, including the director. Yun San requested data on the rainfall, water storage, and floodgate management over the past ten days. The employees, all in navy uniforms, scoured the cabinets and brought out a few files. Since the third week of July, when the rainy season ended, the average precipitation had been only 2.75 inches, and the water was at its lowest level.

"We are following the floodgate-management guidelines," the dam's director said. "On the day of the girl's disappearance, only the minimum flow required to supply water and maintain the oxygen concentration in the river was discharged, as per the dry-season guidelines."

The director was embarrassed. If someone had died in the reservoir or a body had been carried downstream, then that might attract unwanted scrutiny about their dam-management practices. When a serious incident occurs, people always try to find a cause. If they can't find one, they make it up.

"It was just like any other day," he said. "We had supper around seven thirty and finished checking the machines, including the VCR, by eleven thirty. I fell asleep in the duty room a little after midnight."

The man on night duty on the day in question held his dark-blue hat in his hands and answered Yun San's questions politely. Yun San asked again.

"Try to remember. Did you see a suspicious person or a high school girl near the reservoir?"

The director, who was listening, replied instead. "The night watchman's job is to monitor the dam, maintain facilities, and manage the floodgates. He works according to the rules, so he doesn't have to be held responsible for things outside his orders, such as monitoring people walking near the dam."

Yun San requested the CCTV footage. There were a total of twelve CCTVs, two on either side of the six floodgates and two fifty yards downstream. However, the quality of the recordings was poor; they seemed merely to be used to check the sluice gates and flow rate in real time. There were no lights installed, so everything was black once the sun went down, and the video was automatically deleted after forty-eight hours.

Yun San and Nam Bora, who were under pressure, began investigating Jisoo's school and her friends. When the survey data came in, Jisoo was found to be quiet and withdrawn. A choir member said, "Jisoo didn't really make a sound until it was time for a trio, when she actually sang." Jisoo's homeroom teacher said that although Jisoo got on well with her friends, she did not hang out with them after school, but that this kind of introversion was characteristic of exemplary students. She seemed afraid that Jisoo might appear problematic.

Yun San sensed that Jisoo had opted for deliberate isolation, rather than just being friendless. Although she was a lonely child, it seemed as if she didn't want her loneliness to be noticed. Apart from this, there were no other striking statements or evidence.

The squad expanded their search to cover a wider area, including three blocks of the main road around Hamil Middle and High Schools, and the new city beyond Borim Stream on the other side of the ridge. Roads, buildings, basements, the reed bank along the river, and the forests on both sides of the ridge were also searched. Now they were looking not for Jisoo but for Jisoo's body.

During the investigation, the ivory phone in Howard House was as quiet as an ancient relic. There were only occasional calls from insurance salespeople or political parties.

Heejae's eyes were sunken, and Seonwoo's clothes hung loose on her gaunt body. They didn't even open their eyes at the loud ringing of the alarm clock. They were afraid to face each day's punishment. When they were forced to wake up, the absence of their child made their heads spin like a hangover.

Time was eating away at their lives.

At noon on the fifth day after Jisoo's disappearance, the phone rang loudly at Howard House. Neither parent dared answer it. They just looked at each other. Finally, Seonwoo picked up the phone.

"You must both come now."

It was Yun San's voice. Seonwoo could not ask what was going on. Heejae snatched the receiver from her.

"Sergeant! Have you found her? Did you find Jisoo?"

"Yes, we've found her."

Yun San put the phone down and stood there stiffly, looking at Nam Bora. Jisoo's body had been found in the middle of Borim Stream, over a mile from the dam. As the discharge volume was reduced due to the lack of rain, the water, which was usually over four feet deep, had become shallow, so that part of the body, snagging on a stone after being carried downstream, was exposed on the surface.

The person who found her was a middle school student who had been cycling to school along the riverbank. The boy had first assumed the body was a mannequin abandoned in the river. But when he waded in with the plan of rescuing the mannequin and dressing it up in a tae kwon do uniform to serve as a sparring partner, he recognized the mud-stained school uniform.

When Yun San had arrived at the scene, barricades had already been set up and a police squad deployed. Three members of the forensic team, their pants rolled up to their knees, were bent over in the middle of the stream, peering into the water, taking pictures, and gathering evidence.

"The forensic team wants us to stay out," Nam Bora said as she waded out of the water. "To avoid compromising the scene . . ."

She had set off immediately after receiving the report. The bottoms of her pants and one of her shirtsleeves were wet: she seemed to have slipped on a rock and fallen while fishing about in the stream. She opened her damp notebook and reported the facts.

"The body was found lying facedown. There will need to be tests, but there are no visible injuries. It's unclear whether the body was there from the beginning or whether it was abandoned elsewhere after death. It seems like it got caught on a rock after being carried downstream. The water is shallow because it's the dry season . . ."

"Anything else?"

"I couldn't see clearly, because I was keeping an eye on the forensic team. But I'm fairly sure the victim is barefoot."

"Both feet?"

Nam Bora nodded and asked, "Could it be suicide?"

Yun San took off his sunglasses and looked at the river. There was a possibility it was not a crime.

"We'll have to wait and find out."

For Yun San, any investigation into a death was a process of eliminating questions and possibilities one by one, rather than simply discovering who the killer was, and in this way, it was a process based on the consistent relationship that always exists between life and death. Even if it was suicide, the motivation and method had to be clearly demonstrated. Nam Bora changed her wet socks in the patrol car parked on the riverbank. Vans from local newspapers and broadcasting stations had flocked to the scene, and reporters carrying cameras ran along the river. The sound of water running over the shallow riverbed was unceasing.

Yun San was at a loss for how to tell the child's parents the appalling news. He was helpless when it came to informing them that the worst had become a reality, asking them to come to identify the body of their loved one, holding them back when they rushed to embrace their daughter with hoarse cries, and supporting them as they collapsed before their wretched child.

Jisoo's face as she lay flat on the stainless-steel table showed both large and small scratches. The torn lower lip was bruised, and abrasions were visible on her chest. Her tangled hair was bleached by the sun in places.

The first thing Heejae felt when he saw his daughter was her sense of betrayal: *I shouldn't have trusted you. I'm only eighteen years old, but I pretended to be a grown-up. I believed in you like a fool . . .*

"Could you please confirm that this is your daughter?"

Yun San spoke hurriedly, studying his notebook. There was nothing written there, nothing to write down. But he couldn't bear to see their grief-stricken eyes.

"I'm sorry," Heejae said, "but that's not my child."

He stared at his daughter's swollen face as if she were a stranger to him. He believed the situation unfair. When he'd asked the police chief to put more manpower into the search, he had never imagined her body would be found. Without a body, his daughter would not be dead. Nothing happened until something happened.

Yun San did not think Heejae was lying. He was just unable to accept reality. Yun San turned to Seonwoo and asked again.

"Could you please check again?"

Seonwoo clutched her chest as if she had been stabbed by a dagger, and remained motionless for a long time. She seemed afraid that someone would say something, or look her in the eyes. She seemed to be pondering what to say if she had to speak. Then she collapsed on the floor. Nam Bora assisted her to a chair and waited, applying a cold towel to her forehead. Seonwoo stared at Jisoo with dull eyes.

"That's right. That's the wristwatch on a red leather strap that I bought for her sixteenth birthday."

Seonwoo's face twisted, but she didn't burst into tears. Women, Nam Bora thought, were stronger than men. It was obvious Seonwoo was braver and more honest than her husband: she accepted her child's death by acknowledging her belongings. Unlike her husband, who was denying his daughter's death, she faced the overwhelming pain head-on.

"What's going to happen now?" Heejae asked with a blank look.

Yun San thought Heejae had the right to ask questions, and that Yun San had the obligation to answer them. It was a duty established the moment they accepted that the body in front of them was Jisoo.

"The missing-person case now turns into a murder investigation, and the case is transferred from our team to the violent-crimes team. As soon as an investigation unit is formed, they will focus on the results of the autopsy. Please go back home. I'll call you when there is more news."

This was the standard answer, and Yun San felt ashamed of it. He couldn't find any words to comfort them. Heejae coldly shook off the hand Seonwoo laid on his shoulder, as if his wife were to blame for his daughter's death.

To Seonwoo, it felt vaguely as if her daughter's absence had happened a long time ago. She had not felt like this in the beginning, but now Jisoo had been absent for what felt like an eternity, so long that all her memories of her seemed to have faded. If she had a daughter, she must be in the classroom for her seventh class period. What was the seventh class on Wednesdays?

A special investigation team had been set up in a temporary shipping container on a vacant lot about thirty yards from the main police station. Due to the increasing number of people working the case and the limited budget, the space had been commandeered with difficulty, as a last resort.

The violent-crimes division was headed by Kang Ilho, serving as team leader, with Choi Daegon, who was just back from suspension, together with detectives Kim Insik and Yun San. Nam Bora joined them as family-liaison officer. At the first investigation meeting, Yun San reported on the progress of the case from the day of Jisoo's disappearance to the discovery of the body.

"The victim, Jang Jisoo, was eighteen years old, and she was a second-year student at Hamil High School. She didn't come home after leaving the house on the morning of August twenty-second, five days ago. She was found dead around eight forty a.m. on the twenty-seventh."

Yun San let Nam Bora brief the others on the missing-persons stage. Nam Bora opened a chart and reported the victims' activities on the day of her disappearance in a toneless voice, as if she were reading from a textbook. Kang Ilho then emphasized the importance of the incident, mentioned the new government's wish to eradicate violent crime, and reminded everyone that the victim's father was a trusted businessman and an important person in the community.

After the inquiry, reporters gathered outside the shipping container. The detectives looked trustworthy in front of the cameras, like actors onstage. Kang's expression, which seemed to be inspired by cheap action movies, was dignified.

"I have nothing to say at the moment. We will simply do our best to catch the criminal. That's our job."

The autopsy report arrived two days later. The body had been decomposing underwater for five days, so there were no high expectations. Yun San scanned the dry medical language of the report.

Trauma: 42 cuts and bruises throughout the body, caused by human assault or impact with underwater obstacles due to shallow flow and currents.

Blood: No toxic substances detected.

Internal medical findings: Detection of algae plankton and micro-dust in alveoli. Water in the stomach.

500 ml or less plankton detected. No signs of organ rupture.

The cause of death was drowning. According to the autopsy, Jisoo's wounds and lung residues indicated that she had been carried downstream after she died in the reservoir. Considering the state of decay, the depth of water in the basin, and the flow rate of the stream, the time of death was estimated to be the evening of the day of disappearance. Yun San's gaze, as he read facts that had already been guessed by the investigators, suddenly came alive.

Urinary findings: Detection of a small amount of semen in the body. Genetic identification required.

Two thoughts came into Yun San's head simultaneously: first, that the investigation would have to start all over again, and second, that the investigation might end sooner than expected. So far, they had no account of the victim's sexual relationships, thanks to her wealthy upbringing, claims that the victim was a model student who had never caused problems, and her parents' tendency to paint their daughter as a child. But what if all that was just appearances? What if her parents didn't know who she was?

A lukewarm breeze flowed from the inefficient air conditioner on the wall and heated the inside of the shipping container. They would have to see Jisoo's parents again. They had to dig up facts the parents didn't know about their daughter, and before that, they had to tell the parents what they didn't know. How do you tactfully reveal the discovery of semen in someone's daughter's body?

After a brief moment of thought, he decided, *You can't.*

When Yun San and Nam Bora arrived at Howard House, Seonwoo had just woken up. She had meant to doze for only a moment, but before she knew it, the sun was low in the western sky. Heejae brought her out to the garden, where the two detectives were waiting.

Seonwoo sat at the garden table and looked at Howard House bathed by the setting sun. Loose joints, holes here and there, faded roofs, peeling paint, and broken paving stones under the porch—all defects and blemishes she had never noticed when she thought life was perfect . . . She was shocked that the house she had lived in for so long could look so unfamiliar. Everything she had known before seemed to have disappeared, as if she had returned home after a few decades of space travel and found it had been a million years in earthly time.

"Was Jisoo an introvert?"

Heejae tilted his head to one side at the question. He seemed to be wondering what Yun San meant, and hesitating because he was not sure of the answer. "What do you mean?" he finally asked.

"The friends we have met remembered Jisoo as a model student with excellent grades," Yun San explained. "I think she was friendly to most of her classmates, but she didn't have a friend who was close enough to answer my questions in detail. Usually, people around that age have one especially close friend."

"Isn't having many friends proof of good socializing skills?" Heejae asked. "Jisoo had excellent leadership skills and was keen on extracurricular activities."

Heejae added that Jisoo had been a class leader since elementary school, a member of her class's relay-race team, and a soprano in the church choir.

Yun San explained again.

"Her circle of friends was wide, but it was surprisingly shallow. She couldn't open her heart to close friends and didn't have anyone she talked to. I'm sure you've heard this before: being close to everyone means not being really close to any one person. It sounds like Jisoo had a problem with friendship."

Heejae rolled his eyes. Yun San thought that the animosity he expressed suggested that Heejae's view of his daughter was contrary to objective facts. He might have seen his daughter as he wanted to see her. He might not have known much or might have known nothing about his daughter. Or known wrongly.

"Did Jisoo have any difficulties?" Nam Bora asked, looking at Seonwoo. "About going to school, grades, and so on?"

Seonwoo's answer was firm. "No, her grades were always at the top. Even if she had a problem, she was not stupid enough to do what you think she might have done."

Seonwoo's subdued voice was sharper than any criticism. Yun San, who was listening, interrupted Nam Bora and Seonwoo's conversation.

"Did Jisoo have a boyfriend?"

"What do you mean?"

"An autopsy revealed an unidentified person's semen in her body."

Seonwoo's mouth opened wide. This was a greater shock than if her daughter had simply disappeared or died; she felt fearful. Heejae's eyes blazed like burning coals. He wanted to run to his daughter's room and ask right away, *It's not so, is it, Jisoo? These people have got something wrong, haven't they?* But his daughter was not in her room.

Yun San looked at Heejae with pity. When a child has a problem, parents always look for a good explanation or reason. But here, they couldn't grasp the issue itself: that a child without a problem is a problem. Yun San tried his best to look as friendly as possible.

"We've asked for a DNA analysis, and we'll check the result. We're investigating every possibility—"

Heejae, whose hands were on his waist, was shouting even before Yun San finished speaking. "Every possibility? Look, my daughter was brutally raped and murdered. What other possibility is there?"

Seonwoo grabbed the edge of her cardigan to hide her trembling fingers. Both husband and wife, Nam Bora thought, had just had the shock of their lives.

Yun San did not give up. He kept asking questions about Jisoo before and after her disappearance, whether her attitude had changed, and if so, how, whom she was close to and whom she hated, or who did not hate her. But he couldn't discover anything new.

"May I take a look at Jisoo's room again?" he asked, judging that there was nothing more to be gained here. Seonwoo cautiously refused Yun San's request.

"Well, you saw it last time," she said. "We, her parents, do not enter her room recklessly either. She was a sensitive kid and we trusted our daughter."

Recognizing her anxiety, Nam Bora stepped in. "Maybe we missed something," she said. "You wait here, sir. I'll go up with her parents and be right back."

They entered the house, leaving Yun San in the large garden.

Heejae felt strange barging into his daughter's room without permission. Although she was his daughter, he always asked her if he could enter.

Nam Bora went over to the window with its curved sill. Beside it, four small frames hung next to each other. They were photos of Jisoo taken around Howard House and the nearby hills last year. Jisoo on the terrace, smiling, her big teeth showing. Jisoo waving her arms and legs like a balloon doll while watering the lawn and avoiding water droplets. Jisoo in her school uniform, looking straight at the camera. Jisoo in the far right-hand picture, hugging her knees, her feet on a chair, in front of this very window.

Jisoo was smiling broadly in all the pictures. Heejae hadn't noticed these pictures in his daughter's room before, and he seemed embarrassed that someone had made his daughter smile so much. "I've never seen her smile this way since she was a middle school student," he told Nam Bora. "She was a kid who didn't smile at all."

Nam Bora asked Heejae for permission and then opened Jisoo's drawers. Something was inserted between the pages of a workbook in the bottom drawer. It was a picture of Jisoo looking at the camera with a bright smile. The wind blew her hair over her face, and the hem of her skirt fluttered lightly. There was a bluish outline in the lower left corner. Whether it was a lake or a river, it was clear that it was a sunlit stretch of water. The dam was visible in the background.

"When was this picture taken?"

Seonwoo, who had been looking closely at the picture, spoke up. "I don't know exactly, but she bought that polka-dot blouse in June this year, so I think it must be after that. Every couple of months, the whole family stays in the villa for a few days, and the last time we went there was at the end of June."

"According to this picture, Jisoo recently went to the dam with someone else."

Even before Nam Bora finished speaking, a sharp realization shook Heejae's body. A thick vein popped in his neck, and a slight twitch appeared around his eyes.

"Lee Jinman, the Hamil Schools manager, used to take pictures of my family. He has an old Leica camera that he inherited from Dr. Howard." Heejae spoke hurriedly, as if he were being pursued by something.

"What was his name again?" Nam Bora asked.

"Lee Jinman. He has two sons at home."

While she wrote the three names *Lee*, *Jin*, and *Man* in her notebook, Nam Bora kept an eye on Seonwoo's subtle expression. Seonwoo was clenching her fists. "They are good, sincere children," she said.

Heejae refuted her claim immediately, his voice cracking. "One of them could have stolen his father's camera. Or maybe they were together. Only look at this picture. It proves that those wretches invaded this room that *we* couldn't enter freely!"

Nam Bora changed the subject, interrupting Heejae. "How about your daughter's relationship with Lee Jinman? Were they close enough for her to stand in front of the camera in such a carefree, easy manner?"

"He's been kind to our children," Heejae said. "His kids as well. But I didn't know he went to the dam with her. If I'd known, I wouldn't have let them go. Did he really take her around without us knowing?"

"I don't know yet; there's nothing confirmed," Nam Bora said.

Heejae took a step closer and pressed hard. "Then when will we know? When are you going to find out who did this to our child?"

Nam Bora closed her notebook. "You have to give us time. It's only by stirring things up and even annoying people that we can find out the truth about your daughter's death."

She slipped her notebook into her pocket. It was clear the next step for the investigation was to meet Lee Jinman.

"We'll find out what happened to you," Heejae whispered, staring at his daughter's smile. His eyes were blazing. "We'll find out what they did to you."

The mysterious death of a powerful person's daughter was enough to generate public curiosity. Improper speculations about how the terrible incident would affect Heejae and his dreams of entering politics, as well as curious sympathy for the bad luck that had come to his perfect family, were rampant. Jisoo's report card was published in the press, and Hanjo's painting was published with an article introducing Howard House.

"Now what are you going to do?" Suin shouted, throwing the newspaper on the desk with Hanjo's painting clearly visible. Since Jisoo's disappearance, Hanjo hadn't noticed time pass. Her death had contaminated his life and changed everything. He alternated between anxiety, waiting, fear, and anger. Sometimes, they hit him all together.

Without giving him time to mourn Jisoo's death, rumors began to circulate among the students that his paintings had something to do with her death. It was unfair, but he couldn't blame his peers' curiosity about the incomprehensible incident. He tried to act normally, as if it had nothing to do with him, but did not know how to, and his hesitation only increased their misgivings. He tried recalling how he used to act when his friends had talked to him before, and attempted to act in the same way now, but that only made him feel yet more unnatural and awkward.

"What's wrong with you?" he told Suin now. "I just painted Howard House."

"Don't be silly. Everyone knows you painted Jisoo. You won the prize in the school art exhibition with that painting, the top award in the high school art competition, in front of the whole school. And you still claim you don't know who the girl was?"

Hanjo realized that nothing he said could convince his brother, and was seized with helplessness.

"That's why I . . . Are you saying I did something?"

Hanjo tried not to stutter, as if doubts would disappear if he showed he didn't care.

"What? Why are you acting like a guilty man?"

"Because you're treating me like a guilty man."

"I know you're not that kind of person. But do you think other people know this? Of course not. People don't know who you are. Do you know who detectives look for first when a woman dies? It's a man, her husband or ex-husband, her boyfriend, whoever she usually went about with."

Hanjo was suffocating. There were rumors in school that he had been dating Jisoo. Jisoo was quiet, but she was very friendly toward him. If they met in the hallway, she would approach him without hesitation and talk to him, or visit his classroom to borrow a textbook she had left at home. Regardless of the facts, they were considered a school couple. The claim was definitely groundless, but he hadn't hated it or felt bad. There were times he'd wanted the rumors to be true. If he had known this would happen, would he have corrected those rumors?

"I'm not Jisoo's boyfriend, and I've never flirted with her," Hanjo shouted.

"What were you doing that night?" Suin said, in a soft, dry voice. "The day Jisoo disappeared."

"I was painting in the studio."

"Did anyone see you there?"

Suin's eyes flashed like the filament of an incandescent light bulb. Hanjo hesitated. "Nobody," he said. "What's wrong with that?"

"If no one saw you, you won't be able to establish an alibi. But is it true that you were alone there?"

Hanjo's gaze shifted. Had Suin noticed the lie? He hadn't been alone in the studio. There had been someone else. But he couldn't say that. Suin tightened his hooklike grip on his shoulder.

"Get ahold of yourself. You weren't alone. Tell me who you were with!"

Hanjo felt calm; he wanted to tell the truth. He was about to reply *Jisoo*, when Suin suddenly spoke.

"You were with me."

"What?"

"Don't you remember? We'd been there since five thirty that evening. After you finished sketching Howard House, I came to help you with your math assignment."

Hanjo realized his brother was giving him a solid alibi to help him out of a tight corner. He felt immense relief. Suin hadn't turned his back on Hanjo; he blamed himself for putting his little brother in danger.

Suin was still speaking. "What was your math assignment?"

Hanjo was speechless. Suin answered his question gently.

"It was the solution to how to use a quadratic formula in a cubic equation. I gave you three exercises. It was around ten forty p.m. when you got home. I arrived a little later after organizing my books . . . I mean, we were there all evening, in the studio. Drawing a picture, solving a math problem . . ."

Suin's voice was calm, and his tone was full of conviction. He made Hanjo *want* to believe that it had happened like that, even if it hadn't actually. The story was full of Suin's trademark confidence and arrogance, but people seemed to love Suin's arrogance more than they loved Hanjo's humility and politeness. Desiring to be loved by people, Hanjo went along with his brother's story.

"Yeah, we got the call from Howard House shortly after we got home, saying that Jisoo hadn't returned. And then we walked around looking for her . . ."

"You remember. All right. Don't ever forget. No matter who asks, just say that. Just the way it was . . ."

His brother's story went round and round in Hanjo's head as if in a roundabout. Yes, as it was. Five thirty, annex studio, sketching, math assignment, cubic equation, quadratic formula, ten forty . . .

The words were not sincere, but they would build a new truth. Their brotherhood was based on falsehood, but that falsehood would unite them more strongly than anything else.

The next day, Nam Bora visited Howard House and found Lee Jinman taking care of the rose garden. Flashing stems. Strong, sharp thorns. Flowers so thick that they bent branches, velvet-soft petals.

Jinman, dressed in overalls, took off his thick gardening gloves to greet her. They reminded Nam Bora of baseball gloves. Apparently trying to assuage her suspicions about his free time, he stressed that he was tied down in the garden at all times, and even a moment's neglect would ruin it. Nam Bora asked him to be as specific as possible about the day of the incident.

"It was as usual until I got a call from Howard House," Jinman said. "I was just going to bed when I answered the phone and then went running up to Howard House with my two boys and my wife. The boys and I wandered around the hill and riverbank looking for Jisoo and only came back at dawn."

Nam Bora took her notebook out of her pocket and wrote down the time they had returned home.

"I'm just trying to see if I missed anything. During the day? So in the afternoon . . ."

"I worked all day replacing the water pipes in the school auditorium. I had to finish it before school started, because it meant cutting off the water supply. From ten a.m. onward, I was digging up the old pipes with five workers, and we finished around six p.m."

"Did you come home right away?"

"I finished cleaning up, then stopped by the building-supplies store. I had to ask them to bring me new water pipes by eight thirty a.m. the next day."

"How long does it take to go from the school to the store?"

"It's about ten minutes' walk."

"What about after that?"

"I left there around six thirty and walked home. I had a simple dinner, but I was so tired. I left the TV on, and I dozed off on the sofa for a while before washing up. Then my wife came back."

"Did you happen to see Jisoo that day?"

"On her way home from school, she passed the construction site and greeted me."

"Did she always do that?"

"What do you mean?"

"Did Jisoo usually come to where you were working and say hello?"

"It's because she's very kind and considerate."

Nam Bora went downtown to meet with the workers and visit the store to check Jinman's statement. It had happened exactly as he said; there were no discrepancies. When she went back to the office, Choi

Daegon, who had his nose stuck in a dish of black-bean noodles, stared at her as if she were a stranger.

She didn't know why she suddenly had to clean the house. Over the past few days, Miran had felt compelled to sweep, clean, and scrub Malcolm House for two hours a day to feel better. Taking down the curtains revealed otherwise invisible stains, which seemed to threaten her life. Dust flying from cracks in the floor, threads sticking out from the end of an old rug, long hairs that were apparently hers, pigeon feathers and debris blown in by the wind . . .

Her whole life lay in that messy little house. They lived there, smiling, talking, blushing, caressing, crying, soothing, and shouting at each other. Sometimes bad things happened, but they recovered and grew stronger.

Not that there were no secrets and deceit. Over the last two years, Jinman had had a strong pain in his back, Miran's uterine myoma had grown, Hanjo had used the money intended for reference books on a game console and gone a semester without books, and Suin had taken cigarettes out of Jinman's pocket and smoked them. There were things they didn't have to tell each other, rather than secrets or lies, and things that didn't matter even if she somehow learned about them.

She never blamed her husband for his poor income. He was keen on his work, and money to live on was not a big problem. Even if money was sometimes tight, she managed to find a way. However, Suin's university fees were different. For now, there was no way to send Suin to college unless he got a scholarship. A week ago, the teacher in charge of university admissions had explained the details of scholarships at several Seoul universities. These were colleges that had been founded recently, and so provided exceptional academic subsidies to compensate for their short history.

Miran held an empty laundry basket at her hip and stared at four drawers. The top drawer was her husband's, followed by one each for their two sons, and the bottom drawer was hers. The order represented the hierarchy in the house.

When the children were growing up, clothes from the first drawer moved downward like water flowing. Her husband's jacket was shortened and moved to Suin's drawer, and then moved to Hanjo's drawer a few years later. Over time, the boundaries between the drawers became fainter. Now shirts, jackets, and pants were common possessions, no one person's. The sons wore their father's shirts casually, and the younger brother exchanged jeans with his older brother. When Miran folded up the laundry and put it in the drawers, she often wondered what was whose. But it didn't matter. They shared clothes the same way they shared their destiny.

Nevertheless, Miran was able to distinguish the subtle smells of her different family members from drawer to drawer. She took her husband's work pants from the top drawer, which smelled of old wood and dirt, Suin's school-uniform pants and checkered shirt from the second drawer, and from the third drawer a pair of brown shirts and jeans that smelled of paint and oil.

She put them in her basket.

Before, if she had heard about a woman taking out freshly washed clothes and washing them again, she would have laughed and said, *That's stupid.* But now it had to be done. Three or four times even, not just twice. Everything had to be washed, the collars, sleeves, and knees scrubbed to clear away any traces of that night that might remain.

She didn't know why, but the men of her family had looked very strange that night. They had looked immature, with startled eyes. She couldn't help but imagine it had to do with Jisoo's disappearance. They were tough, smart, or kind, but they all needed her care.

That fateful night, when she came home after ten o'clock, her husband had been alone. He was coming out of the bathroom, still changing his clothes, when she came through the front door. The dim fluorescent light shone on his face.

When she asked, "Did you have dinner?" he stared at her as if she were a stranger. He looked puzzled, as if he had been caught doing something he shouldn't have done. He changed the subject by rubbing his forehead with a towel hung around his neck.

"Both kids are late. I'll have to say something when they get back."

Miran glanced at her husband's muddy overalls lying by the front door. The three men always ignored Miran's pleas to put their laundry in the basket next to the washing machine. Her husband took off his working clothes by the front door, and her sons just threw theirs anywhere. Her husband's pants, half inside out, were thin and transparent. They looked like the husk of a dead cicada.

After a while, Hanjo came in through the front door. Her son's body smelled of paint solvents and sour sweat. Miran said, "You're late. Where were you?"

"The studio in the annex."

Miran was relieved. Now only Suin needed to come back. She quickly stepped through the front door and into the past. Nearby, an insect chirped, and the wind carried the smell of mown grass. The hill glistened silver. In the dim moonlight, the long, thin outline of a man appeared.

"Why are you so late?"

"I've been downtown."

Miran grew anxious. Suin was a child who intimidated his parents. Before she asked Suin something or tried to communicate with him, she always discussed the topic several times with her husband, and they arranged her main points and the order in which she would say them. Even then, if Suin did not answer clearly, she always believed there was good reason for it. There were many things parents didn't need to know, after all, or things they eventually found out without lengthy questioning.

But tonight was different. She needed to know. She had to know.

"I'm asking where you've been!"

She wondered why he had come from the hill, and not from the school. And why the pants he had changed into that morning were damp. And why his face was so pale.

"I had a small argument with someone. It's no big deal."

She wanted to ask whom, and why he had quarreled with them, but she didn't. She didn't think she would get an answer even if she asked.

"Are you hurt?"

"No."

That was a relief. She would find out the rest later. It didn't matter if she didn't know.

"OK, go in and wash up. Make sure you put your dirty clothes in the laundry basket."

Now, Miran put Suin's pants, which had just been ironed, Hanjo's shirt with its indelible paint marks, and her husband's overalls into a washing bowl, added detergent, and pummeled them hard. She didn't trust the washing machine.

Her hands were throbbing because she was rubbing the clothes so roughly. In this moment, Miran realized why she was doing this. It was possible that either her husband or one of her two sons, or all of them, were somehow connected with Jisoo's death.

Nevertheless, she couldn't ask them or push them for answers. What she didn't believe was the world, not her family. From countless movies and TV dramas, from people's complaints and moaning, she knew how unfair and unreliable the world was.

They might be suspected by the police because they were closest to the Howard House family. Someone might start whispering about the relationship between Jisoo and the children. It was true that the sons had been close to Jisoo. Detectives eager to find the criminal might come with glistening eyes. If her kids seemed nervous, they'd start asking questions.

She had an obligation to take care of, reassure, and protect her family. She could not allow anything bad to happen, no matter how small. To prevent it, she would do everything she could. Even the wrong things, if they could not be avoided.

She shook the heavy laundry and hung it on the clothesline. The wind blew the laundry out at an angle. Her husband, Suin, and Hanjo seemed to be flying up, side by side, toward the silver clouds.

Jisoo's remains were buried in a memorial park outside the city. The detectives were reluctant to attend the funeral, making various excuses. Choi Daegon said he had to thoroughly investigate the gangs around the dam; Yun San had to go to the school library to meet Suin. Kim Insik left the office, saying that he was taking an old jeep that often broke down to the repair shop. As a result, Nam Bora, as family-liaison officer, had to attend alone in full uniform.

The mourners gathered for the funeral in the morning. Their backs were bent and their heads bowed. Even Jisoo's friends looked like old people. Nam Bora's cell phone rang at the end of the cremation ceremony. It was Yun San. He told her about Suin's activities on the day of the incident, and ordered her to meet Hanjo and compare their accounts.

Nam Bora left the memorial hall. The midday sun beat down on her head. She took out her sunglasses and walked along the path running down the middle of the cemetery. She could see a boy curled up in the shadow of a hawthorn, visible in the distance, holding his face in his hands. Nam Bora approached the bench where the boy was sitting.

The child's face looked thinner and more haggard than when seen from far off. His white shirt was stained with sweat, and his hair was disheveled. His expression revealed the vulnerability of the youngest child in a family who needed special care. Nam Bora took off her sunglasses and put them in her pocket.

"You said your name was Hanjo, right? I know it's going to be hard. You were close to Jisoo. But it'll be OK. Right?"

Hanjo did not answer. Nothing would ever be OK. The brief moments of this summer would never fade away, and they would define the rest of his life.

"May I ask you a few questions? I simply want to talk about this and that. I might have missed something. Nothing more."

Nam Bora had used the word *simply*, but in an investigation, there was no such thing as *simply*. Every question had a purpose. Hanjo avoided looking at her and moved his lips slightly, but Nam Bora could not hear what he said. He seemed to be both complaining and resigned.

"Was there anyone that Jisoo liked? Or anyone who liked Jisoo?"

She spoke only in questions, not statements, as if following a communications guide for her job as police officer. Hanjo shivered at the thought that he was the answer to both questions. The hum of cicadas troubled him.

"I don't know. We just painted together. Jisoo loved modeling. She felt good when I drew or took pictures of her."

Nam Bora recalled a painting by Hanjo hanging in the living room of Howard House. It was a painting of the house covered with snow. Standing in the second-floor window, Jisoo's yellow silhouette seemed to suggest that she knew she was beautiful, and it had occurred to Nam Bora that the yearning expressed in the picture might indicate Hanjo's feelings as he painted her.

"Did you like Jisoo?"

Nam Bora's question was in the past tense. The fact that Jisoo could never be drawn again caused every joint in Hanjo's spine to ache.

"If I liked her, was that wrong?"

Hanjo hated himself for speaking in the past tense. This situation felt strange, as if it were happening to someone else.

"When was the last time you saw Jisoo that day?" Nam Bora asked.

Hanjo's ankles shook like those of a tennis player returning to the bench after a tough match. He looked at Nam Bora's snub nose, which was slightly grimy.

"I was going to the studio in the morning, and Jisoo was going to school," Hanjo said, still staring at the nose. "Jisoo goes on a self-study program during vacations."

"Was there anything strange about Jisoo then?"

"No, she was just the same, like any other time."

"How was she the same?"

"She was just coy and said what she wanted to say."

"What did she say?"

"She said she couldn't come to the studio that afternoon, because she had work to do. She acted as a model for me during the vacation."

"Where were you that evening?"

Hanjo's forehead was covered in sweat. Though his clothes were shabby, he had a grace that was rarely found in children his age, a seriousness that went beyond his years. Nam Bora imagined that he was a sensitive child, one difficult to deal with. But she had no way of confirming this.

"In the annex studio."

Hanjo struggled to remember his brother's expression and gestures as he'd told him to say this.

Nam Bora asked, "Alone?"

"With my brother. My father said he must help me study math."

Hanjo continued to give specific answers. It was much the same as Suin's statement, as recounted by Yun San. While Suin had explained the solution to the math problem in detail, Hanjo only said he'd helped him study math.

"Are you done? Can I go?" Hanjo asked, looking at Nam Bora with anxious eyes.

"Of course. It's no big deal, so don't think too deeply about it. I'm just asking, that's all."

Nam Bora's answer was casual, but she wondered: Were the brothers really innocent? An alibi from family was generally considered less reliable than that of other people. Still, Nam Bora reassured the boy that it was no big deal, that it really was nothing.

As he walked away from Nam Bora, Hanjo wondered what she would think if he told the truth about that day. That his brother hadn't been in the studio with him. That it was Jisoo who had been there, since he had asked her to be his model during the vacation. That Jisoo had said she would come, but had left by evening . . .

Would she believe it?

For the meeting, there was a stack of maps, charts, and detailed investigation reports on the table. There was a severity about the coffee- and cigarette-stained table that did not allow for weak reasoning or poor logic.

Nam Bora handed out round paper cups of coffee to each detective. Kim Insik began to report, ruffling his thinning, curly, prematurely gray hair.

"There's not much in terms of the victim's relationships. She hadn't had an argument with anyone lately, and hadn't lent or received any money."

Money, politics, and anger were common starting points for detectives investigating murders, whether they were veterans or new. Murder is not a matter of unusual people in unusual situations, but an act by ordinary people in everyday life.

"Hey, the mayoral candidate's daughter got hit on by a lunatic," the boss said. "So find something. What they want out there is a result." He bit down on his cigarette filter and struck a match nervously. Kim Insik let out a small cough at the smoke.

"I met the owner of the snack bar at the start of the riverside walk, and he said he knew the victim. She'd been walking up and down the path once or twice a week for a month before her death. He doesn't remember seeing her on the day of the incident."

"What about any other kids? Did he talk about any other kids that used the path?"

"I checked out some of the kids who seemed to be in trouble, and there's nothing much. They used to smoke cigarettes together around there, but I confirmed they were at a billiard room downtown that day. But there is one high school student who has been cycling along the riverside for about six months."

"Who's that?"

"Lee Suin, the eldest son of Lee Jinman. He was closest to the victim among the boys of his age. Lee Suin's younger brother won an award for painting a picture of the victim. The victim's father also seemed suspicious of the children. I'm afraid we'll have to dig up more information about them."

The old fan on the ceiling circulated the room's hot air. Nam Bora agreed with Kim Insik, but couldn't forget Hanjo's face. There were weak points in his story, and it needed more checking, but she wanted to believe what the child had said. She spoke in a needlessly hasty manner.

"There's no evidence yet that allows us to be conclusive. The children searched for the victim until late at night on the day of her disappearance. I don't know about her father, but her mother seemed to believe them."

Kim Insik, embarrassed, snapped back. "Do you realize that what you're saying is ridiculous? When compassion intervenes, an investigation is ruined. If you want to make a point, give me a reasonable basis!"

"Well, I met the second son of the Malcolm House family at Jisoo's funeral today. Although they were close to the victim, the boys were studying math together at Howard House that day."

Kang threw the still-burning cigarette into the coffee left in the paper cup; it sizzled as it went out. "If I'm not mistaken," he said, "isn't the family-liaison officer's job not alibi investigation but to care for the victim's family?"

Nam Bora's face turned red at Kang's rebuke. She was called the family-liaison officer, but the truth was, women weren't given much to do in an investigation. The team leader assumed a woman couldn't fight a criminal at the scene of an arrest, trace suspects, or interrogate suspects once they were arrested; he believed she would close her eyes or vomit in the autopsy room. Thus, the group regarded her as the team's handmaid, someone who prepared coffee according to the number of people present, for example, or listened silently to the complaints of the victim's family. When the investigation stalled or took a step backward, she would be there to blame.

"And what's more," the boss said, determined to blame her for the sluggish pace of the investigation, "what kind of an alibi can you trust when you say you're just asking? They're brothers. We should consider the possibility that the two of them matched their alibis and that they were accomplices. You shouldn't be looking for reasons to believe a person of interest; you have to come at him with your suspicions!"

Yun San understood Kang's prejudice against Nam Bora—she was new, a woman, and not from the violent world—but he felt the boss was being unfair. Although she lacked tact and experience, she had the qualities of a competent detective. Despite being optimistic and curious by nature, she knew when to be serious and could interpret clues. Yun San cautiously brought the discussion back to the case.

"Don't we need to look at the incident from a slightly different angle? We should look at the victim more closely, since we can't find anything to latch on to about the people around her."

"You're thinking suicide. Look here. Is that how an investigation works? There's no reason to conclude that way, even if the identity of the criminal is unclear."

Yun San's face turned red at the boss's reprimand, which felt close to ridicule. The boss thought that Yun San, although he was a competent investigator, was physically soft, good for scribbling reports on small pickpockets or attempted sexual harassment. It was just a prejudice, but it wasn't completely groundless.

"There were no visible wounds on the body that appeared to be intentionally inflicted," Yun San protested, "other than signs of being swept along or snagged by rocks as it floated down."

"That should be seen as evidence that the victim didn't resist rather than as a clue that suggests suicide. It means the murderer is an acquaintance."

Kim Insik wriggled his eyebrows to show support for the boss's opinion.

"Whether we like it or not, the incident has now gone beyond being just an incident. Citizens are calling for a killer to be caught, and the media are ahead of us in looking for a killer. What happens if we classify the death of a leading politician's innocent daughter as suicide when everyone is watching? People will think that we're incompetent police officers who can't catch a murderer and are blaming the victim to avoid responsibility." Exasperated, Kang knocked on the table with a damp coffee cup. He added in a dispirited voice, "I'm going home. I have a meeting with the commissioner as soon as I get to work tomorrow morning."

"Why are the higher-ups calling you in? We're busy catching criminals," Choi Daegon asked.

"The investigation is slow, and the commissioner's phone is on fire," Kang snapped. "If you don't want to see a bunch of heads go flying, don't argue about this and that. Question everyone. All her family, all her friends, all her neighbors!"

The atmosphere of the meeting room was subdued after the boss's irritable reproaches. Everyone was silent. Nobody was in the mood to talk first. It wasn't until quite a while later that Choi Daegon sighed.

"There's not much we can do. But seeing the boss's face, we'd better do something quickly. Let's try this first . . ."

"What?" Kim Insik asked curiously, expecting Choi Daegon to reveal a new clue or offer groundbreaking inspiration that would mark the turning point for the investigation. Instead, Choi Daegon stared at Nam Bora across the table and said, "Let's have another cup of coffee and think about it first."

Nam Bora looked at Choi Daegon and Kim Insik in turn, speechless. Yun San closed his notebook where it was lying on the table and said, "Coffee at this time of night? Hey, Officer Nam. Go home. You need some sleep."

Nam Bora stood up along with Yun San. It was almost eleven o'clock.

There was a knock on the front door. Jinman opened it cautiously. As soon as Yun San entered the house, he took out a cigarette and lit it without asking.

"You must be proud. Your sons. Your eldest the top student in the whole school and the second an artistic genius."

Yun San spewed smoke and words together. He seemed to be taunting Jinman for having quit smoking.

"Even if the kids are close to the Howard House family," Jinman replied bluntly, "they have nothing to do with this."

"I know. I'm just trying to make sure."

"What's not certain?"

"There are witnesses saying that your eldest son has been frequenting the riverside path. And the girl died there."

"Did you say 'frequenting'? Detective, he's one of hundreds or thousands of people who walked there that day. It wasn't just that day either. I used to go there a lot before, too. Most importantly, our boys were together at the time it happened."

Jinman stopped because his voice was unexpectedly loud and rough. Yun San checked the time by the old wall clock. It was 3:55 p.m. Yun San changed the subject.

"You took pictures of the people at Howard House. Is there any particular reason?"

"I've been doing that since Dr. Howard lived there. The doctor left me an old camera as a gift because I was good at it. Since then, I've taken pictures when there was an event at the hospital or school. And, of course, personal and family photos. To save on the development and printing costs, I bought secondhand equipment and set up a darkroom in the basement. I used the same camera Dr. Howard left me to photograph the current owner's family."

"Did you ever take separate portraits of Jisoo?"

Yun San examined Jinman's expression, adopted an attitude that made it blatantly obvious he was observing him.

"Just Jisoo? The owner, his wife, Haeri, plus the dog, November, too."

Yun San's eyes changed subtly.

"Did you take pictures of Jisoo most often?"

Jinman could not tell if he suspected him or if he was inviting him to express his innermost thoughts.

"I would say so."

"Did you have any good reason?"

"Because Jisoo liked photography. She loved being photographed."

Yun San asked to see the darkroom. Jinman led him out of the house and down narrow stairs next to the porch. Under the stairs, there was a basement about ten yards wide and five yards long. Part of it was a workshop, its shelves filled with thick scrapbooks, glass bottles of various shapes, plastic containers, paint cans, wood and corrugated cardboard, and a statue of Agrippa with a broken nose. Yun San also noticed pruning shears, trowels, and woodworking tools of various sizes.

The darkroom was an inner space closed off by wooden blocks. Jinman walked through the workshop, opened a wooden door, and entered the darkroom. There was the sound of water flowing from the faucet.

Yun San stayed in the workshop and looked around carefully. The titles on newspaper cuttings stuck to a cork panel caught his eye. "How to Communicate with Your Child." "Where Do Artistic Talents Come From?" "Interview with the Top Successful Applicants of the Bar Exam." They were helpful articles for the children's education.

Next to them were more-recent articles. "High School Girl Missing." "Police Investigate Kidnapping." "Missing High School Girl Found Dead: Police Blamed for Faulty Initial Investigation."

Yun San opened a notebook lying on a workbench. Work-related concepts and ideas were organized into various notes, charts, and pictures. There were sketches of drainpipe connections, details about the scope of replacement and the number of workers needed, traces of wage calculations, more sketches of replacement parts for roofing panels and classroom structures . . .

"Even if you're investigating, you can't just go searching through other people's notebooks."

Jinman had suddenly appeared and snatched the notebook from him. The book opened as it fell to the floor, revealing a colored-pencil sketch. It was a view of the reservoir as seen from the side of the dam with the sluice gates. Judging from the tree branches covered in fresh green leaves and the low water level, it had been painted recently. Yun San suddenly wondered if Jinman had manipulated him into looking at the notebook. If so, what was he trying to induce him to think?

"You have a previous conviction," Yun San said, flipping through his notebook. "Before your marriage, when you were twenty-six years old?"

He asked this casually, as if it were unimportant. Jinman's expression hardened and grew sullen. Yun San raised his head and stared at Jinman. It was an eerie look, as if a snake had reared its head inside Yun San. Jinman brushed a hand over his haggard beard.

"There was a minor dispute with the labor manager at the sewing factory where I worked."

"The other person's cheekbone was broken, and three ribs were cracked. A twelve-week medical certificate was submitted to the court. How can you say that it was a minor dispute?"

"But both of us were injured."

"You were sentenced to one and a half years in prison for violating the law on violent behavior, weren't you? You were unemployed after you got out of prison; then you started working at the Hamil Schools under the auspices of Dr. Howard."

Jinman hesitated, deciding whether to speak or not.

"That factory made household sewing machines," he said finally. "I was an executive of the labor-union-promotion committee, which consisted of about twenty people. In the process of establishing the union, there was a conflict with the factory manager and the labor manager. Someone had to be responsible for the injury during the physical fight. One of the executives picked me out. I told the police that I had taken the initiative in the violence."

"You claimed to be a perpetrator for the sake of the organization?"

"It was not like that. Even if I didn't lead the rally, I had to be held responsible for using violence. I was hotheaded and young. But why is something that happened more than twenty years ago a problem now?"

"Things like that aren't really hidden, even if you think they are. Even if they seem to be gone, they never disappear."

Jinman could hardly contradict him. A case file with details of his motives, track record, and judgment would be in the police archives.

He was an ex-convict. Such things are usually forgotten, but when an incident occurs, detectives are quick to find potential criminals.

Jinman waited for his family to come home and breathe life into this shabby house. He missed the loud voices, the giggling laughter, the clatter of spoons and bowls, and the noise of the children running up and down the stairs as if it had been decades.

He sat on a wooden chair on the unpainted porch and remembered when the children were young. The bluish Mongolian spots on their behinds, the transparent-seeming veins, the black eyes looking up at him, children's lips pouting like those of a fish . . .

In this house, he had taught Suin how to toddle and taken out Hanjo's milk teeth. Even if there was not much he could do, it was enough for the children to feel loved. After they entered adolescence, his sons responded bluntly or slammed their doors shut as if they were about to break them. Still, he secretly enjoyed the rebellious years of his sons, who had grown fed up with his nagging.

"Of course children don't listen," he would tell his wife. "That's proof that they're finding their own way in life."

His easygoing words would make her glare. His wife had certainly lost her tongue these days. He had wanted to talk to her that night when she came back. They were a family, and deserved to know each other. They had a duty to do so.

He had never needed his family as he did today.

He had emptied half the bottle of soju when he heard Suin's footsteps on the grass. That straight forehead so unlike his own. He couldn't believe this dazzling boy was his child. It was clear to Jinman that he favored Suin. But that didn't mean he didn't love Hanjo. He did his best to give each of his sons enough love, not letting Suin know that he was his favorite or Hanjo that he had lost his love.

"Why don't you come here and talk to your father?"

For a few years now, Jinman had been wary of asking anything from Suin, even to run errands. In front of his son, he was a small, humble, and insignificant man.

"Is something wrong?" Suin spoke as if soothing his father.

Jinman wanted to say, *I feel as if I've been left alone.* Instead, he emptied his glass of strong soju. The detective's questions lingered in his mind. The detective had expressed doubts about Jinman and his two sons, including Suin's alibi. His eyes had gleamed when Jinman said Suin had gone over the hill looking for Jisoo in the middle of the night. Those harsh eyes that were bent on finding clues and evidence to blame Jinman's children.

Even though he had worked so hard to take care of his family and build trust with his neighbors, Jinman couldn't handle the fear he felt at this moment—the fear that something was rushing toward this house at full speed and would destroy everything he held precious.

"The detective came again, asking where Hanjo was that evening."

"What did you say?"

"I said he was with you."

Jinman looked at his son as if asking if he had done well. Suin was annoyed by his father, who always fretted about what he thought. His father was neither knowledgeable nor virtuous. He was just a man who managed to live by the petty work of his hands, a manual laborer who, on hard days, would start snoring before nine o'clock, the moment he put his spoon down on the table. He was a father on whom Suin couldn't rely, because he was affectionate without offering wisdom or concrete plans. Suin couldn't expect dignity or deep insight from his father, and it broke his heart. But Suin couldn't show his annoyance.

"Well done," he said, "because that's true. Don't worry too much."

Jinman didn't know what he shouldn't worry about, but he was relieved to hear his son's assurances. Suin looked considerate, perhaps because of his high forehead.

"He asked me about you, too. Someone saw you by the reservoir . . ." Jinman's face was flushed with alcohol. "Did you go there that day? You know, the reservoir."

"I told you. I was with Hanjo."

In the evening sunset, his son's face glowed red like a flawless jewel. His son, Jinman thought, was more mature than he was.

"Yes . . . If you're sure, I'm sure."

Someone was practicing the piano badly in the school music room, and the sound drifted up the hill. Suddenly, Jinman couldn't shake the thought that the house was too small for his son. He knew, although Suin had never said as much, that his son had always longed to leave this shabby house. He dreamed of running away from poverty and a bleak future, and carried a deep anxiety that he would never escape from his proud parents and his status as the son of a handyman.

Now, after one semester, his son would be going to Seoul. He would go to college and pass the bar exam and become a judge. This child deserved to achieve and acquire, achieve and enjoy. No misfortune must ever touch this child.

Suin spoke again. "I know what he's thinking. But it's not true."

The sun shone in a red cloud of dust over the western city. The church spire and the arch of the school auditorium were honey colored. Hanjo appeared at the foot of the hill. He was walking along with long legs that made Jinman wonder when he had grown up like that. He jumped up and called his son's name. "Hanjo! Hanjo!"

Standing with his back to the red sunset, the child smiled. Then he shouldered his bag and started running.

After obtaining a search warrant, the investigation team took two boxes of photos, films, sketches, and newspaper clippings from Lee Jinman's studio. The pictures were mainly landscapes taken around the hill and downtown, including photos of the missionary houses. There were also various photos of the Howard House family, including at school events, and Easter and Christmas events at the church. The photo of Heejae smiling broadly with his hair combed straight seemed to have been taken for election posters.

A significant photo came from the second batch. It was a picture of Jisoo smiling as she leaned against the safety railing of the sluice gates. The calm water glistened over her shoulder.

"This is it! Jang Jisoo went to the dam with Lee Jinman to take a picture," Choi Daegon shouted, waving the picture he had just picked out from the pile.

"I'm sure she's been there many times, not once or twice. Don't you see the different clothes in each picture?"

Kim Insik pointed at the prints as he spoke. A dress with a pattern of waterdrops, jeans and a white piqué shirt, a sky-blue shirt with a checkered skirt . . . The shoes were white tennis shoes, black shoes, pink canvas shoes. The length of the hair and the shape of the bangs were also different, so it didn't look like a simple change of clothes on the same day. Lingering snow and spring plants on the surrounding ridges revealed clear seasonal changes.

Choi Daegon snapped his fingers. "He lured the victim to the scene that day using a photo shoot as an excuse. They'd been there several times before, so she went to the appointment without any suspicions."

"Wouldn't it seem weird to suggest taking photographs at night?" Nam Bora interrupted. "And with no witnesses . . ."

"There was sunlight when the girl went to the scene. On a summer evening there would still have been sunlight even close to eight p.m. There were no witnesses because there are few people on the path to the dam."

Yun San nodded as he listened to Choi Daegon's explanation. If Choi Daegon hadn't been able to explain his theory, Yun San would have stepped in instead and arranged the story to suit the facts. It all fit. But he couldn't rid himself of a feeling that something was wrong.

Lee Jinman had the absentminded air of someone who didn't think about the world too deeply or notice its deceptions. Even now, he didn't seem to realize the dire situation he was in. It was a naivete bordering on stupidity.

"No matter how hard I think about it," Yun San said slowly, "the motive doesn't fit."

Choi Daegon's nostrils twitched, and horizontal wrinkles appeared on the sides of his nose.

"The motive only emerges once you've caught him and put the screws on. Now that the pictures are out, he's dead meat."

Yun San thought it would be hard for Lee Jinman to escape.

Lee Jinman was arrested a little after eleven a.m. the next day. When two police cars drove through the school's main gate, Hanjo was in his second class of the day. Sitting near the window, he was watching an English teacher explain the history of the American Puritans. He didn't write anything down, because listening was enough. He could understand everything the teacher was saying.

The police cars did not use their lights or sirens. Three men and a woman got out of the cars and crossed the tranquil playground. Hanjo couldn't concentrate on the teacher's explanation. He didn't want to know *why* the police had come to school. He only wondered if his father knew about it.

When the bell rang for the third period, he climbed to the rooftop instead of going to the classroom. He sat on a railing overlooking the playground. The detectives were headed straight for the water-pipe-repair site. Jinman was preoccupied with measuring the location of the water pipe with a tape. He wasn't aware of anything.

Kim Insik approached Jinman, and they laughed together as if they were exchanging jokes. Perhaps because of his beard, which he hadn't shaved for several days, Jinman's expression was dark as he smiled.

Standing behind him, Yun San and Nam Bora did not smile. They were all somewhat awkward, like the actors on a stage.

When Choi Daegon pulled back the hem of his jacket, the handcuffs at his waist glinted. Jinman stood stooping, like one of Rodin's *Burghers of Calais*, and removed the thick sleeve covers from his arms. His body looked small. He was frowning, as if trying to come up with something to say. Kim Insik pressed Jinman's shoulders back and handcuffed him. He must have felt pain, but he did not resist or struggle.

The detectives grabbed Jinman's arms and moved toward the far side of the playground. They strode slowly, as if they were rowing with difficulty across a sea of light. In this moment, Hanjo felt that he would regret it for the rest of his life if he stayed here. He jumped up and ran down the stairs two by two. He could see the clear blue bands on the police cars parked on the far side of the playground.

"Father! Where are you going?!"

Hanjo's shout stopped the detectives in their tracks.

"What are you doing here?" Jinman yelled at his son, who was running nearer. "You're not in class?"

Hanjo managed to stop just before he ran into a police car. His breath was in his throat, and his heart was constricted.

"Tell me where you're going," he said. "If we don't talk, Mom's going to be mad."

Jinman did not speak. Hanjo wondered if his father thought he would understand, whether he spoke or not. Yun San grabbed Hanjo's shoulder tightly enough for him to feel pain.

"We're going to have a quiet talk with your father. Don't worry—he'll go back home if everything's all right." Yun San's voice sounded soft but harsh.

"But why is he handcuffed?"

"You punk. Where are your manners?" Choi Daegon said, grabbing Hanjo by the collar with a hooked hand. Jinman's face drained of color. He looked clumsy, like an amateur actor trying to project dignity.

"Stop," Nam Bora shouted. "He's only a child."

Choi Daegon let go of Hanjo and got into the driver's seat. Nam Bora soothed Hanjo in a soft, gentle voice. "Don't worry. Your father won't have any problems."

Hanjo wanted to believe her. All this was nothing, and he hoped he could go back to his old life, even if it wasn't perfect. Jinman's sleeves were twisted from how tightly the detectives held his arms. Kim Insik pressed his head down with a palm and pushed him into the car. Looking out through the open car window, Jinman said, "Hanjo, tell your brother. It's nothing, so tell him not to worry."

Hanjo couldn't decide whether his father's words were a request or a scolding. The car started with a jerk, kicking up a pile of dirt as the wheels spun free. Through the rear window, the back of his father's head looked blurred. The hair on the top of his head was sticking up. Was his father scared? Was he lost in thought?

"No! I won't! You come and tell him yourself this evening!" Hanjo shouted as the police car drove away. The zelkova tree in the playground gave off a scent of thick sap, and unfamiliar birds flew up into the white, bleached sky.

By the time he got home, Hanjo was on the verge of exhaustion. He felt nauseous but didn't have the strength to throw up. Every corner of the house where he had been born and raised was as unfamiliar as if he were seeing it for the first time. Family photos taken by his father, his brother's prize certificates hanging on the wall, his father's worn-out work clothes, the old TV set, and the cabinet that had lost its polish . . .

He went upstairs and threw himself onto his bed. The sagging springs creaked and squeaked. In his dream, he was being chased by wild animals, either wild dogs or hyenas. The beasts surrounded him, their snouts pressing close. Their nostrils were spouting hot steam, and their slippery saliva touched his face. He tried to run away, but his legs wouldn't move. An animal with a long snout transformed into the face of a detective with a long chin.

Hanjo opened his eyes. It was dark outside the window and hazy in his head, as if his mind were foggy. When he came downstairs, light was streaming out through the half-open kitchen door. He could see his mother curled up at the table. Her hair had lost its sheen, and her arms drooped like the wings of a broken bird. He saw a half-empty bottle of soju on the table. Hearing him come down, his mother looked at him.

"Ah, it's Hanjo. We should have dinner, right? There's still rice left in the cooker from this morning, so take some of that."

Her voice was crushed and hard to understand, as if she spoke with a twisted and swollen tongue. His mother's face, with its bloodshot, red-rimmed eyes, was unfamiliar, as if it were reflected in a warped mirror.

"No, wait a minute," Miran said. "I'll take care of it."

His mother drank most of a glass of soju and headed for the counter. As she moved, the soju glass toppled over, and the remaining liquor dripped onto the floor. His mother swayed and fell with a short, dull thud. Blood started to seep through her frazzled hair. She seemed to have cut the back of her head on a projecting plank or a nail. His mother passed out for a moment, then opened her eyes and smiled.

"Hanjo, are you hungry? I have to prepare a meal for you . . ."

Hanjo carried his mother on his back to the main bedroom. She was as light as a paper doll. He laid her on the bed, wiped her damp hair, and pressed a gauze pad to the wound to stop the bleeding. He wondered if she should go to the hospital, but decided not. His mother said again she would cook for him, then asked him to eat with his father when he came back, then asked him to go out and see if his brother was coming, and then fell asleep while asking what day it was.

It was cool and quiet in the room. His mother's breast rose and fell regularly in the dark. Every time she exhaled through her half-open mouth, a thin groan emerged. Sometimes she frowned and muttered something he couldn't understand. Perhaps she was having a bad dream?

As he looked at her, he realized his mother was vulnerable, in need of protection.

He wanted to wake his mother up. Her bad dream would disappear if she woke up. Life would go on, and she could believe this shabby house was still safe. But he didn't do it. The glow-in-the-dark needle on the desk clock flashed blue. It was 8:35. If his father hadn't been arrested, this was when the whole family would have sat around the dinner table.

Leaving the room quietly, he went back to the kitchen and wiped away a dry spot of blood. Suin, who had just come back from school, where he had stayed late to do homework, took off his school jacket and hung it on the back of a chair.

"Brother! They took Father away. Two police cars came. There were four detectives."

Suin searched his bag, took out a cigarette, and lit it. Hanjo wondered when his brother had started smoking, but he did not ask. Later, when the chaos had subsided and everything returned to normal, he would ask.

"They can't do anything. Even if they wrongfully accuse Father of a crime, it will all come out in court."

Words and cigarette smoke seeped together through Suin's lips. His distorted smile matched his sharp eyes, and he looked mean. Hanjo didn't know if he was just desperate to comfort himself, but he chose to blindly believe what his brother said. Suin could always overcome Hanjo's confusion with boldness and cold confidence.

"Father stayed still when they handcuffed him. If he's innocent, he should have gone wild, but he couldn't say a word."

"If Father didn't say anything, we shouldn't say anything either."

Suin's words were a command and a warning: even if Hanjo wanted to know his father's crime, he should not try to find out. Hanjo felt as if the world he had been living in had broken and transformed into a new world, one that was different from the kind and warm reality he'd always known.

Hanjo longed for someone to pat him on the shoulder and say it would be OK. But his father was in jail, his mother had collapsed drunk, and his brother didn't have the guts for it all. He realized in this moment that he was the only one able to comfort himself. He closed his eyes tightly, squeezing back the tears, and hugged himself.

The case of the murder of a high school girl in Isan was closed. Very soon, Hanjo couldn't remember the events—and even if he remembered them, it was all a mess. Too much had happened in too short a time.

During the police investigation, their father had confessed to the crime. He said he had taken Jisoo up to the dam by saying he would take a picture of her and, after molesting her, had pushed her into the water, where she drowned. He stated that there had been no physical torture or coercion during the police investigation.

A battle ensued at the trial. Their lawyer insisted that their father had not visited the reservoir on the day of the incident. He presented a report that described the TV show their father said he had watched that evening. He also secured testimony from a construction-materials dealer who had phoned Malcolm House around nine p.m. and spoken to Jinman. The trial seemed to be tilting in their father's favor.

Then, at the trial's third session, a prosecution witness gave decisive testimony. At around eight p.m. on the day of the incident, he said he had seen their father walking along the riverside in a flustered state. Their father did not deny it. The construction-materials dealer, who had been expected to provide favorable testimony, refused to testify in court, as if burdened by public opinion. In the end, the defense lawyer had to change his innocence plea to a plea for leniency.

The prosecution demanded the death penalty for their father. The judge sentenced him to life imprisonment, defining it as a brutal crime by a beast with a human face who had deliberately lured and killed a minor who needed protection. It was an inevitable sentence, because he already had a criminal record of violence and there was keen public interest. Their father refused to appeal, despite the lawyer's recommendation.

Their mother did not visit their father, even after the sentence was confirmed. She was drunk on the day the dismissal notice came from the school, and when their father's trial began. From then on, she did nothing but pour alcohol, drink from her glass, and fall asleep on the table, the table where they had once sat talking, laughing, and enjoying themselves with a dish of chicken in the middle.

Hanjo sat on his narrow bed and looked through the window at the darkness. Maple branches shook in the wind and scratched at the windowpane. There was a crackling sound from the drain in the wall. Had his father really killed someone? Why had the target been Jisoo? What had he killed her for? If it wasn't true, why hadn't he pleaded innocence?

The moon, gnawed on one side, cast a silver shadow on the clouds. Everything was gone, but here in the darkness, he could still think of his favorite things. For example, spring-afternoon sunshine, cabbage-white butterflies, summer showers, dazzling white canvas, unused tubes of paint, pictures on white walls . . .

He was scared and excited that even after the things that had sustained his life were shattered, he had the ability to imagine beauty inside himself and the desire to create it.

Hanjo

Sunlight cast distorted polygonal shadows on the paint stains covering the floor of the studio. He had overslept. Rothko whined, hungry. Hanjo scratched his pet's head and filled the bowl with food, which Rothko rushed at and gobbled noisily. The dog, who had lost his main caregiver, had matted fur and smelled bad. As his master patted his back, Rothko carefully studied the bloodshot whites of his master's eyes, the bags below them, his lips with their layer of dead skin, and his disheveled hair.

It had been two days since Hanjo's wife disappeared. Life without her was a mess. Hanjo had felt as if he were Orpheus as he had gone down the stone steps to his studio. He couldn't even look at a canvas, let alone paint, even though he stayed in the studio all day. Outside the studio window, everything was as cold and quiet as water in a swimming pool. Loneliness, helplessness, anger, and despondency surged through him constantly. His characteristic stutter, which had not been heard for a long time, had reappeared.

He did not report his wife's disappearance to the police. She hadn't gone missing; she had just left. It was he, not the police, who had to solve this problem. He had to find her, meet her, and soothe her.

His wife's novel revealed her hostility, but it also contained her pity and her love. Maybe his wife was giving him time, an opportunity for him to read the manuscript and contemplate his next steps, to look back and reform himself, to rethink his existence and repent.

Hanjo typed out a text message on his cell phone with clumsy fingers. I want to meet you and talk to you. That was all. Showing resentment or making pathetic appeals wouldn't help. He could make a phone call, but she wouldn't answer. Besides, he had nothing to say if she did pick up.

In the afternoon, he sat on the bench in one corner of the garden. Time on the hill, far from the world, passed slowly. He remembered the little things she did for him and the things he did for her, the gifts they gave each other because they adored one another, their acts of love and devotion.

He had never doubted his wife's love. There was no need or possibility. She was beside him the moment he needed her, and avoided him before he even knew that he wanted to be alone. She never objected to his opinions and didn't blame him for being wrong. She simply persuaded him over time until he changed his mind or found a better way. She made him a better human being without making him feel inferior or guilty about it. She made him feel like a good man, a good husband, a great artist, loved by everyone. Those were things that couldn't be done without love.

But why? Hanjo wanted to ask his wife. *Why do you want to plunge me into the quagmire of scandal and infamy? Why did you not tell me about your anger and hostility, instead of writing a novel?*

His wife would check the text he sent; he knew that. He waited for her reply like a terrorist waiting for a time bomb to explode. He was in a hurry, but he remembered that it took time to understand an incident and solve a problem. He struggled not to think of her while waiting. He was afraid he would resent her, afraid he might get angry.

The sun heated the window frames as the sunset colored the walls. The curved lines of the tiles above the solid pillars were submerged in darkness. His wife's message arrived a little after nine. It said: *Steel Life, tomorrow at 3 p.m.*

Hard, businesslike, and not at all warm. It became clearer that his wife had left him, not disappeared. Surely she could have stayed. Even if she could not love him, she could have continued by his side, even hating him or being mean to him. Some days she might be grateful to him and on other days complain, and so they could have grown old, grown sick, and died together. But she hadn't.

Hanjo decided not to argue when he met her. He would accept whatever she said unconditionally, and plead with her to come back. Then he suddenly recalled his wife's text and felt discouraged, realizing that his thoughts were naive and optimistic.

His wife would neither press him nor accuse him. She would quietly reveal his weak points and let him deal with the pain. He would be unable to refute what she said or excuse himself by saying it was not like that. He would be unable to move on by saying it had been a single mistake in the distant past. He would just have to watch everything fall apart.

Steel Life was a café at the beginning of the riverside path, where they always walked together. The single-story building located on a narrow strip of land between the road and the river was mainly visited by couples who wanted a quiet place. They sold tea and light food during the day, and cocktails in the evening.

He and his wife often stopped there to enjoy brunch or drink coffee on their way out for a walk. Around dusk, a single light would turn on in the house on the other side of the river, and his wife liked to look at the dim glow reflected in the water.

Today, there were very few customers on the riverside terrace in the late afternoon. His wife was sitting at a table close to the water, with a view of the river. It was the seat they always sat at whenever they stopped at the café. In those days, he'd thought that the sunlight, the people, the river, those moments spent facing each other would last forever.

Hanjo struggled with his impatience to say something. If he could, he wanted to confess his mistake and apologize. But he couldn't be sure what he was being accused of. He hesitated for a moment, then opened his mouth.

"That manuscript . . ."

His wife looked at the red roofs of the houses across the river. The wind caught at her scarf, which was printed with a pattern of blue waves, white foam, and seashells. It was a gift he had bought her two years ago, but it was faded because it had often been worn, and the corners were wearing thin. His wife spoke.

"The novel's going to be published next month. It's called *Your Lies About Me*."

There was a persistent sound of a basketball bouncing on the ground. Students wearing green and yellow vests were playing basketball at the riverside sports park.

"That's a good title," he said. "It's all lies to me."

"Even if the title says *lies*, people will try to find the truth. I don't suppose you will, but even if you want to claim libel, you can't, because the title already states that it's all lies."

It was a clever trick. If he admitted that the contents of the book were true, he would admit his disgrace, and if he denied it, there would be no reason for him to urge her not to publish the book. What choice did his wife expect him to make? Either way, the result would be the same.

"You're going to publish a book about us without a single word of discussion?"

He hadn't meant to criticize her, but his voice had risen. He realized this was a mistake, but he couldn't control his feelings. Two glasses of iced coffee were placed on the table by a waiter with oiled hair.

"About us?" his wife said quietly, looking at the drops of water pearling on the glass. "Not at all. It's about me. It's about my man. It's about me loving. At least it's true because it's my story. You're way off the mark."

Hanjo wondered if she was the same person he knew, or thought he knew. Once they had been central to each other, the pillars that supported each other. But now he was nothing but an insignificant stranger.

"It's also my story before it's yours," he said. "I was the one you loved, and I was the one who loved you. Your love includes my privacy."

Hanjo was bitter that he had to use *love* in the past tense. She shrugged instead of answering. She seemed to be indicating that she didn't know what he meant, or that it didn't matter. He felt the danger inherent in his wife's relaxed silence. To be exact, it was the danger that his wife's book contained.

"Don't worry—it's a novel. It's true that it deals with our love, but the main character is a fictional character, not you. No one will know it's you, because there's not a single line about you."

She took off her sunglasses, put them on the table, and leaned forward. It seemed that she intended to show her eyes clearly to him. The only person for whom his wife had written this book was he, not an unspecified number of readers.

"Even if there are perfect secrets, there are no almost perfect secrets. If one person knows, everyone knows. Why do you want to ruin my life after all these years of silence?"

She took a biscuit from her handbag and threw it into the river, as usual. From under the shade of the dark bridge, five or six mother ducks and their ducklings came flocking.

"Your life?" she said. "Come off it! It was my life. I was your maid-servant, lover, nanny, and stand-in. So you're nothing without me. Believing that it's your life is just a fantasy. Don't you know that?"

Hanjo could not deny it. He hadn't forced her, but it was true his wife had been completely sacrificed to his artistic ambition and his desire for her body. She was his absolute helper, supporter, guide, and guardian. In the eyes of the world, she was invisible. Even when he appeared in public, her name and status as his wife were all she had. This was because of her dedication and his selfishness. Even now, it was clear he still cared more about himself without her than about the wife who had left him. But this was a secret between the two of them.

Somehow, he had to soothe his wife. If there was a misunderstanding, he had to solve it, and if there was a mistake, he had to beg. But he had no skills to charm or persuade her. The only thing he could do was mumble like he always did.

"I'm sorry if I gave you a hard time. I didn't realize you were in such pain because of me, my faults, and some unintended mistakes. I sincerely apologize. But I'm just . . . I just loved you."

His wife reached out and stroked his face as he struggled to explain. Fingers like ice cubes touched his bare skin. She spoke in a low voice. "Loving me was not your mistake. I loved you the same way."

"Yes, we're not enemies. I'm the man you loved."

Hanjo took hold of her hand, expecting a little mercy. But his wife pulled her hand away.

"Certainly something has to be done. You're the perpetrator. So I'm the one to be comforted and the one to punish."

At the edge of the river, a frog made a splash in the water. A bird chasing a flying insect flew low over the surface. The shadow of the bird spreading its wings glimmered in the river. The water was murky and had a faint smell.

"I didn't harm you emotionally or ethically," he said. "I didn't look at other women or cheat on you. I respected your advice about my work. But you have written something dangerous that might destroy me. This is cold violence in our peaceful, everyday life with no anger or hatred. It's not like you at all."

His wife did not answer. She didn't seem angry and looked indifferent, as if she didn't know him at all. Had she suddenly decided her lifelong commitment to her husband was a fleeting one? Only then did he feel guilty for taking her love for granted.

Hanjo picked up a small stone from under his feet and threw it into the river. The stone, unable to fly that far, fell to the shore with a clack. He asked, hoping she wouldn't answer, "I don't know what you want—me to leave you, or you to leave me?"

His wife still kept quiet. She seemed to be deliberately staying silent so as not to give him favorable information or relieve his guilt.

"Yes," he said, "let's have a cooling-off period for a while, if you want. I'll move out and you can come home."

She shook her head, because she reckoned it was not fair for her husband to be kicked out. It was obvious what would happen if he left home, since he was humiliated and helpless: he would end up drunk in some shabby room with empty soju bottles rolling around, whining in self-pity. Justifying herself like a wrongly fired farmhand, she shouted, "You stay in the house. You're the one who caused the pain, so I'm the one who has to suffer."

She had found the words to hurt him. She wanted to tell him how immoral he was and how much she hated him. But if she explained *why* she was doing what she was doing, then he would feel better: instead of confused and upset, he would feel at peace knowing that he deserved punishment. She didn't want him to be at peace; that would be a bad sign. So instead she said, "I love you."

Hanjo was puzzled at her words, but he could not ignore a truth that had been proved his entire life. Even if he knew nothing else, he knew this: she loved him. It was as clear as water. He cleared his throat. "I love you, too."

The sun fell on the rippling water and broke into various colors. Shadows of the willow trees by the river cast black stains on the water. She couldn't help laughing. Her husband was a moron.

Suin's office was on the twelfth floor of a tall building in the Seocho-dong Legal Town. When the elevator door opened, Hanjo saw a sign that said HWASEUNG LAW FIRM. The receptionist guided him to the conference room. Suin worked as an office manager at a law firm with three lawyers.

Unable to concentrate on preparing for the bar exam due to his tight finances, Suin eventually failed to become a lawyer. He worked part-time throughout his college years and after he graduated, but then his finances only got worse, and he worked on various building sites. When he was already over thirty, caught between a rock and a hard place due to a series of failures, he started working as a clerk in a small lawyer's office and moved to this current law firm after several transfers.

Suin, as he entered the conference room, looked more like a lawyer than even a top-notch lawyer. Dressed in a wrinkle-free shirt and a high-quality suit, he was in good shape. His face, thanks to the care he took of his skin, made him look three or four years younger than his little brother. It was unimaginable that this was Hanjo's elder brother who had sat opposite him in the kitchen of the small, dark Malcolm House such a long time ago.

On the day they found his brother's name among those accepted for Seoul National University's Law School, Hanjo remembered, the family had sat at the dinner table for the first time in a long time. Come to think of it, it wasn't so long after their father was arrested, but it seemed like a lifetime had passed.

"I have something to tell you," their mother had said.

She had hesitated for a long time before speaking out. Ever since their father had been taken away, she hadn't stopped drinking. Alcohol was their mother's painkiller, sleeping pill, and nutritional supplement. Meanwhile, half her flesh and hair had disappeared. Hanjo seemed to have lost half of his mother.

"I'm going to Jinju," she said, slowly. "I'm going to get my health back by helping Sister Martha."

Their mother was planning to return to the House of Siloam, where she had grown up. Sister Martha, with her thick, horn-rimmed glasses, had founded this orphanage in Korea at the age of twenty-seven, and now she was turning seventy. Their mother produced a bankbook with worn edges and a wooden seal. She laid them on the table. Her gesture was cautious, like that of an independence fighter delivering secret military funds.

"Your father and I saved little by little. You two will be able to stay in Seoul for a while. Suin will have to earn extra money for the tuition, but there's nothing we can do about it."

Mother licked her dry lips. Her complexion was pale, and her cheeks, which were completely hollow, showed veins in places. However, she was not drunk that day, and her eyes were clear.

"Don't worry. We'll get by," Suin said.

His words were intended to reassure their mother, but it sounded like he was snapping at her. Suin, who never showed strong feelings to anyone else, often shot barbed words at his mother. He would never have said that if their mother were drunk. Hanjo thought that his brother was intentionally trying to break his mother's heart.

"I hope you can," his mother said softly, "but how?"

The incandescent light bulb on the ceiling sent out a cold, lonely light. Their mother's skin, as she clenched her fists until it hurt, was as thin as a windowpane, and the backs of her hands were covered with veins. Her cardigan, which had once fit her perfectly, thin though she was, now hung as loose as a sack.

"I won't enroll in Seoul National University," Suin declared. "But don't worry. The rich won't leave me alone."

Their mother wanted them to leave her son alone.

Suin continued, glancing at his father's empty chair, where the armrest was worn smooth, "They obviously know what would happen if they let poor, smart kids go free. They'd rather make them crawl under their feet before they become troublemakers as dissidents, union leaders, or intelligent criminals. They'll look out for me, like throwing scraps to tame a fierce dog. I'm going to take the bait from the rich, and pretend to be obedient."

Hanjo wanted to ask when the whole family could live together again, but he swallowed the words. Even if they could live together, it would be a different life than this, so it was a pointless question. Their mother's lips trembled as she forced out her words.

"If you hate your father, you can blame me. But you shouldn't blame yourself. Just don't do that. There are unlucky people, stupid adults, and . . ."

Their mother pressed her hands to her temples as if she had a migraine. It seemed as if she was trying to think of what to say next, once the pain lessened. She was struggling to find the words to convey her love and reassure her children, words that wouldn't sound absurd or forced and that would give her sons courage to endure others' judgment and carry on with life. Should she say, *I love you—I love you so much, I love you so much, I love you even if it kills me?* This was the truth, but it was inappropriate in the present situation. If she said that, the boys would think she didn't believe they could look after themselves.

Ultimately, the words she wanted to say didn't exist. If they did, she didn't have the ability to find them.

"I can't stand this headache. I must go to my room and lie down. I want to tell you more things that will help you . . ."

The floor creaked as she crossed the room; it wasn't the sound of old wood, but the sound of a weary mother. Hanjo did not blame her.

His mother was not a weak or irresponsible woman. Her burden was so heavy that she just didn't have the energy to take care of her children. When he thought of his mother's vulnerability, his heart broke, and when he thought of his mother's helplessness, he felt pity.

Suin's insight into the rich was surprisingly accurate. Here and there, people were saying that the children of criminals should not be punished for their parents' misdeeds; they should not be abandoned. Teachers and parents stepped forward to support Suin's talent. Everyone in Isan saw Suin as another victim of Lee Jinman's crime.

At the end of winter, the brothers left Malcolm House. Hanjo stared out of the truck window at the place that had once been their home. Red tiles bleached gray, rusted grooves everywhere, the worn-out front-door handle, the yellow-stained porch . . . The tip of his tongue felt a sting, like a spark from an electric wire.

"What's going on? You've suddenly come to see me . . . Did you beat someone up? Or did you get hit?"

Suin pulled back his shirtsleeve and looked at his watch as he spoke. Rather than checking the time, he was indicating that he was busy. Hanjo took out a brown envelope from his backpack. Suin urged him to speak quickly with a flick of his right index finger and middle finger.

"It . . . it's a novel," Hanjo said, flustered. "My . . . my wife wrote it."

The stuttering, which had disappeared more than thirty years ago, had come back. Hanjo's stuttering had begun around the second grade of elementary school and continued until he entered middle school. He did not do it in every conversation but when he tried to avoid saying what he wanted to say or when he was telling a trivial lie. It was particularly severe when talking to specific people, including Suin.

"She wrote a novel?" Suin asked. "Hey, that's something to celebrate. But why did you want to see me? If it's an invitation to a celebration party, you could just have phoned, surely?"

Hanjo stammered some more.

"No . . . no. It's not like that. I . . . I don't want the book to be published."

Suin whistled softly. Whenever Hanjo stuttered as a child, Suin used to whistle—like an experienced dentist whistling during treatment to reassure the patient. The whistling didn't help his stuttering, but it filled the silence between Hanjo's halting words.

"You said it was a novel?" Suin asked calmly. "Why are you so impatient about a fictional story, if it's not an accusation or nonfiction?"

"There's a problem with the story."

"Calm down. Nothing's happened yet. Whatever happens, it won't be a big deal."

"The main character is twenty years older than the woman."

"Who can blame adult men and women for falling in love in this world?"

"The problem is that the main female character is only a high school girl. The main character is a married man, and . . . I'm the main character."

"Really?" Suin asked, leaning forward.

"Ah . . . no. Only in the novel! My wife was a college student when I met her. Or if she wasn't, I believed she was. But . . . but she's turned things around to get the reader's attention."

Suin whistled quietly again. He approached life with the belief that people were no good. Lawyers expected everything to work out, but the office manager had to keep the worst in mind.

As Hanjo said, there was no problem if the story was moderately racy so as to attract the reader's attention. However, from a legal point of view, the story had a low flash point. It was a crime under the Children and Young Persons Act if the woman was younger than nineteen years of age. Depending on the circumstances, statutory rape might be involved. In that case, the sentence could be more than five years' imprisonment or even a life sentence.

Suin didn't say the words out loud. He wanted to reassure his brother. He whistled softly again. Hanjo was irritated.

"Can't you stop whistling? It's really annoying."

Suin stopped and stared at his brother's big body. Now even whistling couldn't soothe his brother's anxiety. He tried to keep calm and said, "There's nothing to worry about. She's not going to sue. If she were going to sue you, she wouldn't have written a novel. The statute of limitations has long expired."

"The problem is not the accusation, but that the novel is being published. The rumors will ruin me."

"Yeah, the bomb is ticking, so we'll have to stop the clock somehow. If we can't stop it, perhaps we can slow it down . . . Let's buy some time by applying for an injunction banning publication. In the meantime, you'll have to figure out what she wants and come to an agreement. Next time, frighten her with a big lawsuit. We'll have to try to stop its publication."

"If that doesn't work?"

"We'll go to the media. Newspapers, broadcasts, the internet, word of mouth . . . We need to mobilize all possible media. We'll have to be prepared for damages at that stage, but we won't be fatally hurt. But we will have to completely slaughter our opponent."

Hanjo didn't want his wife to die. All he wanted was to live *with* his wife. Suin reached over the table and grabbed Hanjo's shoulder.

"The legal battle won't end unless one of you dies. You can't spare your opponent and survive as well. Don't start at all if you're not confident."

Suin stood, plunged his hands into his pockets, and whistled. Then he stopped and shook his head, perhaps recalling Hanjo's scolding. "Sorry, sorry. I didn't even realize I was whistling . . ."

Suin had never taken his brother seriously when they were children, and it was no different now that they had left their hometown. But he did not find Hanjo's plea annoying or unpleasant. He might be cold and arrogant, but he genuinely wanted to help his younger brother this time. "Don't worry," he said, with absolute confidence. "I won't let anything happen to you."

Suin's smile transformed his face, making him seem young and beautiful. It was as if he were a boy again, lighting up Malcolm House. Hanjo felt relieved. Suin had something he didn't have: he could always sense danger and was bold when confronting it. Even as a child, he was not swayed by fear, because he knew danger fed on fear. Hanjo wanted to believe his brother was still like that.

Soojin

Living as the son of a murderer was not easy, but it was not impossible. Over the years, Hanjo had learned the rules of living as a murderer's son without anyone teaching him. He knew how much he should talk about himself to someone he liked, whom he shouldn't love, what he should do, what he shouldn't want . . .

When people asked about his childhood, Hanjo would say vaguely that it had been normal, nothing special. People might think he was hiding something, but they didn't pry. In this way, he was able to live a relatively normal life. Yet when the sound of the clock ticking was unusually clear at night, the past held him by the ankles and would not let go.

When the two brothers arrived at Seoul Station after leaving their hometown, they were greeted by homeless people with hollow eyes and shabby clothes. These people were the victims of the IMF's sharp claws. Newspapers and TV channels reported almost daily arrests and suicides of incompetent officials and corrupt entrepreneurs. All were simultaneously victims and criminals, victims and perpetrators.

After living for a month in the students' study room, the brothers secured a semiunderground room with mold on the walls. At night, they huddled together in the cold room without light and cursed the darkness that kept them locked in. Softly, they told themselves this was the price they had to pay to become better people.

The following spring, Hanjo was accepted into an art college. He had considered skipping university altogether and joining the army—the brothers didn't have money for the tuition fees anyway—but Suin convinced him to get a degree. Suin said he would earn the tuition by working as a live-in tutor.

The entrance exam involved drawing foil trays, screws, hangers, and staplers with twelve colored pencils, distinguishing between cold and heat. Hanjo used only black pencils to depict the objects in detail, and shading to express heat and cold. When asked by the interviewer why he didn't use color, he replied, "Color changes from time to time, so form is important; form is the essence of things." It was a perverse answer, intended to produce a fail, but he was accepted instead.

Although he was able to pay the tuition fees with the money Suin gave him, Hanjo was unable to do what other college students did. He never got a driver's license, went on group dates, enjoyed festivals, or had a regular girlfriend. All he did throughout college was teach as a part-time instructor at a cram school and offer private tutoring lessons. He found this existence difficult, and he lived day to day by dreaming of a better future, even though he didn't know what kind of future that would be.

Suin, who had become a resident tutor with a family, became thinner and thinner every time they met, until by the end of the summer vacation, he had become a completely different person from the one Hanjo had known before. His white skin had turned pale, and his cheeks were hollow as if they had been gnawed. His eyes bulged, and something shady flashed in them. His face, which expressed a wish to escape from his painful past and a longing for a new life without shame, was as fierce as a boxer's who ran away with a swollen face as soon as the bell rang for the last round after eleven rounds.

Somehow, they never mentioned Howard House. Hanjo couldn't even remember its structure. He had erased it from memory, in case he recalled the sorrow buried in his heart. It was only after he stopped imagining Jisoo's face and Haeri's smile that he felt like he had shaken off the past. At the same time, the relief was tempered by a sense of futility, as though he had lost his bearings together with his memories.

The following summer, Hanjo took a leave of absence from school and enlisted for his military service. When he left the guard post at dawn, the stars above his head glittered in the dark as if they were fragments of his shattered life. Precious people had disappeared, important things had turned into nothing, and good memories were tinged with horror. Secrets and lies settled in his body like the ashes of old pain.

Hanjo remembered his mother, who had become the wife of a murderer, with more heartbreak than his father. It was after Hanjo was born that his mother first fell into depression. It began with mild symptoms. In the autumn, there was insomnia and lethargy. After that, his mother began to drink. Then she needed prescriptions for sleeping pills, and by the time Hanjo entered elementary school, she would put sleeping pills in her mouth and wash them down with a glass of beer mixed with soju. Nevertheless, his parents tried to accept each other's weaknesses and were faithful to each other.

When spring came, his mother's symptoms became lighter. In May, she mostly lived in the garden, where flowers bloomed all day. His parents were like a friendly pair of parrots. His father became more talkative when he mocked his mother with a silly voice, and they kept looking at each other, as if they were trying to show him how much they had loved one another before he was born. However, as autumn deepened, his mother would sink into depression again. Like a snail hiding in its shell, she would retreat and drink.

After a while, his mother left to work in an orphanage run by Sister Martha to help her quit drinking. She returned two years later. Hanjo didn't know how hard it was to quit drinking, but he felt that his mother, who had shaken off her addiction, was strong. These were the best days of his childhood. She prepared his breakfast, stayed up late watching TV with him, and waited on the porch for him to come home at night. It was nothing special, but those ordinary days were happier than any other time before or after.

By the time Jisoo disappeared, his mother was addiction-free and active. After Jisoo disappeared, though, his mother fell into a swamp. Hanjo wanted to avoid her eyes. They were eyes filled with contempt for the world and resentment toward her children. It occurred to him that his mother hated them.

One night, he couldn't fall asleep. There was a light glow on the stairwell from the kitchen downstairs. He heard the sound of water from the faucet, the noise of bowls clashing, and the regular creak of the floor. And, quiet yet sharp, his parents' voices . . .

His father usually hung around the kitchen while his mother washed the dishes. He also usually got up from the table and walked around the house when he was trying to persuade his family of something. What was his father trying to convince his mother of?

Hanjo lay on the floor and listened. He couldn't hear very much, because his father kept his voice low. He could hear certain words: *detectives, photographs, hate, college, trial, happiness,* and also his mother's voice talking about Siloam and Sister. Suin's name came up as well. He waited for one of them to speak his name, but they didn't.

Afterward, Hanjo could not guess what his parents had said that night. It was certain they had mentioned Jisoo. Perhaps his father had confessed the crime to his mother and asked for forgiveness? It was unclear whether his mother had forgiven his father, but it was clear she had turned a blind eye to his faults. Perhaps she thought it was not her responsibility to judge her husband.

Their discussion that night revolved around not what they had done but what they had to do. Under the incandescent light in the kitchen, his parents tried hard to predict the fate threatening them and to prepare for it. His heart ached when he thought about his parents desperately discussing their sons' futures without having time to regret and atone for their crimes, without blame or anger for the husband's sins, without grieving for their broken lives.

Once their father was arrested, their mother shut herself away in their house to protect her sons from the disgrace of being labeled a murderer's kids. Was this the future their father and mother had desperately planned that night? Far from being bright and hopeful, it was a dangerous future in which no new promises were made and old ones were broken.

In the chilly night air at the DMZ, Hanjo frequently recalled his father's stubby eyebrows and his mother's thin, trembling lips. He resented them, but he couldn't hate them. He felt no anger at his father for succumbing to evil. It was as if it had nothing to do with him.

Now Hanjo had to pretend not to know his parents—like Peter, who denied Jesus three times. As if they had never given birth to them or sat together at the dinner table, laughing. He suddenly felt cold at the thought that he was the only one who felt sorry for himself. He fastened the top button of his military coat and pulled his chin down.

He wanted to get drunk.

Poverty was not just an idea; it was accompanied by physical suffering. Cold and hunger, odors and filth. Hanjo comforted himself by thinking it was good to have small ambitions and not be too optimistic about the future. His wish was just to live a normal life like a normal person. Such a trifling, humble wish.

He graduated from college, but no opportunities awaited him. He was already over twenty years old and still lived in a small basement room and worked as an assistant instructor at an academy. As he painted in his unheated room late at night, using leftover pigments that his students had used and discarded, he reflected that his life was as useless as a dried-up, crushed tube of paint.

The paints he picked up were all somber and dull colors. He believed that bright, shiny, and vivid hues were fundamentally out of character for him. As he warmed his frozen fingers under his armpits and studied the sketches he had painted only lightly to save supplies, he felt proud of himself: it felt like a miracle he was able to paint at all. He liked the smell of thinner, which made him feel dizzy, the smell of paint mixed with emulsifiers, and the elasticity of the tight canvas.

There was no need to fight memories while painting; there was no past in the pictures that occupied him—no killer father, no drunk mother, and no dead Jisoo. Through the magical power of color and form, he escaped from pain.

He was still young; his life was not yet a failure. He wanted to paint how irregular the world was with conflicting colors and lines, and how fragile relationships could be. He wanted to express how hitting rock bottom in life was nothing special. But becoming an artist was a different matter from being a painter. It needed something more than talent: the right workshop, the money to buy paint and materials, and the time to concentrate on working . . . It was not that there were no artists who had suffered from poverty and still showed extraordinary talent. The problem was that Hanjo had no faith in his talent. He always feared that poverty would wipe out even his humble abilities. It made him afraid to paint.

He needed a hill to lean on: Hamil Hill. In May, it was covered in green, and at night, it exposed its soft body to the sky. There were only terrible memories left, but Howard House was still a source of joy, frustration, aspiration, and sorrow. He didn't know why, but he felt he could paint there. Howard House was his muse, like Giverny for Monet, Arles for Van Gogh, and Fontainebleau for Millet.

Hanjo recklessly called his old art teacher from high school. There was no one else to call and ask about life. The teacher did not ask how he had been. Hanjo asked if Malcolm House was still empty.

"The Malcolm and Howard Houses haven't been lived in since you left," the teacher told him.

He added that Jisoo's parents had died in a car accident the year after Hanjo left. Hanjo felt guilty for not knowing this.

The teacher seemed hesitant to explain why the houses were empty. It was obvious to him that no one would want to live in a house where such terrible things had happened. But for Hanjo, who was broke and had nowhere to go, the terrible house was his only possible destination. He forced himself to ask, "Could I go back to Malcolm House, by any chance? I could pay a little rent every month, even if it's not much. I can do simple repairs or maintenance myself."

The teacher said that they were still having trouble finding managers for the missionary housing. "Some people came, but couldn't make it through the full moon," he said, adding that he would talk to the principal and try to get the foundation's management committee to agree to the hiring.

Two weeks later, the teacher called him.

"The committee has made its decision. Empty houses deteriorate fast, so they need someone to manage them. Stay at Malcolm House to begin with, then move to Howard House as soon as you can. Don't worry about the rent. I'm glad we've found the right person."

The expression *right person* sounded as if the committee had been poring over his qualifications. The reason why he was the *right person* was probably because he was the son of a former caretaker. Ten years later, the status of the past remained as clear as a tattoo carved on someone's body.

Nevertheless, it was above all fortunate. He didn't know how long it would last, but he had a house to live in. Even if it had long been empty and was old, it would be fine if he repaired it. He might be able to find teaching jobs in a couple of art academies in downtown Isan. It would take time, but he would be able to continue painting.

He opened his suitcase in the small room and began folding his smelly clothes.

Malcolm House was located in a dip in the hillside, barely standing up, like an old man who had reached the end of his life. The fence was old, the paint was peeling off, and there were scratches on the outer walls. A rusty weather vane turned squeaking on the roof. The ruined garden and the caved-in roof felt like his own life.

Everyone who had lived in this house had vanished. By the time she had returned from the House of Siloam, his mother did not know who she was. This was because of alcohol-induced dementia that lasted for four years. His mother's death was not surprising; she hadn't been truly alive since that fateful summer.

His mother's cremated remains were buried near Seoul. He had thought his father would find his mother when he was released, whenever that happened. But his father was never to find her. The following winter, acute pneumonia meant that Jinman did not see another spring.

Hanjo flopped down on the gray, bleached wooden chair on the porch. A slightly short left back leg made the chair rock and squeak. Perhaps his father's slipped disk might have been due to this shaky chair. Hanjo pulled a rusty key out of the mailbox hanging from a porch pillar and opened the front door. It was a door made of zelkova wood that his father had decorated with carved black wedges.

Now he would live on this hill and have this terrible house. Its broken parts would be rebuilt, and damaged parts repaired. The weak ground would be reinforced, and peonies, crape myrtles, daffodils, and irises would be planted along the garden boundary. And he would paint pictures. He had that talent. And even if it wasn't so, he had no choice but to believe it was true.

He was hungry when evening came, but he couldn't cook so much as ramen, because the electricity and gas had been cut off. Hanjo went up to the second floor with a candle. When he turned the rusted clasp and opened the window, the wind blew in. The moonlit hillside led up to Howard House. Bats nesting in the rafters squeaked.

Howard House, with all its lights out, was like a grave wrapped in darkness and silence. At that moment, there was a sound like a nail being pulled, and the second-floor window of Howard House burst open. The moon shone sharply on the windowpane. The large cedar tree beside the house cast a shadow over the window, but as the moon came out from behind the clouds, the window was revealed more clearly—then, almost at the same moment, it was closed from the inside. It was as if Hanjo could look inside the sky-blue casement window and see the high back of the bright-brown chair, the white sheets on the bed, the glossy wardrobe, and Jisoo's colorful summer clothes hanging inside it. The excited voices of the Howard House family seemed to come alive again.

Then a gray figure glimmered beyond the window. Although it was difficult to make out, it looked like a human figure. Judging from the way it wavered near the top of the window frame, he assumed it was someone tall, with a long neck.

Jisoo? Hanjo was horrified; he whispered her name. It was a preposterous idea. Jisoo had liked the window, but how could a dead girl come back to her room?

Beyond the moonlit window was darkness. He raised the candle and shouted, "Is anybody there?"

There couldn't have been. To the best of his knowledge, no one lived in Howard House. All the people who had once lived in the house had left and could not return. Nevertheless, he could not forget the silhouette he had just seen.

Was it a picture of an actress that someone had pasted on a windowpane? Or was it a shadow cast by the moonlight on the glass? If so, how had it disappeared in an instant? No, he had seen nothing.

When Dr. Howard went back to Atlanta and left Howard House empty, rumors of ghosts had circulated among the local children. Hanjo had argued with them, saying, "There is no such thing as a ghost, and even if they exist, they don't hurt people." But now he wondered whether the absurd rumor was true. A ghost was living in Howard House. Someone who loved the house so much, they couldn't leave even after they died.

Hanjo stuck his head out of the window. The sky was colored silver, and clouds billowed like waves. The wind, like a whip, forced the grass to lie down on one side to sleep. At last, he felt relief that he had come home. He would start cleaning up as soon as dawn came.

One fine day, Hanjo wandered down the hill into the city. The city was lively, and people passed him on the streets, dressed in bright clothing.

Among the store owners, he saw familiar faces. They seemed older or more tired than before, and some even limped. Hanjo didn't talk to them, and they didn't even pretend to know him. He was relieved that no one recognized him, but his relief was made bitter by the fact that he was completely isolated from others.

Three days later, the electricity and water supply were reconnected to Howard House. Hanjo carried his two suitcases up the hill. Nine of the twelve bulbs in the old chandelier did not work; the filaments were broken. On the wall was the picture of Howard House that he had painted in school.

The Howard House in the painting looked like a sailing boat passing through a huge storm, swamped by wind and rain. The wind blowing from the left side was borrowed from Turner's work. Paintings such as *Snow Storm: Steam-Boat off a Harbour's Mouth*; *The Fighting Temeraire, Tugged to Her Last Berth to Be Broken Up*; and *Dutch Boats in a Gale*, which showed dignity in the face of disaster, seemed to be meaningful in his humble life.

Howard House was unfamiliar, like a work painted by someone else, not himself. He even had the feeling that the painting itself had died a long time ago and that it was only a ghost of itself now. The wind shook the windows loudly and shouted, *Lee Hanjo, why are you here? You left as someone who would never come back.*

The next day, it rained, and he cleaned the house. In the afternoon, after work, the rain stopped and the sun shone. Long-forgotten landscapes came to mind, as if the scales that had been covering Hanjo's eyes had peeled off. Jisoo's upstairs room, the first-floor hall, the study that echoed with Beethoven's piano sonatas, Haeri's rapid steps up the steep stairs, and the love of a couple who had peeked through the curtains one summer night—all these memories surging like a slow, breaking wave.

Once every few days, a mailman came, and once a month, a man came, read the gas meter, and left again. They wore blue uniforms and were silent. Through the ceiling, you could hear the drooping branches of the cedar brush against the roof. If the weather was good tomorrow, Hanjo would trim those branches.

The house was like an old man moaning about his aches and pains. All the time, water pipes leaked, drains clogged, rust stains peered through peeling paint. Hanjo wrestled with the decay, picking up a wrench and hammer and fighting back. One day, he was forced to call a repairman when a blocked drain proved too much for him. As the repairman tightened the pipe with a wrench, he said, "It's really good to have someone living in Howard House. After all, no matter how nice a place is, if no one lives there, it's a haunted house."

He was short but sturdy, and wore a working jacket with a woolly collar. Hanjo's father's face overlapped with the repairman's kind expression. His father replacing water pipes in Howard House, his father mending the roof, his father applying cement to the broken stairs with his hands, his father hammering away at the broken window frames . . .

"If a ghost lives in a haunted house, does that mean I'm a ghost?"
His joke made the repairman smile, screwing up his tiny eyes.

Hanjo did not pay attention when Kim Soojin first set up her easel on
the nearby hillside from which Howard House was clearly visible. He
assumed she was a member of an amateur art club who did not know
the house was haunted, and he was also busy working on a house that
had been left empty for such a long time. She came every morning for
more than a week and left just before sunset. It wasn't until a few days
later that he properly noticed her presence.

That day, the sky was overcast. She came up the hill a little after
nine with her materials. She set up her easel on the side of the road to
escape the wind, fixed her canvas, laid out her brushes, pencils, and
paints, twisted up her messy hair, stuck a pencil in to hold it firm, curled
up, and lit a cigarette. Its smoke swirled away in the wind.

Hanjo strolled down the hill. He wasn't sure if the object of his
curiosity was the woman or her painting, but suddenly he wanted to see
them up close. The woman fixed her eyes on Howard House and kept
moving her brush, as if determined to ignore him as he approached.

The Howard House in her painting looked much more dilapidated
than it really was, due to the antique colors she used and her shading.
The porch steps had collapsed, the roof was drooping, and the porch's
pillars were tilted. The windows were covered with dust, and the door-
posts were rotting at the bottom.

"This roof . . . Don't you think it's drooping too much?" She kept
her eyes on the painting as she pointed at the canvas with the tip of her
brush. The branches of the cedar tree, bent by a strong wind, hung over
the dusk-colored roof.

"A little bending isn't a bad thing," he said. "The flow of time is
made clear."

"That's why the house looks so foolish."

She coughed as if she were holding back laughter. There was no sign of her earlier concentration, or of her somber, single-minded focus. It was a sudden change of emotions that might or might not be real.

Kim Soojin gave the impression of being healthy even though she was very slender, perhaps because of her shoulders, which were angular, as if she were carrying bricks on them. There was an energy to her. The arms under the fluttering sleeves of her dress were tanned by the sun and looked firm. Her face reminded him of someone, but he couldn't remember who it was.

"I think I've seen you somewhere . . . Have we met before?"

"I often hear that," she said, dryly. "It must be because I look normal."

Hanjo apologized as if he had made a big mistake, but she didn't seem to think he was rude. Dark clouds were gathering far away in the western sky.

"There's a picture of Howard House hanging on the ground floor, isn't there?" she asked suddenly.

"Why, you seem to know as much about Howard House as someone who's been inside."

"You don't have to go in to find out. I saw it in an old newspaper."

Hanjo grew playful. "Then do you know that the house is haunted? I saw something like a ghost in the window on the second floor the night I arrived. I don't know if I really saw it or just imagined it."

Her brief smile seemed both to accept what he said and to find it ridiculous. The house wasn't haunted; he had simply seen a ghost. He was disappointed because he had expected her to say that ghosts didn't exist, and to insist what he'd seen was an illusion or a delusion.

The cool breeze began to bring a smell of rain. Hanjo said, "It's going to pour. You'd better come and shelter inside the house for a while. Otherwise, you'll be soaked."

She quickly wiped her brush, folded the easel, and followed him up the hill. The rain had started and began to thicken as they reached the porch. Once inside, she looked around the house, shaking her slightly damp hair.

"There's the picture, but there's no ghost," she said.

"I don't know. It'll show up after nightfall . . ."

Rain fell in torrents outside the window. Lightning flashed, as if ripping open the black sky, and thunder shook the windows.

She spread out her sketchbook and drew lines with pencils of different thickness and hardness. Horizontal and vertical lines intersected like a grid. Sharp diagonals and slanting lines made the page look as if it had been slashed by a knife. The sound of pencils brushing over paper mingled with the sound of rain outside the window. He watched quietly as she swept the thick, soft pencil leads down from the top of the paper, left to right, carefully and without hesitation, then sharpened the pencil tips on fine sandpaper. The sketchbook was filled with lines and geometric figures that randomly intertwined at different angles.

The rain stopped when the wall clock showed eight o'clock. She went to the washbasin and washed her fingers, which were shiny with graphite.

Hanjo remembered reading somewhere about art therapy, where drawing lines was an effective treatment of hyperactivity syndrome. Did she also take refuge in painting in order to endure harsh pain or sadness? If so, what memory was she trying to escape from?

She was unlike anyone he had ever met before. She chatted without hesitation, then fell silent for a long time, laughed freely, then quickly turned cold like a stranger. All her expressions felt simultaneously feigned and sincere.

She reminded him of an actress with dozens of masks, constantly changing her face. The unpredictability was exciting, giving life to their conversations, but it demanded much energy from him. Confronted with such a wonder, Hanjo often forgot who he was. He was willing to obey her and surrender to her beauty. He wanted to let her control, manipulate, and ruin him at will.

They wandered aimlessly through sunlit streets. When they were tired of walking, they sat at a café terrace and looked at each other. Sometimes, they stood side by side, examining a picture they had taken turns drawing in a single sketchbook, and giggled. There was a pure happiness in these childish, simple acts.

They talked incessantly, about the city, about the house, about things that had changed and not changed. But they remained silent about the past, as if they had promised not to ask each other about their childhoods. Hanjo did not talk about his father, and she also ignored his history. Sometimes, when they talked about his school days, he gave only short answers, then blatantly refused to tell more straightforward stories or answer questions. He was one of those people who hid his pain because he didn't believe he would be comforted if he showed his wounds.

For them, only the other was important, and only the present was clear. Like figures cut from a picture book, their backgrounds and surrounding characters were absent.

"Have you ever seen a dead body?"

She asked this one afternoon while opening a can of beer. The aluminum tab lifted and gas leaked out with a hiss. He looked at her with the eyes of a frightened boy from ten years ago. Jisoo's wet hair and bare feet came to mind.

"A girl I knew . . ."

"What girl?"

Hanjo wasn't sure whether to continue talking or not. If he did, how much would he have to tell? The air smelled of rusting iron. He drained his remaining beer and said, "She was eighteen years old. She was found dead in a river five days after she disappeared."

His voice was serious and his story sounded like the bitter truth, but she didn't seem to believe him entirely. It was true that there was something he hadn't said: that he never felt free from responsibility for Jisoo's death.

"Did you love her?"

As if eager not to miss his answer, she leaned toward him, her shoulders hunched like a cat's, as if she were obliged to listen because she loved him. He felt as if he were confessing.

"Perhaps it was what is called first love? Or maybe not, I don't know . . . I did love her, but I hated her just as much. Either way, if it weren't for her, I wouldn't have started painting."

His words, a mixture of truth and lies, sounded vague even to himself. He couldn't figure out why he was telling her something he had never told anyone, and what he himself had forgotten. If he had to name a reason, it must be because he had been waiting to share his dark memories with her. If their pain looked similar, it could confirm their love.

There had been no progress in Hanjo's work. The white, empty square of canvas enclosed him like a prison cell. He didn't know what to draw or how to draw it. The act of creating something seemed to be beyond him. At some point, he grew terrified his brush might contaminate the pure white canvas.

If he painted like someone saddled with debt, he would create only dead paintings, lifeless, meaningless, and devoid of beauty. Every sunset, a deep sense of futility and helplessness flooded over him.

Still, she wondered what he was drawing, and wanted to see his paintings. But he had no paintings to show her, finished or in progress. He was just a poor would-be artist who could not break into the market, a good-for-nothing without even the slightest will to paint. He could not stand it any longer and confessed his incompetence to her.

"I have a little problem."

"What kind of problem?"

"I don't know why, but I can't paint. Or rather, perhaps I should say that I know the reason but don't know the solution."

The light from the window cast a distorted rectangle on the floor. She answered firmly, "Don't worry—you'll find a solution. I'm sure I'll love that painting."

Her voice, certain without reason, evoked in him an instinctive wish to believe her. Hanjo quietly laid his hand on her breast. He could feel her heart beating inside her ribs, like a small red bird flapping its wings. When he moved his hand down to her waist, she twisted away. The thought of being rejected by her opened a deep chasm in his breast.

She had not considered herself his model at the beginning. But there was not a moment when he wasn't drawing her. Whether they were facing each other without a word or they were talking, they focused on each other's expressions and gestures, then drew one another in a sketchbook or on a sheet of paper.

Then one day, she stopped drawing and posed quietly for him. She was dressed in a white shirt and jeans, but he unthinkingly drew a nude figure. She looked at the picture and said, "That's a fake. I never posed for you nude. How can that be me?"

He hurriedly apologized, saying it had been unintentional and that he was sorry. She went home without replying. The next day, she still looked angry. "Don't try to paint me according to your own imagination," she said. "You have to draw me the way I look so that you can show me as I really am."

"Yes, just as you are, as you look . . . I can draw that. I want to."

A few days later, she posed nude in front of his canvas. Something was glimmering between her white thighs. Was it a sunset shadow? A paint splatter? He looked more closely. Cut marks, which seemed to have been made with sharp instruments on multiple occasions, were intertwined like red cords—thick, thin, short; long scars and serrated ones; white, red, gray, or pink wounds; hard keloid marks and healed cuts along the veins . . .

It wasn't only the thighs. Dozens of scars of different shapes, colors, and sizes were revealed everywhere. Hanjo felt neck-wrenching spasms. He didn't dare stare at such horror. He wanted to look away from her body, her wounds. Even if he longed to ask what had happened, he was afraid to hear the answer.

But fear soon turned into intense curiosity. It was not just his desire to know but a sense of duty that compelled him. Perhaps she had been abused by someone close to her as a child. Was that why she never talked about her family?

"Who was it? Who did this to you?" His voice broke.

She looked at him with calm eyes. "Nobody. I did it."

He felt as if he had been hit in the chest with a shovel. Foolish questions flickered through his mind. Whether the tool was a knife, an awl, a weapon specifically designed for self-harm. Whether she was afraid when she cut herself, whether it hurt, how she endured it if it did hurt. Whether she was still cutting herself . . .

He resigned himself to never knowing the answers.

"Now I'm OK," she said. "I'm fine now."

He stroked her shoulders and thighs with his fingertips. He didn't want to ask her why. He would simply listen to her when she wanted to talk. If she didn't want to talk, it didn't matter if he never heard. No matter how horrific her past was, he couldn't help loving her.

He didn't know if this was an absurdly naive belief. It could have been an excuse allowing him to turn a blind eye to the problem and escape. Nevertheless, he did not want to hear the details. Maybe it was a deadly fact that would tear them apart, and everything would be fine as long as it stayed hidden, like a mine that wouldn't explode unless you stepped on it.

An idea flashed through his mind, so quick he almost didn't catch it. He wanted to draw her. He was sure he *had* to draw her. He even thought he had lived his whole life only for this chance. The wounds were a pattern drawn by her soul, age rings that recorded her life. By drawing her scars, he would soothe her pain, and the painting would heal someone else's wounds. It was a shallow idea, but he was also convinced it would succeed commercially.

Hanjo started sketching. Regret that his life so far had been only a shell and hope that real life was starting arose simultaneously. Now he seemed to have become the person she wanted, someone who clearly knew what to draw and how to draw it.

Her concentration as a model was amazing. She never grumbled or grew irritated, nor did she complain of pain. She had the patience to maintain the same posture for hours, and the concentration to remember her previous pose. Hanjo focused on using her whole body's fine muscles and her messy hair to express her essence.

The time he spent painting her gave him a feeling of ecstasy, as if they were making love. Every landscape was seen anew, and every object held a vivid essence. He felt like Lazarus, emerging alive from the grave.

Sometimes, when boring news appeared on the television, Hanjo talked about moments that he could recall without sorrow. The park where he'd gone on a picnic when he was in elementary school, a model monkey wearing a uniform guarding the entrance to the zoo, and the smell of animals as he passed by a rusty fence . . .

She talked about her mother and father, who had died one after another when she was a child, and her uncle's house. She was scolded by her teacher for not doing her homework because she helped her stubborn cousins study.

"When I was in the third year of middle school," she said, "I suddenly realized that I couldn't remember my mom and dad's faces. No matter how hard I tried, I couldn't recall them. At that moment, I thought I had become an adult."

He understood what she said as clearly as if the words were his.

"I never tried to remember my father's face. It was not that I couldn't remember it but that I didn't want to remember it. I didn't get close to anyone . . . because I didn't want to say that."

A thick tendon bulged in Hanjo's neck. Perhaps because of the tragic events he'd experienced as a child, he had difficulty forming relationships with others. It was a complicated and slow process for him to get acquainted with strangers, and most relationships ended before they even started. But he wanted to tell her his painful past. He spat out his words as if they were clots of blood stuck in his throat.

"My father was a murderer. He killed someone when I was in my second year of high school, and then gave himself over to death."

He spoke calmly about the rubber shoes his father had worn on Hanjo's first and last jail visit after his father was arrested. All the time he was talking, he felt a mixture of anxiety that their relationship would be broken and expectation that she would understand everything.

She set the TV remote she was holding down on the table and, after a moment of silence, asked, "You believe he did it?"

Hanjo could not understand the question. Which part of his story did she want to hear more precisely? About the father murdering an eighteen-year-old girl from a neighboring house, dumping her body in a dam, and being arrested before his son's very eyes after acting as if nothing had happened? Hanjo blinked his eyes and asked, "What else can I think if I don't think that?"

"He was your father, wasn't he? Suppose someone else was the real culprit, and the police arrested him instead, as a scapegoat. Haven't you ever thought that? Not once?"

Part of Hanjo was eager to believe her argument. If what she said was true, he was afraid of the other question that would inevitably arise. Who was the culprit, if not his father?

"Father confessed, the prosecution presented evidence, and the court ruled. All the social systems and functions worked properly. Why would the police have falsely accused him?"

"People are stupid. They pretend not to see the obvious or are afraid to speak. Then when the police, the media, or politicians say something, they believe it without a doubt. That's how Uncle Malcolm became a murderer."

Her voice and manner were so natural that Hanjo replied without thinking, explaining that things didn't change even if you thought about them, that you couldn't restore faith in what had been discredited, that you couldn't undo the past. Then, when he had finished speaking, he felt that the air inside the room had changed subtly.

"Uncle Malcolm?" he whispered. "Did you just say Uncle Malcolm?"

Near her collarbone, a blue vein appeared to swell, the vein that holds back tears and gives the body strength. Hanjo remembered a sunny afternoon in the Howard House garden—the two-pronged vein on the neck of a child who fell from the railing and burst into tears. Jisoo's heels, colored green by crushed grass.

"You . . . are you Haeri? No, it can't be. You're Soojin, aren't you?"

Hanjo turned toward the old family portrait on the piano, his surprise mingling with his embarrassment. There was the girl in the picture, her protruding forehead, low nose, chubby cheeks, and angular chin. A playful, smiling face without her front teeth . . .

In this moment, the fog between them lifted and everything became clear. Hanjo stared at the woman in front of him. She didn't avoid his gaze. After a while, she said, "After my mom and dad died, I was adopted by my uncle. He even changed my name to help me forget the shock quickly. It wasn't a bad idea. It was my mother's family name, not that of a complete stranger."

Only then did Hanjo vaguely understand her life and her wounds. Her growth from child to adult was not natural but shaped by tragedy. How could he not understand what this girl had gone through, having suffered such cruelty and tragedy at the age of eight? The very thought was enough to make him want to weep. He felt sorry for Haeri and felt pity for Soojin.

Carefully setting the pain of the tragedy aside, they did not resent or reprimand each other. They simply asked and told each other about that summer as if they were trying to find lost fragments of memory one by one and make a sculpture. She said *Hamlet* had been lying open on her sister's desk at a particular page.

"I've read that page hundreds of times. Even now, when I close my eyes, I can recall the lines where the queen tells of Ophelia's death:

'There is a willow grows aslant a brook,

That shows his hoar leaves in the glassy stream;

There with fantastic garlands did she come

Of crow-flowers, nettles, daisies, and long purples . . . but long it could not be

Till that her garments, heavy with their drink,

Pull'd the poor wretch from her melodious lay

To muddy death.'"

She recited Queen Gertrude's lines in a gentle voice. He felt joy at sharing a part of his life with her, a fragment of his soul. It was an intimacy like that of family meeting after long being parted. Now he could understand her pain and felt sure he shared it.

The clear white moon hung from the window frame like a cut-out. The black branches of the cedar stretched out vigorously, and the pointed leaves rustled. A gray feral cat passed silently over the lawn.

They usually worked all through the afternoon, while the light was good. Hanjo was eager to capture the pure curves of her body. It was not a compulsion to draw but a pure desire to draw. So far, his paintings seemed not to have been paintings at all, and she felt like the first and last painting in the world.

As the sun went down, he let his weary eyes and stiff hands relax, and she stretched her rigid muscles. Then they shared hard, salty spaghetti. The sweet addiction of perfect isolation fascinated them.

One day, it was late evening. The temperature had dropped sharply as raindrops scattered. When the soft raindrops touched it, the ground emitted dry heat like a sigh. After nearly two hours of nudity, Haeri shivered. Hanjo put his hooded shirt over her shoulders.

The back of the leather sofa, which had gone off-kilter and hardened like a tree stump, creaked. He poured hot coffee from the pot and handed it to her. Steam rose from the cup like a mist. Their faces were close enough to touch. Each could feel the slightest tremor of the other's breath.

"I love you," Hanjo said.

Hanjo wanted her to say she loved him. But her lips were frozen. His throbbing heart drove all the blood in his body to one place. Haeri replied reluctantly, "I love you, too."

She didn't seem to be entirely lying, but she also didn't seem sincere. He had already stopped at that point a few times before. Each time, he felt he couldn't read her mind. Maybe it meant that she needed more time rather than that she was refusing his love. But how much time? He didn't want to be indecisive anymore.

He kissed her. He fingered each of her wounds like an old scholar reading a book word by word, as if in that way they could understand the pain they each held within them, as if they were giving birth to new flesh on the stained scars.

"Wait, stop," Haeri said. "Stop."

He hesitated over whether to stop or not, but thought of an excuse, words that could hide the shame of being rejected and asking for forgiveness. A phrase popped out of his mouth, the silly words men say in such situations: "I love you. You love me, too, don't you?"

His plea for love sounded like a threat to her. Haeri didn't answer. She didn't realize he took her silence for a passive acquiescence or a tacit consent.

Anyone can dream of becoming rich and earning a fortune; imagining is not a crime. However, stealing other people's money or robbing a bank is a crime. No matter how much someone may love another, forcing them to do something they dislike is the same. But, in this moment, only the fact that he wanted her was filling his body and soul.

"I love you. I love you. Tell me you love me."

This was all he could say. That was all he wanted to hear. No matter how harsh fate was, no matter how persistent the past was, he thought he could overcome them with that one word.

Haeri pushed him away. He felt a sharp pain from the marks her fingernails left on his chest. Her refusal felt like a denial of his entire existence. An uncontrollable rage arose within him. It wasn't at her; it was his anger at himself for being rejected by her. Unthinkingly, he pushed Haeri down on the sofa and muttered, "Why not?"

At that moment, his father came to mind. He knew now why she had rejected him: he was the son of a murderer, a man who had killed her sister. This was his punishment. The relief he felt at being free of his past and being understood by her had created the illusion that he was forgiven.

He hugged her so tightly it hurt. At that, the strength drained from her tense body and a gleam of resignation flashed through her eyes. He kissed her eyelids. He felt convinced that he loved her more perfectly than he had loved anything else at any point in his life.

Only later did he regret what he'd done, hundreds or thousands of times, realizing that he should have stopped. He also realized how self-centered and violent his behavior was that day. But at that moment, it was all about loving her.

Now he would love her even more deeply, even just to be forgiven for his mistake. And he would draw her. Of all women, this one woman was proof of life, a woman who enabled the world to be recognized through her existence—just as da Vinci painted Lisa Gherardini, Modigliani painted Jeanne Hébuterne, and Chagall painted Bella Rosenfeld.

Now he was not afraid of empty canvases. Painting her was the only way to approach her and the act of loving her. He wanted to express her beauty, pain, and desperation in an image of light, nobility, and life. He observed her with a zeal that was close to obsession, guessing her proportions and calculating the painting's composition. He also explored techniques from Greek sculpture, medieval religious painting, and Renaissance paintings, as well as studied the characteristics of the different paints and oils and the effects of various materials.

When *Ophelia: Summer* was finally completed, Hanjo led her to the canvas without hesitation. The girl in the painting, whose face was covered by a translucent veil that half concealed, half revealed her, was lying partly submerged. On the surface of the shallow stream, water weeds grew and a blue sky spread out overhead. Beyond the broken branches, Howard House could be seen far away on a green hill.

The water was still, and a peaceful smile lingered around the girl's mouth as she lay with her eyes closed. Wreaths made of flowers, their ribbons dangling in the water like aquatic plants, lips singing her sorrows, cuts and scars visible here and there . . .

Haeri felt strange. Even when she saw herself dead, she didn't feel scared or disgusted. It was not the soft and pure Ophelia of *Hamlet*, but Ophelia with the traces of a harsh life all over her body.

"I think I know what to draw now," Hanjo said. "My thoughts have become clear, as if a road has opened in front of me that wasn't there before. I'm going to apply the four seasons to Ophelia. Autumn as light, winter as ice, spring as mud."

Haeri kept her eyes on the canvas. "So you think we're going to be together until fall, winter, and next spring?"

"Of course, and if we can't be together, if we break up, I'll keep on drawing you and drawing you."

Hanjo hugged Haeri with all his might.

It was a week later that Haeri stopped visiting Howard House. She disappeared as if she had never been there. There was no sign of her in the house, where she had always floated like air, nor in the studio, where she had posed bathed in sunlight. He did not know what had happened, and could not believe it. He couldn't decide whether to be angry or sad, because he couldn't accept that he had lost her.

Hanjo went all over the place like a madman. But he couldn't find anyone to question about her whereabouts. Only after she disappeared was Hanjo surprised to learn he had never asked for her phone number. He had never needed to call, because she was always there for him. What selfish illusion had that been?

It was his long-standing habit to think about situations calmly and to accept things philosophically. He was sometimes told that he took other people's jokes too seriously, so that the atmosphere became awkward, or that he was inflexible because he misunderstood other people's metaphorical expressions. He was dismayed at his stupidity in not having been able to abandon such unpleasant attitudes, even toward his beloved.

He wondered countless times why Haeri had left. He struggled to recall her words and actions before she left, and pondered the meaning of her most trivial expressions and gestures one by one. Why on earth had she left? Where had she disappeared to? Why had she loved him, and had she really loved him?

Among them, the most heartbreaking question was why she hadn't even left a short note behind. She wasn't soft enough to hesitate to notify him of their breakup. He didn't have the kind of personality that might make her fear he would cling to her, begging for forgiveness for having done something wrong.

Did she think that a farewell would be more than he deserved? Or was she trying to punish him for his irreversible mistake by leaving without a word? Perhaps she could not accept the fact that he was the son of her sister's murderer. When he had asked why she loved the son of the man who once made a morass of her life, she had replied, "I thought of the Malcolm House people as family. So even after the incident, I didn't feel any anger or hatred toward Uncle Malcolm or yourself. Every day I waited in Howard House for you to come back. I really thought that would happen. My family was dead, but you were alive."

Haeri's words awakened sorrow, but he could not easily understand them. It was only right that she should hate the murderer and forget his son, but she hadn't. It must have been because of her loneliness at being left alone and her longing for the past.

They used to sit side by side each day, looking at the afternoon light and the setting sun. She liked him to stay beside her, and he would keep his eyes fixed on her like a faithful dog. They would prepare and share humble meals together.

The fact that she wasn't around weakened Hanjo. It was not just a feeling of emotional loss but withdrawal symptoms with physical side effects. He had indigestion, insomnia, and a lethargy that made it difficult for him to continue his daily life. He didn't wash his face for days, replaced meals with canned beer when he was hungry, and didn't turn on the lights when it was dark.

While they were together, he'd thought he understood her pain. But now it was clear that it had been an illusion. She seemed to be staring at something in the air, not at him, in the moments they were facing each other. Even when he believed they loved each other, he had often felt excluded from her life.

Ultimately, he didn't understand anything about her. No one can rid themselves of the memory of another person. No one. It is the same as saying no one can overcome the truth.

It was a year later that Hanjo left Howard House. The truck was loaded with six or seven boxes and the four *Ophelia* paintings. Painting was the only comfort that sustained him amid the pain of Haeri's absence. Although she had left him, she still existed as the model he had to paint, his Ophelia.

Having obtained the basement of a shabby building in Seoul's Myeongnyun-dong for a small monthly rent, Hanjo began doing odd jobs, painting construction sites and signboards part-time . . . Then, as manager and instructor at an art academy, he survived each day by giving private lessons. In those days, living without any expectations, he recalled the word *hope* like a long-lost vestigial organ.

He arranged to meet Suin about three months after he came to Seoul. Suin had just started working for a law firm, and when he entered Hanjo's basement studio, Hanjo saw that his brother had shaved his dark beard clean and oiled his bushy hair to create a sophisticated look.

They had rarely met since college. They knew, even if they didn't talk to each other, that each was a mirror reflecting the other's pain, that they should not think of one another, in order to protect themselves from horrible memories. No matter how or when they met, they always had to drink quietly, then go their own separate ways.

When they met, they were as awkward as cousins who saw each other once every few years. There was so much to say about the past that they couldn't express, and there was nothing to be said about the future. They paid close attention to their words, avoiding anything that would remind them of their past tragedy. They kept their guard up even when speaking about mundane things. They feared how words could turn into deadly weapons.

Yet there was an eternal question poised on Hanjo's lips, a question he had always wanted to ask his brother after that summer night but that he always swallowed. A secret that he would never know unless he asked now. He downed a glass of soju and said, "I don't know why, but I feel I should have said that I was alone in the studio that day."

Suin jumped as if he had been burned, then struggled to regain his composure while Hanjo poured more soju into his glass.

"But why didn't you?"

"If I had said that, the detectives would have grabbed you and questioned you about where you had been and what you had been doing."

Suin let out a long breath, as if that would drive the embarrassment from his body, and as if it would enable him to handle the complicated problems ahead of him. "I wanted you to be safe," he said. Thick veins stood out on his temples. The effort to make his words sound true was visible.

"I was safe."

"If you hadn't said you were with me, you wouldn't have been. You were young and scared and didn't understand the situation."

"Yes, I was stupid back then!" Hanjo shouted. "That's why I did such a stupid thing!"

Suin looked tired, as if he had aged ten years in a flash, and yet looked as pale as the boy who had escaped that summer night.

"Did a stupid thing? What did we do?"

"You don't remember? We lied about being together, and we've been silent for over ten years."

Hanjo realized he had not moved forward from that summer night. He would never be able to escape.

Suin nodded resignedly. "Yes, I lied and made you lie, too. But what are we going to do about that now?"

"I . . . I need to know." Hanjo grabbed Suin's forearm. "You . . . Where were you? What were you doing then?" He wanted to trust his brother. He wanted to believe that he had not used him as a shield.

"Yes, I was there," Suin spat. "In the villa near the reservoir. I don't know if you don't believe it or don't want to believe it." It was as if he were talking to himself, almost whispering. He said, "Jisoo liked me then."

A huge rake dug a deep furrow in Hanjo's heart. He was afraid that his brother was telling the truth, that the person whom Jisoo loved from the beginning had been Suin, not him. He had been a sacrifice offered so that she could gain his cold brother's love.

"But why did you make me lie about being with you?"

Suin's face turned pale. What was he afraid of? Of telling the truth? Of his younger brother knowing the truth, or of his younger brother not believing what he said?

"I had to protect you then."

"You weren't protecting me—you were just trying to protect yourself."

"Maybe . . . No, it's not true," Suin stammered. "Jisoo was modeling in your studio that afternoon. That means you're the last person who saw Jisoo. I thought that neither of us would be suspected if I said I was with you."

Hanjo felt relieved by his brother's words, as if all those years had been nothing and the consequences of the lie had nothing to do with him, although Suin had deceived him and used him for a lie. He held up the bottle of soju to finish what was in it. Suin snatched the bottle from his hand.

"Stop. Do you want to be like Mother? Do you want alcoholism to ruin your life?"

Hanjo didn't look at his brother. The sketch on the canvas he had been working on became blurred. He tried to prevent the tears from running down his cheeks.

"Brother . . . ," he asked softly. "Did you . . . did you love Jisoo, too?"

Suin thought for a moment, then put a hand on his shoulder. It was strong and rough, but warm.

"Is that important now?"

"Isn't it important to you?"

"Hanjo, there is no answer in the world that offers the truth and is sweet to hear. Even if I don't know anything else, I know that we did not commit a crime, that we're not stupid or ignorant. That's all."

Suin's voice was serious and full of confidence, but it was not the answer Hanjo had wanted to hear. Another question lingered on his lips. But the words, frozen hard on the tip of his tongue, refused to emerge. He wanted to ask, *Did you kill Jisoo?*

After Haeri left, Hanjo completed a series of fourteen *Ophelia* paintings. Except for the four pictures he had worked on at Howard House with her as a model, they were a series of smaller paintings. He did not want to give up on his dream of having an exhibition, even though the works were not really up to such a high standard. It would be better if he could sell some of the paintings, but it would be good if they simply made a favorable impression on the people who mattered.

After eight rejections, he was able to book a gallery that had recently opened in the suburbs. He rented it for a two-week-long exhibition, expecting no optimistic results.

During the exhibition, the number of visitors could be counted on the fingers of one hand, and not a single painting sold. The gallery owner, Seo Inmoon, who had a round face and round horn-rimmed glasses, with not one sharp angle in sight, had given the exhibition the creepy name *Death and the Maiden*.

But then Seo Inmoon, who seemed to be always complaining about everything in a shrill voice that did not match her teddy-bear-like figure, shouted in excitement on the day after the exhibition closed, "You've hit the jackpot! Someone says they're going to take the four large *Ophelia* paintings!"

He half wanted to believe her and half could not believe her. Was this Seo Inmoon's idea of a bad joke because she felt sorry for not selling a single work?

"I don't know the identity of the buyer," Seo Inmoon added, giggling. "However, when someone picks up a newbie's work, it means they have an eye for things. Either they're extremely wealthy or they're a chaebol-owner's wife or a venture businessman who's made a killing."

Hanjo wanted to tell Haeri the news, say that she had stimulated him, drawn out hidden talents, brought him good luck through an invisible umbilical cord. The paintings were footnotes to her existence and a courtship addressed to her after she had left him. Through those paintings, he admitted his sin, confessed his love, and begged for forgiveness.

"Even if people tell you to get lost, you mustn't give up," Seo Inmoon said. "You have to grab people by the legs of their pants. That's basic in running an art business, the mutual trust between the artist and the client."

Seo Inmoon, pocketing not only the rental fee but also her brokerage fee, was flustered at how risky the exhibition had been and how fortunate she was to sell four paintings at once in a gallery in the suburbs.

"This is just the beginning. Let's make a bigger show for the second exhibition, OK?"

Despite Seo Inmoon's fussing, Hanjo could not shake off a premonition that this miraculous moment would be the high point of his life. Beyond *Ophelia*, he would never be able to paint again, nor would his works sell if he did paint.

His premonition was correct. Despite Seo Inmoon's urging, his work remained sluggish. His paintings failed to establish new themes and techniques, and were of all different sizes, styles, and subjects, which made it difficult to organize them into an exhibition.

The twenty-four paintings in his second exhibition, which was held only after several obstacles were overcome, looked unfinished. The works had a patchwork quality, with different colors covering other colors, and remained unsold after the exhibition.

Haeri's absence drained all the light from him. Hanjo was an unknown artist wandering on the outskirts of the art world, and he was soon forced to return to teaching middle and high school students preparing to enter art college. He was becoming needier, darker, and weaker. He didn't know how many years it would take before he could escape from this life. Perhaps he was doomed to stay locked up in it forever.

"It's me, dear. Haeri. Let's meet on Saturday. I'll tell you what's going on when we meet."

The voice on the phone felt as remote as if it were coming from a Jurassic valley. After telling him when and where to meet, Haeri hung up without waiting for his answer.

That Saturday afternoon, they sat facing one another on a sunlit café terrace. Perhaps because her hair was shorter than before, she gave off a boyish vibe. Her stubby nose had become sharper, and the protruding cheekbones gave her a lively air. The dimples that formed when she pressed her lips together had deepened. She seemed to have grown an inch or more taller since she'd left him, but maybe that was because she had lost some weight. She was as full of self-confidence as ever, but seemed more passionate.

Haeri took a sip of iced coffee through a straw and produced a pink business card printed in Korean and English. *Soojin Kim*. Kunst. *Senior editor.*

Kunst was an art magazine that did not have many subscribers, but had established its own market with a unique perspective and sharp eye.

"I've been working there as an editor since I was a senior in college. It started out as a poorly paid part-time job, and now I've become full-time editor."

That evening, Haeri escorted him as far as his home and showed no hesitation about meeting again the next day like lovers. It was as if the time they'd spent apart had been cut out of the film of their lives, and the reel spliced together again. When he considered the pain and loneliness he had experienced after she left, it felt like a betrayal, but when he met her again, none of what he had planned to say came to mind.

"It's good to see you doing so well," Hanjo finally said, bitterly. "I know you left to do that, but . . ."

Haeri smiled broadly. She seemed to be vividly and purely pleased that they had met again. She didn't talk about the past or mention why she'd left him. It was as if it had never happened and there was no need for her to ask how he'd been, or be curious about what he'd been doing since they broke up.

She talked about her articles, her interviews, and the art market, which had been struggling since the recession. Then she said she would interview him, without asking if he was still painting. It was not a request for an interview based on plans and procedures, but an impromptu and unexpected notification.

"What are you talking about?" Hanjo said. "I'm not a promising young artist; I don't deserve an interview."

"It's not that you don't deserve it; you just don't have pride. Have more confidence in yourself. You sold four paintings in your first exhibition, didn't you?"

"It was the first and last piece of luck in my life. The second exhibition was a disaster. Now I'm making a living by directing students' studies. I have no time to work, no motivation, and no money to paint."

As he spoke, it struck him that he was already being interviewed by her.

"A painter is an artist even if he doesn't paint," she said. "By the way, can I order a bottle of beer?"

Hanjo called a waiter to order, then said, "If you feel sorry you left me without a word, you don't have to. It was hard, but I've forgotten."

It wasn't true. It was an innocent lie designed to hide his humiliation. But her reaction was unexpected.

"Forget? How could you do that? I've never forgotten you . . ."

Haeri stared at him with a puzzled look, as if the person who had left without a word was not she but Hanjo. He couldn't believe what she said, but he didn't want to conclude it wasn't true.

The waiter put a bottle of beer misted with drops of water on the table. As he talked about his work in Howard House and his first exhibition, Hanjo realized that it had been the peak of his life. He didn't want to say anything about the long, subsequent decline.

It was past eight o'clock when they got up. He took off his jacket and hung it around Haeri's shoulders, over her blouse. He still had a lot to talk about.

Hanjo's studio was a semiunderground studio of some eighty square yards. There was a thin mattress on the icy floor, and an old table that was the only piece of furniture. The back of the chair was covered with clothes, and four empty soju bottles were lying in front of the bathroom door. He busily swept the mess together and pushed it under the table.

"You don't have to clean up," Haeri said. "I like it being messy. It makes me think you can't do anything without me."

They exchanged stories like fairy-tale lovers who had been separated for a hundred years. Haeri's every word sounded as memorable and vivid as the lines of the main character in a play. It seemed both natural and surprising that neither she nor he had changed.

Haeri kissed him. Her hair tickled his cheeks and neck. Before they knew it, they had penetrated each other's bodies like plow blades penetrating soft, black soil, warm and soft, elegant and strong. They stayed united for a long time, like children who had come back to their old home.

Her article in the October issue of *Kunst* mainly consisted of cold criticism rather than excessive praise for Hanjo and his work. It was not a groundlessly favorable review. He was introduced as a painter who, after his second exhibition, could no longer paint. In the article, he appeared to be a wounded herbivore on the verge of being eaten by predators, the last individual of a species that had been wiped out and was close to extinction in an ecosystem dominated by the law of the jungle. Nevertheless, she did not neglect the animal instincts he still possessed. It was an accurate article, without exaggeration or underestimation.

This was Haeri's talent: the power of getting what she wanted, even though it made her uncharacteristically cold. Writers, gallery owners, and artists visited her, and exhibition catalogs were piled high on her desk. Her unique eye and intense drive had earned her the company president's full confidence and the industry's attention.

Hanjo clearly realized that she could pull him out of the dark, that he could never leave her, and that he wanted to be subjugated by her. He was indescribably proud of the fact that he had been chosen by the woman everyone wanted.

The following spring, he moved his things into her two-bedroom apartment: two large trunks, a desk and some books, his bedding in a bundle, and about twenty small paintings. As they painted the room sky blue, they chuckled at the sight of their faces splashed with paint. There was more affectionate familiarity between them than between siblings. It was a closeness that lay beyond physical desire or artistic passion. They understood each other, both having lost precious people at the same time. It was as if they were sick with the same disease.

They skipped from one day to the next as if they were crossing over stepping-stones. Joy and happiness were contained in their small, bright room. In the morning, sweet sunlight like ripe tropical fruit poured down onto the narrow veranda. They listened to each other's regular breathing and laughed at each other's unwashed faces. He stroked her scars as if underlining an incomprehensible sentence.

But he was still an unknown artist and old enough to feel a generation gap between them. Why did she love him? If marriage was a business, why was she investing in him?

"You have something hidden inside you," she explained. "It may be an undiscovered talent or a hidden secret, but I'll draw it out. If that doesn't work, I'll cut your stomach open."

Hanjo didn't know what he had inside him. He didn't know how to get it out, no matter what it was. But, faced now with this woman he loved, he grew condescending. "You're going to kill the goose that lays the golden eggs?" he said. "No, don't ever think about cutting my stomach open."

She watched his frowning eyes, his twisted lips, and his hand brushing the canvas. Though he was reticent in speech, slow in action, and often submerged in his vague thoughts, he was not a stupid or lazy man. Inside, he was full of desires intent on tearing his breast open and rending his heart apart.

"I'm going to use all the people I can," she said. "Mobilize the media, and satisfy the buyers. You'll become famous and I'll make a profit. How about it? Aren't you happy?"

"I'm happy. Or at least if I'm not happy, I can try to be."

"Look out of the window, dear—the sleet has turned into real snow!"

Haeri was already running out of the front door. He grabbed her padded coat from the hanger and followed. She ran around in the snow like a bird trying not to get caught. He stretched out the hem of her coat like a net, caught up with her, and hugged her. Her face was wet and her eyelashes glistened with sparkling snow. Her ears were red and the veins in her cheeks were exposed. She was such a bright mass of joy that he was blinded for a moment.

His heart was about to split with happiness, like a log under the blow of a sharp axe. The simple fact that she was alive in front of him became a source of amazing joy.

Some kinds of love have the power to reconstruct the past, the ability to restore a broken life. He had forgotten about happiness a long time ago—it was hard to recover its shape, color, and texture—but at that moment, he felt that he deserved it.

With only fifteen days left before the wedding, Hanjo called Suin. Suin was not annoyed, but he didn't seem welcoming either. Suin noted down the date, time, and place of Hanjo's wedding.

"Congratulations. I'll be there. I'm busy now, so I'll hang up. We've got a client waiting for us . . ."

Suin, who had married three years before, had a two-year-old son, and a second child was due the following spring. Hanjo had first met the woman who would be his sister-in-law at a dinner about a month before the wedding. She said she was teaching math at a middle school in Seoul. Dressed in a white blouse and black pants, she was quiet and her face was not very expressive. She was neither big nor small, and had no earrings or necklace. Her appearance, so ordinary that she stood out, was rather unexpected.

When she was away for a moment, Hanjo asked, "Do you like her?"

Suin answered without hesitation. "She's OK! Why do you ask that?"

"I don't think she's the ideal type for the brother I used to know when I was a kid . . ."

"My ideal type is just my ideal type," Suin said, smiling. "Women who stand out or are great don't hang out with me. But I think she looks good with me. I guess it's because I love her."

Suin's tone reminded Hanjo of something he had once said when sitting on a chair outside a convenience store. It was the day Suin failed the bar exam again and gave up his dream of becoming a lawyer.

"I'm going to stop now," he told Hanjo. "For a guy like me, taking the bar exam is presumptuous greed."

"Why would you say that? You just didn't get lucky. Start over again."

Suin shook his head. "You think I'm smart, don't you? I thought so, too. When I first failed, I thought I was unlucky, and the second time, that I didn't have enough time to prepare because I was working part-time. I made a different excuse every time. I've been in the army, so I don't have any money . . . But at some point, I realized that the problem was me."

Hanjo could feel a quiet sorrow in Suin's drunk and subdued voice. He contradicted him. "What problem can someone as smart as you have?"

"It's true that I'm smart, but I'm not smart enough to be a lawyer. I was just a good student in a small town."

Hanjo felt heartbroken at his brother's helplessness. Suin sounded tired of poverty and his bad luck; he had never shown that before.

Hanjo raised his voice. "Don't you know? You were the pride and hope of our family. Everyone has been dreaming your dream together with you . . ."

"I know, but I'm giving up. I don't have anything left to burn. My parents are dead and my dream is gone."

"But what are you going to do now?"

"I have to earn some money. Maybe by getting a job in the office of an old friend, doing odd jobs, or working as a broker . . . If I work hard, maybe I'll get to be an office manager."

Suin's faint voice reflected his lost dreams. It didn't matter if he couldn't become a lawyer; he would be satisfied if he could just live a normal life. Hanjo was heartbroken about his brother's dead dreams, but he was relieved that Suin had found peace of mind. After all this time and all he had been through, he sincerely wanted his brother, who was obliged to be the son of a murderer and an alcoholic, to enjoy ordinary happiness as this woman's husband.

Suin became an office manager and saved money doggedly. He did not hesitate to assist lawyers by interviewing and writing letters to clients, as well as bringing in new clients or even proceeding with the litigation himself instead of hiring a lawyer, which was illegal. This ability to work on the border between illegal and barely legal meant he was fired thrice, but each time he managed to find a better job. A couple of near arrests for violating the laws that regulated lawyers and for fraud had also come out well in the end. Except for the fact that he didn't have a license, he had nothing to envy a lawyer for.

Now no one knew that he was the son of a murderer who had made the headlines a long time ago. Even if someone knew, they wouldn't be able to talk. Even if they spoke out, it would not matter.

Four works from the *Ophelia* series were hanging on the wall of the gallery, which had been empty for a while since it was not exhibition season. Instead of a wedding dress, Haeri wore the white sleeveless dress that she wore to exhibitions or parties. Hanjo wore a new black suit with a bow tie. More than twenty guests roamed about the room quietly, like goldfish in a fishbowl.

Choi Inyong, president of *Kunst*, was a woman in her midforties with dark-rimmed glasses. She made a cold impression at first glance, but the fine wrinkles at the corners of her slightly drooping eyes made her look milder. The gray hair showing in places demonstrated that she was not afraid of growing old; it didn't matter to her if people knew her age. Her graceful movements, like those of a bird, quickly drew people's attention and dominated the room.

"It's an impressive painting. Tell the new bridegroom . . . I'm sorry, but I don't understand. What a waste of talent to produce a work like that and not have a proper sequel."

After surveying *Ophelia: Autumn*, she looked at Hanjo and smiled. It might have been congratulation or accusation, but there was no trace of malice in her expression. She had the gift of ensuring that even a sharp comment did not offend. She had an aloof smile and the quiet authority commonly found among successful people.

"It's OK. He's going to be painting from now on," Haeri said. "I'll make it happen."

She chewed on a cheese canapé as she spoke. She seemed to be blaming him and comforting him at the same time. Inyong turned back to the painting like a child who seemed resigned after being scolded. There was something of a lovers' quarrel in their words and expressions. Hanjo was proud of Haeri, because he believed she would not only protect him from Inyong's attacks but also transform him into someone strong.

"That's right," Inyong said. "I want a great work and a writer to make it great. Then we can make history. You make your husband an artist, he makes the work, and I make it great, then he produces an even greater work . . ."

The two women smiled at each other. In the art world dominated by money and influence, discrimination and gambling, Inyong was a lioness. Her skill and acumen meant she could name a long list of famous artists she had discovered. What if she could add him to the list?

Hanjo took a deep breath. It was time to declare war on fate. He was no longer alone. He had a wife. They would build their lives comforting each other about their past. And he would paint: pictures where multiple colors would break like waves, evoking emotion; pictures where the color would fill the viewers' eyes; mirrorlike pictures that would show anyone standing in front of them a secret self they did not know.

Hanjo wanted to declare it to the whole world: *Look, I'm free. I've broken free of tragic murder, the grief of losing all I loved, the insult of being called the son of a murderer!*

"Let's go back to Howard House. I want to go there and be happy like in the old days. And you can paint again . . ."

Haeri spoke like Constantine the Great deciding to move the capital of an empire to Constantinople. Under the trust agreement, ownership of Howard House had transferred to her when she turned eighteen; it was the foundation that had allowed Hanjo to stay there as a caretaker.

The reason behind her decision was clear. Hanjo, who was in deep depression after the failure of his second exhibition, needed new opportunities. He accepted her wish easily, with a sense of duty, feeling that she could do anything she wanted, as if it were for her and not himself.

They returned to Howard House like the prodigal son returning to his father's home. As they parked in the overgrown garden and got out of the car, tall weeds brushed their knees. A few roof tiles were broken, and the stone walls were covered with moss. Even though it was daytime, mosquitoes and gnats came rushing to trouble them.

Haeri spent the deposit money from her Seoul apartment repairing the main building and renovating the annex. After a full thirty days of construction work, the interior of the house was complete in a simple style of white walls and black tiles with blue highlights. They had eliminated the ground floor of the annex studio so that it now had an elevated ceiling that allowed for larger paintings, and it was made brighter by the light filtering through the long horizontal windows.

Like a suit handmade by a master tailor, Howard House fit them perfectly. As the old house regained its solidity, Hanjo's potential was also restored. He would be able to paint anything there.

However, the expectation of being able to paint and the act of painting were two different things. Contrary to Haeri's belief in his talent, nervousness gnawed at Hanjo day by day. People were impatient. Customers, critics, and collectors were so impatient to see finished works that they kept urging him to stop before he felt that a picture was ready. But still he felt like a flash in the pan, already outdated—a painter whom people looked at once, then turned away from, nothing more than a physically and mentally depleted man. In the meantime, new artists' paintings caught the eye of customers.

When his wife went to work, the empty studio was a void. He doubted whether he had the right to paint, and didn't believe he had the ability to do so. He heard nothing from his brother, as before. Sometimes, the knowledge that they loved each other faded. Sometimes, he couldn't even be sure they had ever really loved each other.

Hanjo had fallen before he could even savor the kindness fate had unexpectedly offered him. Despite promising not to, in the afternoons, he turned to the bottle. He was no longer an artist but a drunkard. Alcohol was not a solution to the problem but a way of forgetting it, and it was the most wretched way of life he knew—or, rather, a way of death. When his mother died in the nursing home, made senile by alcoholism, he had reflected that it was fortunate her brain had stopped working before it broke down more completely.

Before his wife came home, Hanjo hid the bottle, and without any particular intention or expectation, he painted over a canvas.

"It's all a mess. I can't paint anything. There's nothing I want to draw."

His drunken eyes were blurred, and his voice trembled with self-hatred. Haeri didn't believe that. Even though she did not trust the human being Lee Hanjo, she believed absolutely in his talent. His incompetence, indolence, self-righteousness, and whims she regarded as the essence of his talent.

"You're still painting. No matter what, you're still painting something on the canvas. Look at this color and texture! It's a combination that can't be obtained without discouragement and pain."

When he was listening to Haeri, Hanjo became a different person. It was as if there had never been a moment since his birth when he was not a genius, an artist who would amaze the world. So he didn't abandon the canvas, even if he couldn't paint. He didn't let go of the brush, even if he was drunk. As long as she watched, he could paint. Even if he could not paint, he did not lose the desire to paint. He wielded his brush until the light of dawn permeated the dark skin of night. Then, when the windows became gray, he stretched out beside her, straight as a knife, and fell asleep.

The idea of carving thickly coated layers of paint came by accident. As opposed to the traditional technique of painting on canvas, this style involved revealing layered colors by cutting through thick paint spread on wood panels with a sharp tool, and then sandpapering it.

The finished work was a combination of various wedge-like and wavy shapes. In terms of effect, it was reminiscent of the pointillism of Seurat and technically resembled the wedge-shaped writing of Mesopotamia's cuneiform. The amorphous colors revealed through the crevices in the surface layer, which were like scars, allowed for various interpretations and reminded viewers of specific objects.

"I'll have to give the pictures a name," Haeri said, nodding her head in time to Brahms's piano sonata. "Something that anyone can think of at a glance. After all, people like labels, don't they?"

Hanjo shot her a sour look. "Is that really necessary?"

"How about 'wedge paintings'? It makes you think of the Sumerian cuneiform writing carved on clay tablets, right?"

"That's not bad."

"You'll see. People will call you the Master of the Wedges."

Her voice was calm but patronizing. He kissed her on the forehead in excitement. At last, he seemed qualified to bring her a better life.

Fourteen wedge paintings were selected for the *Wedgehogs* exhibition held at Gallery Kunst the following autumn. Of these, four large paintings were ambitious works that deconstructed Howard House at different points in time using the style of amorphous wedge distribution.

Gallery Kunst was a concrete building that felt unwelcoming at first, with its rough framework. The ceiling, which was more than four yards high, gave it a grand atmosphere, and the three sections of the exhibition hall formed a smooth S-shaped line. Haeri hung the paintings on the bare concrete walls without painting them or attaching the paintings to panels. The colors of the pieces were more prominent because of the rough concrete texture of the background.

The technique of scratching and digging into layers of paint to reveal other colors and the evocation of time and memories received favorable reviews. It was the unexpected result of *Kunst*'s influence and Haeri's ability. On the other hand, some criticized the works, claiming that the wedge paintings were aesthetically and technically substandard. One critic wrote that this technique was merely a clumsy replica of long-past abstract expressionism. To the depressed Hanjo, Haeri said that no matter how negative the article was, it was better than no article at all.

"Wait and see; you'll swim hard and survive like a loach in a pond where the catfish are loose."

True or not, Hanjo was persuaded. Newness was a concept that was interpreted rather than presented. It was not that abstract expressionism was not new but that it simply did not *look* new. Therein lay his newness.

In just three days, the large work *Howard House 2* was sold. Rumors spread that the anonymous buyer was the head of a conglomerate, attracting attention from enthusiasts. Soon after, two more *Howard House* works were sold, and orders for three large-scale works that had yet to be produced were placed.

"I made a mistake," Haeri said as the two-week exhibition was ending, as if just remembering something.

"What mistake?"

"I should have set a higher price for your work . . . I thought you were a great artist, but I was wrong. You're going to *become* a great artist."

His wife smelled sweet, like freshly squeezed fruit juice. She laughed, jokingly grumbling that she would need a secretary to manage his schedule.

Following her advice, he began to develop the techniques and themes of "wedges" and to work on a larger scale. While he was engrossed in his work, she prepared for the next exhibition in two years. Invitation letters were delivered to regular readers of *Kunst*, presidents of major movie companies, entrepreneurs with good liquidity, and people carefully selected from lists of art lovers. She invited not only figures from the art world but also big names from film and fashion, highlighting Hanjo's new works in line with their respective interests.

The works sold for more than double the price of the previous exhibition. Four large-scale works were sold in advance to a large company to decorate the lobby of their new headquarters, which was still under construction.

When he was invited to appear on a program about art travel by a broadcasting company, Haeri accepted without asking him. When he seemed reluctant, she encouraged him, saying that today's artist was not a creator but a person who talked to the public.

His radio and TV appearances brought a popularity that was different from his success as an artist. People who were not interested in painting also became aware of the painter Lee Hanjo. Young people who were indifferent to art purchased his prints, and a famous fashion designer used a motif of the colors in his work on her clothes. An art college invited him to be an adjunct professor. Curators and gallery owners flocked around him; reporters, producers, and students came crowding. His talent was recognized as being at a price worthy of the market, and the name Lee Hanjo was recognized all over the world.

The art market dominated by business perspectives was a beautiful mirage, a combination of capital and desire. Cold reviews of a work, painters' clichéd self-defenses, violent fluctuations in the prices of paintings like companies on the stock market, aggressive sales campaigns and personality-based marketing . . .

Hanjo wanted to survive in this environment as much as he wanted to escape from its hollowness. So he attended parties or gatherings that he didn't want to attend. Mostly, they were drinking sessions where people boasted about themselves secretly or openly, or showed off their arrogance disguised as humility.

When he came home, he felt as if he had been beaten, even though nothing had happened. Sounds kept ringing in his ears. The noise of glasses bumping, of a chair being pulled to a better position, the whispering voices . . . At one party, he remembered the words of a collector in his forties who was whispering to the chief curator of a large gallery, fondling a glass of champagne. "How can they live together like that when they don't fit together? Should we consider them a combination of wealth and talent?"

The curator's reply was inaudible. The collector went on: "There's a rumor that Kim Soojin is in a certain kind of relationship with Choi. Believe it or not, they're saying that she's her mistress . . ."

"Who would ever believe that? But certainly the wedge paintings are a combination of Choi's influence, Kim Soojin's ability, and Lee Hanjo's talent."

Hanjo unfastened his bow tie, stuffed it into his pocket, and escaped like a runaway. It wasn't the first time he had heard unpleasant chatter about his wife, or faced moments when a noisy atmosphere suddenly grew cold at his appearance, where people who had been talking excitedly suddenly seemed awkward when he said hello. One weekend afternoon, he carefully asked Haeri if she had ever heard such talk.

"People talk about us because they envy us. They create stories, inflate them, and twist things, then think it's so. The truth is that no one has the talent you have, and no one can love you as I do."

Haeri was like an elementary school teacher comforting a bullied child. Hanjo thought of Rastignac and Julien Sorel, young and foolish characters in French novels who were sponsored by rich ladies and were destroyed in their pursuit of success. He decided to be indifferent to the distasteful phrase *male Cinderella*, because it was true.

One Saturday morning, they sat side by side on the garden bench. In front of them was the weekend edition of a newspaper Haeri had bought at a newsstand. There was a photo of him printed alongside an interview, and Hanjo stared, puzzled, at his disheveled hair and slightly crooked lips.

He thought of the headline on the day after his father was arrested: "Arrest of Killer of High School Girl." Underneath the large print was a picture of a man with tangled hair, swollen eyes, and tight lips, an anxious killer trying to pull himself together. His father looked unfamiliar. The article was a mix of the facts Hanjo knew and didn't know. The police were investigating the murder of a high school girl in Borim Stream; the criminal arrested was Lee Jinman; he had previously served a year and a half for violating the law on violence; photos of the victim were found in the criminal's studio. It was hard to tell where the truth lay and what was false, but newspaper articles had the power to make themselves believed, even when they were untrue.

"The fact that our father went to prison before we were born . . . ," Hanjo asked his brother that day. "Did you ever hear that?"

Suin shook his head indifferently.

"Is it true?" Hanjo asked again. "Is it true that our father lied to us?"

"He didn't lie; he just didn't tell us, did he?"

"He was lying, because he didn't tell us everything. Some silences . . ."

Hanjo was trying to recall the words that had followed when Haeri laid a hand on his shoulder and pointed. At that moment, there was no trace of a shadow on her face.

"The interview picture looks good," she said. "You're not just handsome; you're an artist."

In the picture, which showed him staring straight ahead, he gave the impression of being a man who didn't need good luck. Therefore, he appeared to be an exception to the rule, an independent person far removed from the laws governing the world at large. His photo in the newspaper looked strange and awkward.

"It looks light, childish," he said. "It's not me, just an image of me that people want to see."

"Well, what do you expect? This is an era when images define reality, isn't it? There's something attractive about you. Should I say it's modern? Should I say it's contemporary? There's a desire these days for people who keep their distance from the world and never lose their presence."

Haeri kissed the picture as if she loved the reputation he had created with his talent and not just his physical shell. He wondered if his wife was trying to insult him.

"By the way," she said, "you need to lose some weight. You have to live for an amazingly long time, like Picasso."

It was true that his body had been expanding noticeably over the past few months. His sleek jawline had grown thick, and the hem of his shirt popped up around the waist. He was embarrassed to be over forty and look it, even though he tried to reassure himself that he was as fit as he'd been in his thirties.

Hanjo rolled on the lawn and removed the dried grass from Rothko's back. "It sounds like you're saying I'm growing old."

"It means you're no longer young."

Haeri's cheeks dimpled. His wife, who stood out like a swan among the directors of major art galleries, curators, sophisticated connoisseurs, and picky high-profile collectors, made him feel both proud and anxious. Sometimes, without warning, he felt afraid that she might leave him one day, as suddenly as she had before.

What would it have been like if they'd had a child? He asked himself this at every turning point in his life, every moment when he needed to make a decision. It was only by doing so that he could make the right choices and justify his decisions. He would have been less anxious if they'd had a child, but more confused. He wouldn't have the worries he had now, but he felt sure he would have had more worries.

Three years after they were married, they were still childless. Nevertheless, they did not make any artificial efforts to conceive. They thought they could have a child whenever they wanted one. The child existed in their imagination, in their conversations, and in their love-making. They wondered whether the child would be a boy or a girl, whom it would look like, what name to give it, what birthday gift it would like, whether the child would draw well or not, and whether, if it wanted to became a painter, they would try to dissuade it?

As the years went by and no child appeared, they chose not to feel empty but to be each other's child instead. So they made silly demands, and consoled and satisfied each other's needs.

It was not that he had never had a chance to be a father. On an island in Thailand, where they went on a summer vacation three years after their wedding, Haeri calmly announced her pregnancy. How could she tell him such an important fact so casually? Even though he didn't expect much motherly love from her, her nonchalant attitude offended him.

During her pregnancy, he adored her like the Virgin Mary. Then, six weeks later, the child vanished from her body. His sense of loss for the child he had never seen created a deep void in his heart. The unborn baby's cries echoed in the depths of his soul. When he set aside his pain and told Haeri, "You can have another one," she shook her head.

"No," she said. "That won't be possible."

From then on, at every important moment in his life, Hanjo asked himself the same question: What if the child had lived? Maybe he would gurgle and toddle, then go to elementary school and come home with knees raw from playing soccer. But that child had left their side. When he finally accepted this, he turned to painting like a soldier going to war.

"I need to paint," he told Haeri. "Better paintings, finer paintings."

"That's a good idea. It's a necessary idea."

He pushed the side of his face against hers, which was moist as if she had just washed it. The curves of their two faces interlocked like pieces of a puzzle. "I don't care if you don't become a Picasso," she said. "You just have to become yourself."

She seemed determined to make his life his most successful work. Her honest desire to dirty her hands for his worldly success was the source of her fierce energy.

Finally, Haeri tendered her resignation from the magazine. Her sudden withdrawal, when she had been so passionate about her work, more than anyone else, inspired various rumors inside and outside the company.

"There's a lot of talk about you," Hanjo said. "Some people say you're going to be working on a big project with the backing of a wealthy sponsor; others think you're going to do my management work in earnest."

He sounded both disappointed that Haeri had left the magazine without talking to him about it and curious about her future plans.

Haeri looked away. "Why are they so interested in other people's lives? If they lived their lives to the fullest, they'd all make money and be rich . . ."

"I'm curious, too."

Haeri's eyes shone like a child's when preparing for a surprise party. "I think it's time for me to do what I want to do. There's something I need to do . . ."

Hanjo didn't ask any more questions. Whatever it was, he believed she would use her ideas and skill. She had a fine understanding of art and an excellent eye for talent. She could also judge situations coolly and objectively, without being swayed by emotion; nor did she act impulsively or jump to conclusions. She would do well in anything she chose to do. Nevertheless, he was hurt by the thought that she was hiding something from him.

After she quit her job, Haeri spent most of her day in her second-floor study. Her favorite brown armchair in his studio in the annex remained empty, and the discolored leather only brought back memories of how she would sit there watching him quietly for hours on end, like a girl who believed that just being present would make him paint better.

When the sun went down and he went back into the main house, the sound of her tapping on the computer keyboard could be heard clearly. It didn't stop even late at night. Hanjo would wait for his wife to come to the bedroom, then, when she did not come, fall asleep alone. It occurred to him that she was trying to push him out of her life.

When he opened his eyes in the middle of the night and found she was not beside him, he felt as if they were separated by a great distance. If she was immersed in a task, he would spare no effort to support and help her, but he could not rid himself of the anxiety that her interest had turned away from him. He was afraid she was fed up with his talents or thought they were exhausted.

Suddenly, he felt anxious that the success he had achieved might disappear like a mirage. There was no rule that yesterday and today must be the same, and tomorrow no different. People lost their jobs, got kicked out of their homes, were killed without warning. Even so, he comforted himself that he deserved his success now.

One weekend, when out for a walk, they sat side by side on a riverside bench. Haeri was dressed in wide brown pants and a fluffy blouse decorated with blue petals. The wind blew her wide trousers around her legs. She smiled at Rothko, who was ignoring her.

"Sometimes, Rothko is more mature than you," she said. "He comforts me, and sometimes, if I want to be alone, he slips away . . ."

When he heard his name, Rothko looked up. He showed teeth sharp like thorns, but he seemed to be smiling. Should Hanjo feel a little bit jealous? He stroked the dog's head as if he were a boy precocious beyond his age.

"What are you so busy with lately?"

He was careful not to reveal his impatience by his tone. His wife answered the question calmly, as if she had been waiting a long time for it.

"I'm writing. It's personal. I hope to publish a book."

"Personal writing? About what, I mean?"

"Don't you know there's nothing left in my personal life except you?"

It was true that his presence was absolute in her personal life. Even though he hadn't thought about it specifically, it was only natural that if someone wrote about him, it should be his wife, no one else. She was his partner and lover, judge, prison guard, and coolheaded secretary. She wrote his interviews for *Kunst*, introduced his work, and wrote about it in various media. There was a cold evaluation of his work, but there were also touching revelations about the person he was. Hanjo wondered how she would depict him.

"So what are you going to write about me?"

"A story about the you that you don't know, and the me that you don't know. It's an autobiographical, nonfictional novel, and nothing at all . . ."

Hanjo wondered what he didn't know and what she *thought* he didn't know.

"I sometimes don't understand what you are saying at all. Is it because I'm too stupid? No, you're too smart. Anyway, I'll be your first reader, right?"

Haeri stroked his cheek with a cold hand instead of answering. His dry skin rustled.

"Of course. That's why I'm writing."

Her voice subsided calmly. Her body, long and thin, looked curved as if held in a large glass tank. Behind her, people passed slowly like fish.

Sitting by the river as the sun set, they looked at each other as if they were looking in a mirror. They found their past, their pain, and their memories reflected on each other's faces. They didn't even notice that darkness was approaching.

Hanjo

The application for an injunction to prevent publication was futile. *Your Lies About Me* was put on display in the fiction section of large bookstores. Sales began to increase after it was mentioned under "new publications" in several media outlets. Flustered, Hanjo shouted into his cell phone.

"The . . . the book is all over the bookstores! Do you know what the ad says? *I was nineteen then. And he was forty.* It's obviously hinting at statutory rape. You said you'd do everything you could. You told me that you would mobilize the media, submit a list of contents, file a lawsuit, so what have you done?"

Suin understood Hanjo's impatience, full as he was of a sense of betrayal. He took a deep breath and spoke soothingly. "Calm down and listen to me. As I told you, we could have sent the publisher a writ indicating that we would take legal action if they pushed ahead with publication, or we could have applied for an injunction to block publication."

"But why didn't you do anything?"

"It's not that I did nothing—I kept my eye on the trends. Only think. Do you think they'd give up publishing because of a mere two-page writ? They would simply stimulate readers' curiosity with noise marketing while they were waiting. An injunction is never granted by the courts unless there is a direct, explicit, and serious reason. Korea is a democratic republic where freedom of expression and freedom of publication are alive and well, right?"

"Then you deceived me the day I met you, while I trusted you?"

Hanjo sounded like someone suffering from rheumatism, whose nerves were on edge because of the pain. An unfamiliar feeling of sorrow pierced Suin's breast like a needle. He began to whistle quietly.

"I didn't deceive you; I reassured you. Look, the situation is not as bad as you think. No damage has occurred yet. Literally, a novel is just fiction; not many readers believe it's a true story. But if damage emerges, we'll fight. If we're lucky, there'll be no damage."

Hanjo was forced to accept that his brother knew the law better and that there was a particular language used in court. Whether the client was the victim or the perpetrator, it was Suin's job to come up with a strategy capable of winning the case. If it was a fight that could not be won, the focus should be on minimizing the damage.

"Would you be speaking so calmly if you were the one involved? What should we do now? Should we wait patiently until rumors start to spread and the reporters rush in, sensing a scandal? Or what . . . ? What?" Hanjo struggled to find the right words.

Suin put an end to the conversation. "I'm busy right now. There are clients waiting in the interview room, so let's meet and talk. After work today, or tomorrow, or the day after tomorrow . . . I'll come to your house after work. I'll be there around eight thirty."

Suin hung up. He wasn't someone who waited for the other person to hang up first. Even though he knew it could be considered rude, he thought it was effective rather than uncomfortable. It was thrilling to make people think they could expect nothing from him and so give up, because that way he could confirm he was superior to them.

He was poor but smart and tough. He also knew how to read the way the world worked and decipher life's complex blueprints. Although he might not be a lawyer, he could finally live like a normal person. It had been his dream to become an ordinary man, and live a normal person's life.

When he rang the doorbell at home, his wife and two sons would come running to the front door. Their eldest son, who was already in elementary school, changed his dream every few days, from becoming an astronaut to being a tangerine farmer, and the second son wanted to be the puppy they were raising so he could eat freely.

Suin believed that this was the life he had always wanted. It was clear he had achieved self-satisfaction, happiness, and a flawless peace. Nevertheless, he was tormented by doubts that he did not deserve this happiness. He couldn't help worrying that the warm lighting, the abundant food, his beloved family, and the constant laughter of his children were bounty stolen from someone else.

Perhaps it was not really happiness—or if it was happiness, it was a false happiness gained in exchange for hiding the truth. A vision of someone shouting, *You don't deserve this joy!* occasionally seized him.

Suin leaned against the cabinet and drank a full glass of whiskey. His throat burned and the strong liquor made him tingle. He remembered the day he'd lost his younger brother, when Suin was seven or eight years old. Hanjo was very young and could not even read yet, but insisted he accompany Suin to the library. Suin told his little brother several times that if he got lost, he should stay just where he was and not go anywhere.

It wasn't until evening that he noticed Hanjo had disappeared. While he searched the reading rooms and hallways, then wandered down the street, the sun set and night fell. An hour later, he found his brother standing in front of a record store. Hanjo wasn't crying. He just looked at him with big eyes.

"Let's go home," Hanjo said. "It's cold here."

Hanjo walked meekly homeward, as if he had forgotten he had lost his way. Suin wondered how his brother could be so calm.

"Weren't you afraid?"

"I was afraid."

"Yet you didn't even cry?"

"I knew you were coming. You said you'd come if I stayed where I was if I got lost."

Suin thought of Hanjo waiting for him in his empty studio, his younger brother standing amid dirty brushes and partly finished paintings, a child much bigger than himself. Suin refilled his glass, even though he knew he should stop drinking.

Hanjo, stay right there, he thought. *I'm on my way.*

The novel was in four parts, and dealt with murder, revenge, and betrayal. It was an indictment of Hanjo before the court of public opinion.

The first part showed how the two main characters, the artist and the girl, met and then separated. The artist seduced the girl and then trampled her with the full weight of his authority, a subtle form of coercion and rape.

The second part, which depicted a murder that happened more than twenty years before, provided an important plotline in the novel even though it was only a short ten-page story in itself. The victim of the murder was the girl's sister. Three or four local men connected to the victim emerged as suspects. Among them was the artist himself as a child. The police finally arrested a logger who lived in the forest across from the village, but the story suggested someone else was the real killer.

The third part showed the artist meeting the girl again, when she was an adult. He married the girl and exhibited works that created a sensation with their groundbreaking ideas and techniques. The works were presented under his name, while in fact they were conceived and, to a large extent, painted by his wife.

The artist continued to succeed as a famous painter by ordering his wife to produce increasingly innovative and larger paintings. Although she accompanied him like an ornament to every exhibition, he kept quiet about her talent and role. The wife was known as his "perfect helper," but her role as collaborator remained unrecognized.

The wife grew disillusioned with her husband's hypocrisy, but she couldn't escape their life. She had constructed herself through him. Unwilling to destroy her own achievements, she was forced to live in his shadow. One day, the artist brought home a twenty-year-old woman. Now filled with betrayal and a desire for revenge, the wife set out to destroy him.

The real murderer was revealed in part four. After a persistent hunt by the detective in charge, the artist was found to be the real culprit. When the girl's sister, whom he had secretly loved since she was young, fell in love with the lumberjack, he was unable to control his anger and jealousy. He killed her.

It is always difficult to connect a person with a fictional character, since all fictional characters undergo such extensive embellishment. This was true here as well: Hanjo and Haeri's real life did not map onto the conflict and betrayal in the novel. Novels may reflect reality, but they cannot replace reality.

But no matter what others might think, for Hanjo, the novel was more realistic and deadlier than reality itself. Even if no one else noticed, he knew. It still wouldn't matter if he pretended not to know, but Hanjo couldn't do that. His wife made three things clear in the novel. The main character was a shameless artist who had violated a minor against her will, a thief who stole his wife's talent to gain fame, and a murderer who had killed a neighboring woman when he was a teenager. Before the real culprit was revealed, the wife, who heard the detective questioning the artist about the past, had this monologue:

> *I didn't think he killed my sister; I didn't think he could have. If so, the person I cannot stand is not him but myself. First of all, I can't stand the fact that he killed my sister. Next, I can't forgive myself for loving such a man. Finally, I'm afraid of myself since still I can't hate him.*

Hanjo couldn't figure out how to refute her wild accusations. Did she really think he was a murderer? If so, when had she begun to think so? And why had she become the wife of a murderer?

There are things in the world that cannot be explained and things that cannot be interpreted. People eat with their families, plant seedlings in the garden, and drink happily with their friends—then they die in a car accident, kill themselves, or fall down the stairs to their death. What reason is there for all that?

That morning, his father had left home early, anxious to finish the work on the pipes in the auditorium. All day long, he had shifted pipes with the other workers and shoveled earth. After finishing for the day, he had checked that the materials for the next day's work were ready. And then he had taken Jisoo to the reservoir and killed her? No matter how hard Hanjo thought about it, it didn't make sense.

Nevertheless, he had not been confident enough to challenge the official version, which had scientific evidence and a clear confession to back it up. He couldn't clearly explain why his father wasn't the murderer, and if it wasn't his father, he had no theory about who else it could be. The grief of admitting that his father was a murderer felt easier to accept than the confusion and criticism he would have to deal with by refusing to do so.

So he ruled out the possibilities that his father might not be a murderer one by one. He did not disbelieve the official case reports and court records, and simply accepted the evidence and legal judgment that his father was the culprit. But he had swallowed a great deal of doubt. For example, why had Jisoo followed his father to the dam that day, why hadn't he said anything about what he had done that evening, and why had he admitted to the crime so easily?

After his father was arrested, Hanjo had gone to the police station with his brother. Nam Bora sent the brothers into a room with about a dozen folding chairs on each side of a long table, past the dark hallway with signs reading **DETECTIVES**, **INVESTIGATIONS**, and **ADMINISTRATIVE SUPPORT OFFICE**. Sitting on a hard chair, Hanjo felt that he had committed an unforgivable crime.

Their father came in through the door opposite. Dazzled by the bright lights, he knitted his brows like a shrew suddenly emerging from its hole. He seemed to have become an old man in just a few days.

"What are you doing here?" his father asked. His hair was disheveled and his eyes were bloodshot. He reminded Hanjo of a character in a Western movie—not the main character with the gun who was quick on the uptake and controlled situations but a farmer who needed protection because he was foolish and naive.

"We were meant to come with Mom," Suin said, "but we couldn't wake her up. She's had a lot to drink."

He seemed to have made up his mind to hurt his father's feelings. Hanjo had many things he wanted to ask his father. Had he killed Jisoo, and if so, why had he killed her? And if he hadn't, why was he here? But instead, he asked, "Is . . . there anything you need? I'll bring it next time. Would you like me to bring some socks if you're cold at night?"

His father didn't answer. He held their hands in his, and Hanjo could see bulging knuckles and broken veins. His father stared at his sons' hands, and was surprised by their unexpectedly thick wrists, hard bones, the feisty vigor and vitality that beat there.

"You know your dad loves you, don't you?"

The father observed his sons carefully, as if he were holding a hammer and aiming at a nail while determining the exact angle and position. For some reason, Hanjo thought that he would never see him again.

"Yes, I know."

"That's all you need to know. You guys don't have to love me . . . You can leave now. Don't come back."

Suin never visited their father after that. Hanjo tried twice more after the sentencing, once on the weekend ahead of his enlistment and once on the weekend after he was discharged from the army. It rained both times, and he didn't meet his father on either occasion.

A warder in his forties with a long chin came out and told him his father refused to see him, so he shouldn't come anymore. He said his father was well and asked if he had any message for him. Hanjo replied that he had none. Even though he understood his father, he couldn't help but feel rejected.

It was raining when he left the front gate of the prison. A blackbird was singing on a distant plane tree. The cement wall faded into the distance, and the black guard towers stood tall in the rain. He thought it was fortunate that the wall was high. It seemed that the high wall was not locking his father in but protecting him from the world. The world was too wild and unruly for him to live in it, but he would be safe as long as he was behind the wall.

On the bus back to Seoul, he thought about why his father refused to see him. Was his father afraid, not wanting to be a shameful father before his son by telling him the truth he'd been dealing with alone? Afraid that by doing so he would cause him a lot more pain?

He wanted to forget his father. He wanted to forget the murder by forgetting his father, as if it were a past belonging to a stranger, not to himself. So he erased his father from his mind. The black eyebrows that wriggled whenever he smiled, the hooklike hands that patted hair that was hot in the sun, the smell of sour sweat that rose when Hanjo was in his arms, the smell of dust.

Over the years, he accepted his identity as a murderer's son. Rather than wasting his life searching for the truth, he chose to believe the lie. Truth and all that stuff . . . Just living was difficult enough.

It was close to noon when Hanjo woke up; he had fallen asleep at dawn after struggling with his wife's book late into the night.

The loud and persistent ringing of the phone forced him to move his stiff body. His mouth was dry, and his tongue was as thick as if he had swallowed sand. He picked up the phone lying on the table.

The caller was an art reporter from a daily paper whom he had met several times. The reporter launched into questions about his wife's book without any greetings. It was like he didn't want to give Hanjo any time to think.

As expected, the reporter said he had already finished interviewing the author. It was not difficult to infer who the main male figure was, and there were already readers who had guessed. Hanjo replied that he would respond legally to wild speculation. It was an impulsive reaction that went against Suin's advice to not make any comment to the media. The reporter said that he didn't know the inside story, but if he didn't cover it properly, he would be branded as shameless. He hung up after thanking Hanjo for clarifying that he had nothing to do with the contents of the novel.

It suddenly became quiet, and the sound of car horns, drills, and whistles could be heard in the distance.

The first article was posted on the internet a little after four in the afternoon. "Is the Main Character of *Your Lies About Me* Real?"

The article hinted at the identity of the shameless villain who had abused a nineteen-year-old girl, but didn't say it outright. The writer seemed to be mindful of libel.

Dozens of comments were immediately posted. Hanjo's name appeared on personal blogs, art-related chat rooms, and social media, emotional diatribes filled with disgusting abuse and accusations.

Soon after, his cell phone and the studio phone rang simultaneously. Hanjo felt like a soldier standing in the middle of a battlefield with artillery shells pouring down. His career, his work, his fame, his wife, his happiness—everything that had once belonged to him, all fragmented and scattered.

I wish my wife were here. She would have told me what to do at a time like this. Don't be scared—they're just jealous of you.

Yes, their marriage couldn't be better, even if people were whispering behind their backs. Hanjo loved his wife like a shepherd who had fallen in love with a goddess. He missed every day spent together, when they laughed quietly and talked softly; he missed the insignificant chatter of those moments.

His wife was seldom drunk, and she didn't burst into tears easily. But in this moment, he thought he would like her to be drunk and crying. Of course she wouldn't even be thinking of him. Come to think of it, his wife might not consider this a betrayal of him, since she had never truly trusted him enough to have a real relationship with him.

He filled a glass and let the liquor flow down his throat. His cell phone vibrated. The word *Brother* appeared on the screen.

"Is that you, Hanjo? Are you OK?"

How could Suin think he would be OK? But he didn't want to blame his brother. It was not his brother who had caused all this to happen; it was himself. He was drunk, but he was sober enough to see that.

"Yes, I'm fine. I have a headache. I guess I drank too much."

"I thought you wouldn't answer the phone. You shouldn't. Turn off the phone right now and leave the house. Don't meet anyone."

He could not hear Suin talking loudly in his ear. He was remembering sitting on a rooftop railing and watching as his father was arrested. The bright gleam of the handcuffs on his father's wrists came to mind. Did his father laugh then? Was it painful? Did he look at himself?

"We can't tell when the reporters will be coming, so turn off your cell phone and get out of the house right now," Suin was shouting. "Stay away for a while. Eat something and come to your senses, huh? Answer if you understand me."

He could see things his wife had left behind: a cardigan on the back of the sofa, a coffee cup with a clear lipstick mark on it, a novel by Guy de Maupassant with a leaf marking her place . . . All of these brought a keen awareness of her absence.

"But I have nowhere to go."

He sounded so desperate that he was surprised. The hollow eyes and emaciated cheeks reflected in the window looked like someone else's. He thought he was being punished. His crime was a half-hearted *I love you* that he had uttered without foreseeing his fate. He could hear Suin's urgent voice through the receiver.

"What?"

"Damn it. I don't know where to go."

Haeri

When Heejae said he wanted to buy Howard House, Seonwoo had been dubious. Standing on the hill overlooking the city, this symbol of Isan was not something that should be owned by an individual. If someone claimed to own Howard House, it would take away part of the city's history, the house that every citizen treasured in their mind.

When signs that he was losing his battle against disease intensified, Dr. Howard had written a will in which he instructed that the house be sold to strengthen the foundation's finances. Leaving aside the high price, however, it was not easy to find a buyer who could afford to maintain the almost four thousand square yards of land, including the affiliated buildings. Construction companies wishing to demolish the house and replace it with high-rise buildings also abandoned their plans, because Dr. Howard had specified that the buildings remain intact.

It was Jang Heejae who finally rushed to rescue Howard House, after it had not found a buyer for more than four years. The second son of a hotel owner in the heart of the city, he admired and hated his father, who was a successful businessman. Heejae, being younger than his brother, had constantly tried to show his father he was not a stupid dropout, but he'd failed repeatedly.

After leaving the army, he jumped straight into moneymaking instead of going back to college. Rather than seeking his father's help, he borrowed money from a bank, bought a used car, and started a rental-car business for the hotel guests. He worked as a driver and mechanic, and relied on his natural sociability and affability. Five years later, the number of cars had increased to twelve.

Once the rental-car business got going, he established a maintenance plant. People who bought vehicles during the initial car craze, when they became available for private ownership, were not familiar with cars, and there were a number of accidents caused by poor road conditions. His business kept growing. By the time he passed forty, he had become a well-known local businessman. However, even for him, Howard House was not an easy thing to acquire.

"When I was young," he said to his worried wife, "there were few buildings in this city with more than five stories. Howard House up on the hill was the only building higher than my father's hotel. I wanted to own that monument that could be seen from anywhere in town. Then, I thought, I would have outdone him."

Seonwoo had never seen such a confident man. She felt obliged to answer that she, too, had wanted to live in the house for a long time.

There was another reason Heejae wanted to buy the house, but he didn't tell his wife about it. He was calculating that the symbolic trust and familiarity of Howard House, which contained the history of the nearly century-old city, would be a great asset to him in his political aspirations. Repairing and decorating the old, abandoned house could be a good news story for the local media.

On the day he paid for it, he declared to his family that Howard House was now "our house," as if producing a surprise gift, and then went straight into a large-scale renovation that maintained the house's original shape while repairing almost everything except the basic framework.

The faded roof tiles were replaced with new ones, the walls were reinforced, and insulating glass was placed in old window frames. The crumbling embankment was rebuilt, and the branches of the cedar covering the roof were neatly trimmed. Howard House, which had once been a solid fortress of wealth and fame rather than a home, now also had the beauty that loving care brings.

On the morning they moved in, they changed into white clothes. As the car rolled up the hillside, Howard House's antique tiled roof and redbrick walls were revealed. The daughters were fascinated by the magnificence of the house, as splendid as a castle in a fairy tale.

The children's rooms faced one another on each side of the hallway on the upper floor. Even though no one told her which was hers, Jisoo went to her room instinctively, as if she were being drawn by something. There were a new bed and desk in the room. As she approached the window and pushed it open, the garden and annex came into view, as well as the school and the city spread out below the hill.

An excited Haeri ran into the room and shouted, "Sister! This house is going to be fun."

Haeri was right. Every day in Howard House something exciting happened, like living in an amusement park. There were countless places to hide, explore, and see. The sounds made by an old house, the narrow gaps between the walls, the number and slope of the basement stairs, the box rooms and the space under the stairs covered with plywood, the scent of the cedar tree flooding through the window when you woke up . . .

On weekends, Uncle Malcolm took pictures with his camera, and Aunt Malcolm made delicious snacks. Hanjo drew pictures of Howard House in his sketchbook all day long. He never got annoyed, even when Haeri bothered him, and he made playful faces that only the two of them understood. Haeri never wanted to leave that happy amusement park.

On that fateful day, Haeri had the impression she was playing a strange game she had never played before. Her mom had probably made her think so, telling her that nothing had happened to her sister and that Jisoo would come back like after a game of hide-and-seek.

At ten thirty that evening, when her mother sat on her bed with a fairy-tale book instead of her sister, she felt something had changed. The fairy tale her mother read was "The Swan Prince." The Sherlock Holmes and Miss Marple stories that her sister read were much more fun.

Haeri couldn't fall asleep easily, even after her mother closed the book and swept back her hair. Her sister still hadn't come home. Her mother got up from the bed and put out the light. "Haeri, your sister's late," she said. "She'll be back when you wake up tomorrow morning, so go to sleep now."

But her mom had lied. Her sister didn't come back the next morning. Everything remained the same, but the house turned into a strange space. Dad's eyes were bloodshot and his neat hair stuck out. Mom was lying on the sofa like a pile of loose laundry. The whole house was like a huge machine with broken screws and cogs.

A police car came up the graveled driveway. Haeri looked down from her window as a man in a gray jacket and a policewoman in uniform got out of the car. The short, strongly built man seemed like the slow-moving protagonist of a TV police drama who was always being criticized by his superiors. Haeri wondered if the detectives would catch the criminal in fifty minutes, just like in the police dramas, which followed the same pattern every time.

They would search her sister's room as soon as they got inside the house, as always in dramas. They would find the box of books she used to read, and a cosmetic box with three colored lipsticks and a set of hair rollers. And they would try to dig up her sister's secrets that these items contained. Haeri didn't want to let them do that. Those were secrets that only she and her sister knew. She crossed over to her sister's room without anyone knowing. Before the detectives came in, she took a corrugated-cardboard box from her sister's closet and hid it under her bed.

Now they wouldn't know how Jisoo threw down her backpack as if she didn't want to see it anymore when she went into the room. How she would not study at her desk but look into the mirror and apply lipstick, sometimes sobbing quietly.

Haeri propped her chin up on the windowsill and stared at the tranquil garden. This wasn't the first time her sister had disappeared. Her sister loved hide-and-seek and was good at hiding. Once hidden, she would appear only long after the game was over and Haeri had given up looking for her. When asked where she had been, she would answer that she was hiding.

"Lies. Who were you hiding from?"

"People."

"What people? Bad people?"

"No, just . . . people."

Haeri wondered who those people were. Maybe Jisoo wanted to hide from everyone? Their mom, their dad, her teachers, her friends, maybe from herself.

Haeri imagined her sister was playing a very long, perhaps never-ending, game of hide-and-seek. Then there would be no more listening to her stories in bed or looking at her back as she cried, face down on her desk.

Jisoo's absence subtly changed the atmosphere of the whole city. People thought they would recover if the murderer was caught after the funeral. It was both comfortable and awkward to think this, but that's how life goes on. But they were never able to recover. They had been complete and perfect as a family, but without Jisoo, that perfection was lost, and they were no longer a family at all.

Throughout the following year's election campaign, Heejae lived at the election office. A house without Jisoo had taken some of his life away from him. People sympathized with him for the loss of his daughter, but did not vote for him. During the counting, a TV announcer commented that he did well from the personal tragedy of his daughter being killed, but failed to beat his predecessor, who had run for reelection.

Haeri noticed the remarkably diminished number of words coming from her father and mother. When they talked, there were taboo words that shouldn't appear on their lips, words like *death, police station, sister, detective*. To talk about death, you had to find other words to replace *death*. If you couldn't find any, it was better to stop speaking.

The forbidden words spread like an epidemic. Words like Jisoo's favorite *corn salad*, the "Ave Maria," which Jisoo often sang, *hide-and-seek, Borim Stream*, and *dam* were not available. Finally, the family lost all their words.

At night, voices from downstairs echoed in her sleep. Her father's voice was constantly high pitched, like the squeak of a starving mouse, and her mother's voice sounded crushed and flattened, like a bent nail.

"The debt collectors came during the day. Two gangsters made themselves at home in the living room for more than three hours. Haeri and I were driven into the kitchen, and then her upstairs room." Her mother's voice sounded muffled, as if covered with fabric.

"Bastards," her father said. "They followed me around like a pair of vultures, and now they're going to gnaw at my dead body?"

People were uncomfortable about the murder of a high school girl; they did not want the affair to get any bigger and hoped it would soon be forgotten. To escape joint responsibility for the tragic incident, they considered themselves victims. The perpetrator was her family. They complained that Heejae had moved to Howard House for the election and invited the tragedy.

Her dad began to drink. He got drunk before dark and sometimes came to blows with strangers. He was caught driving under the influence several times, and avoided being locked up in a cell overnight only because a police officer he knew overlooked the matter.

Everything was fine when her dad wasn't drinking. He was friendly and attentive; he laughed and loved his family sincerely. However, when he was drunk, he had a hard time controlling his emotions. When her father, overcome with sorrow, pounded the wall with his forehead, it trembled. Then at one point, there was a dull sound like a water balloon bursting. That was the sound of her dad slapping her mom on the cheek.

At night, Haeri held her breath in bed. Tense hostility and fear swelled in the dark. She could taste the sorrow, as sour as vinegar, and salty. She heard sounds downstairs, dull sounds of friction and rupture, suppressed screams and groans.

Then she heard her dad sobbing. "Honey, are you OK? Your nose is bleeding. Damn it. Here's a tissue . . . No, look up."

She couldn't believe her father was crying. She could not tell whether he was crying because her sister had not come back, because her mother was a wreck, or because he himself had become a wild animal.

Adults were infinitely weak in the face of pain. They tortured each other in the dark in odd ways, then fell into a short sleep when they were exhausted. Haeri didn't want to think about any of them. She picked up a sharpened pencil and stabbed herself in the forearm, then fell asleep licking the blood flowing from the wound, like a fragile baby animal.

When she woke up in the morning, red handprints were clear on her mother's cheeks. Her cheekbones were yellowish with round bruises like the moon. She stared at the world before her with cold eyes, then forced herself to smile when Haeri caught her looking like that. Her mother's tight smile was unfamiliar to her, as if she were a stranger.

"Mom, can't you run away and live where Dad can't come after you?"

Her mom stared blankly at Haeri, as if she were delusional. For a moment, she seemed to be wondering who this child was. Then she opened her arms without saying a word. Haeri didn't want to be in her mother's arms. The mother with her arms held out was not a mother full of love. It was a mother who had lost the object of her love, a mother whose body had half collapsed, a mother who could no longer protect Haeri.

Haeri didn't trust grown-ups. Her sister, who everyone said would come back, had not come back. Everyone said things would be fine, but nothing was fine. She couldn't believe her father, who rubbed his rough, unshaven face against hers and said, "I love you." Still, Haeri hoped she was wrong. She wanted to believe that her mother had never forgotten her, even for a moment, and still loved her.

Their family had never been separated from one another. They had always gone everywhere together, even on vacations. It was only after Jisoo left that they were surprised to learn that they might break up at any time.

One morning, still asleep, Haeri heard someone knocking on the front door. At first, she thought it was a dream, but the knocking was annoying and persistent. When she opened her eyes, the room was hot and stuffy.

There was a woman standing outside the front door who looked vaguely familiar. It was the wife of an uncle she had met several times when she was younger. Her aunt told her to wash her face because they had to go somewhere, then went into the kitchen. After washing her face, Haeri chewed the cereal her aunt placed on the table and asked, "Where's Mom and Dad?"

The aunt went to the sink without saying a word and washed Haeri's empty bowl in running water. It was only after washing the bowl that she spoke.

"Haeri. Your mom and dad are dead."

Lies! All adults lied. Uncle Malcolm, who said he would find her sister, did not do so, and when her sister died, her mother said she wasn't dead. Now her aunt was lying, too.

"Let's go. You're going to greet your mom and dad, so you must choose a pretty dress."

There were a lot of things Haeri wanted to ask her, but now didn't seem like the right moment. She wasn't sure, because it would be her first experience of greeting dead people face to face, but she reckoned she should act like a good girl. So she took out the pink dress and parka her father had given her as a gift on her last birthday.

The hospital was a three-story brick building downtown. About ten cars were parked in the parking lot. An ambulance was marked with the red words EMERGENCY PATIENT ESCORT and a cross. When her aunt spoke her father's name, a receptionist wearing a black tie guided them to the basement of the building on the right.

The ceiling was white, the walls and floors were cool, and the metal surfaces emitted a silver gleam. A man wearing a white mask pulled back two sheets, one after the other. Her father, his hair neatly combed, seemed to be asleep or lost in thought.

Her mother's face was unblemished, without a drop of blood. Her pale smile was so faint, it was almost invisible. She looked as if she were listening to the second movement of Brahms's Third Symphony in the study. She looked prettier than when she was alive. Was it because the shadow of pain had left her face? Haeri hoped her mom and dad hadn't felt any pain when they died, and believed they hadn't.

There was a police officer waiting by the door. "I'm sorry to have phoned you so early in the morning," he said, stepping closer. "As I mentioned, Jang Heejae and Kim Seonwoo had a car accident early this morning on their way home. As they entered the bridge from the riverside, the car struck the railing and fell into the river. The wheels appear to have skidded on some ice. Both were in critical condition when the ambulance arrived."

"Haeri," her aunt said, "is there anything you want to say to your mom and dad?"

Haeri had things to say. She wanted to say that Jisoo was pretty with makeup, played hide-and-seek alone in the garden, and wanted to run away from their disgusting house. The rest of her makeup, the books under the bed that she read . . . But those words would remain secrets between her sister and her.

Haeri thought of what else she should say to her mom and dad. Things she wished they knew, but couldn't say: that she was scared of her drunken dad, but still loved him; that she hated her mom, who didn't take care of her, but wanted to see her again; that her sister was playing hide-and-seek somewhere. But their souls would not understand her words. So she said, "Hi, Dad! Hi, Mom!"

Her aunt looked at Haeri with astonished eyes, as if she had been slapped.

Her uncle ran a small bending factory in the western industrial complex. It was called a factory, but in reality, her uncle was both president and worker, and her aunt played the role of accountant and laborer.

Her uncle adopted Haeri, who had been left alone in Howard House like an abandoned puppy, and set about changing her name. Her aunt disagreed with the decision, insisting that Haeri would inherit a fortune and would thus be fine on her own. But a large proportion of her father's wealth had been spent on campaigning, and only a small deposit remained in the bank. The only saving grace was the small amount of money Haeri received every month from the trust fund.

Howard House was a trust property, so there was no way they could sell it. Even if they could, there was no one willing to buy it. People could not erase the suffering of the family from their memories, and the house was reduced to being the scene of a terrible murder.

Heejae and Seonwoo were buried in the family cemetery in the memorial park where Jisoo had been laid to rest. Haeri wondered if the souls of her family would feel lonely. She didn't think they would. At least they were together.

Her uncle had daughters who were two and four years younger than herself. Her uncle and his wife did not take much care of her, but they did not mind her taking care of their daughters. She brainwashed herself into becoming Kim Soojin, her uncle's eldest daughter.

"Everything went wrong after they moved to that house," her uncle whispered in her aunt's ear. "I tried to dissuade him, but he just did whatever he wanted, and look what happened. That crazy Malcolm House guy destroyed everything."

Haeri didn't want to believe her uncle when he said that Uncle Malcolm had killed her sister. She banished the details from her memory and erased the people. She was afraid of the truth she would have to face as soon as she clearly defined the nature of the incident—the tangled web of hidden motivations and truths, concealed hypocrisy and sin.

Every morning, when she woke up, her swollen eyes wouldn't open properly. She felt as if she had been crying all night long in her dreams, wrapped in an inexplicable sorrow. She couldn't remember what made her so sad.

Her emotional turmoil led to impulsive acts that did not discriminate between men and women, adults and children. Neither teacher nor friend was an exception. She punched and kicked, and if she couldn't get over her anger, she scratched, bit, and threw stones. In middle school, her guardians were often summoned because of her truancy, assaults, and misbehavior. She would often run away from home. She was repeatedly suspended for limited or unlimited periods of time.

Haeri liked the convenience store with its pale interiors. She memorized first the location and then, as she moved up and down the display stands, the price of each item, until her mind grew as taut as a bow in an archery contest.

She could not recall when she started finding strange things in her pockets, small things she didn't need and that she wondered why she had taken. The guilt of stealing other people's belongings turned into a strange feeling of satisfaction. She didn't know what it was, but when she punished someone, she felt it brought her a small reward in return.

When she got home, she felt suffocated by anger and guilt. She thought she had been contaminated by something bad, and felt sin festering inside her. She wanted to become clean, but she didn't know what to do. She desperately wanted someone to slap her, but no one blamed her or scolded her. The only way was to punish herself.

She pricked her thighs with a pointed pencil. The sharp pain spread throughout her body, and her eyes lost focus. Haeri clenched her teeth and pulled the pencil lead back until it broke. The unbearable pain penetrated her like a wedge and drove away the sorrow in her body. Mental pain gave way to physical.

Her implements became increasingly diverse. Sharp, shiny, or pointed objects . . . The wounds on her forearm or calf grew larger and deeper over time, and recovery became slower and slower. The wounds that she did not disinfect properly grew infected, and keloid scars bulged up.

At school, she received only cold looks. The children who stood around chattering in the corners of the classroom during break times would fall silent if she approached.

A week before the summer vacation, when she was in the third year of middle school, a few boys were hanging around in the hallway. Their voices drifted to Haeri, where she sat next to the window.

"What are you going to do during the summer vacation?"

"Let's sneak into Howard House."

"What would you do there?"

"There are ghosts in that house."

"Lies. How can you believe that?"

"That's why I want to go in and check."

Haeri's stomach roiled and she felt nauseous. Were the souls of her family still living at Howard House, unable to leave? Might her dad be sitting on the brown leather sofa, reading the morning paper? Might the smell of the coffee her mom was brewing wake her up in the morning? Might her sister read fairy tales to her at night?

Haeri hoped it was so, wanted it to be so. It occurred to her that Howard House should not be abandoned to those children's wild footsteps. She had to protect her mom, dad, and sister from them, people who didn't know about their deaths or their lives that continued after death.

The vacation would start a week later.

Beyond the iron fence, the overgrown garden was littered with low shrubs and weeds. There were rusty bicycles and broken hangers lying between dry bushes. White, weathered objects glistened under the thick shrubs like the skulls of small animals.

Haeri recalled a dead cat she had seen in a corner of the garden when she was seven years old. The cat's limbs were stiff, and its nostrils were full of maggots. Its half-closed eyes seemed thoughtful. The cat's body was lonely as it slowly rotted. Haeri felt she was doing something wrong by peeping at the cat, which was slowly decaying after repeatedly freezing and thawing during the winter. Then, one day, the cat disappeared. That night, as she sat by her bedside, her sister told her she had buried the cat under the fir tree in the garden.

Haeri crossed the garden, heading for the house. Her ankles kept twisting in mole holes. The front door was locked with a heavy chain and rusty padlock. The first-floor windows were held shut by big nails. She had no key, but it didn't matter. She turned the corner of the house, and a boiler room appeared, a simple roof over a wooden frame.

She curled herself up like a cat and slipped in through the wooden slats of the wall. The door leading from the boiler room into the basement had been Haeri's secret passageway when she'd lived at Howard House. When they played hide-and-seek, Haeri would go out through the front door, then secretly hide inside the house and surprise her sister.

At the top of the stairs that ran along the basement wall, there was a door with warped corners. A beam of light shone through the gap. When she pushed the door open, the familiar scene came back to life: high ceilings, straight walls, glossy floors, large sofas, and bookcases full of books along the walls. White sheets covered the untidy furniture and bookshelves, as if it were the home of people who were soon going to return from a trip.

A brief pause ensued. One second? Ten seconds? She saw something in the light filtering between the curtains. She was not clear on what it was. It might have been more a feeling arising from being so completely alone than a clear reality. Some kind of warmth, familiarity—the feeling of sweetness and pleasure, the faces where all those emotions were concentrated . . .

Her father, mother, and sister were everywhere—above the eaves, at the corner of the stairs, on the terrace railing. She could clearly feel their presence, even if she couldn't talk to them or touch them.

When she pushed open the study door, the rusty hinges squealed. A brown leather chair stood facing the window. It was her father's armchair, a grapevine carved on a back so high that the top of the head of the person sitting in it was invisible. The armrests where her father's elbows used to rest were faded and pale. Haeri talked to her father over the back of the chair.

"Why did you do that? Why did everyone go away and leave only me behind?"

The house was quiet, her breathing the only sound. She stroked the flowers and vines embossed on the dusty chair.

Haeri wasn't afraid when dusk fell outside the window. Howard House with her dead family was cozier than her living uncle's house. In the bottom of the kitchen cupboard, there were four candles and a matchbox that her mother had once bought for power outages. She lit a candle and climbed the stairs. The guttering flame was like the voices of ghosts. *Haeri, how you've grown. Why have you come? We're doing great here.*

If they saw the shadows cast by the candle on the window, the children would run away. Now no child would dare enter the haunted Howard House.

Haeri pulled the box out from under her bunk bed. When she opened the box, there was a faint scent of Ceylon tea. Her sister's things remained intact. Dry lipstick and cosmetics, sunglasses with broken frames, books with folded corners . . . It didn't seem reasonable that her sister was gone but her things were still there. She remembered her sister smiling with peach lipstick on her lips.

"Pretty?"

Her sister's face was unfamiliar with her bright lips. Their mom used makeup, but she was different from Jisoo. Their mother with makeup was still their mother, just a brighter and prettier mother. But her older sister with makeup on was not her older sister at all.

"You're pretty; I don't like it. It doesn't look like you."

Haeri dipped a finger in the dust of the dried lipstick and put it on her lips. She detected a faint sweetness. Was it because Jisoo wanted to be someone else, someone who had secrets, not a nice, pretty, studious sister, not her mom and dad's daughter, but someone only she herself knew? Maybe she put on makeup because she wanted to show herself to herself, no one else?

There was a yellowish, faded spring notebook at the bottom of the box. It was Hanjo's sketchbook. His drawings of Howard House were more vivid and lifelike than she remembered, despite their rough draftsmanship and poor shading. Corroded bronze window-frame decorations, flocks of birds flying over the roof, sparkling beaks and yellow eyes, sturdy cedar branches and loitering cats, faces peeking out and inviting compassion . . .

Haeri's fingers paused at a bookmark inserted in the sketchbook. A familiar yet unfamiliar face caught her eye. The thin chin and quivering lips reminded her of her sister. The curves of the figure's body, which were drawn in a fast line, looked similar to her sister's as she walked as if dancing. Her older sister looking out the window casually, her older sister holding a book, her older sister staring at the painter and smiling . . .

All the vivid sketches were nude. Haeri felt as if a high-voltage current was passing through her. Could he have imagined this? Or was he actually looking at her when he was drawing?

The wax from the melted candle piled into the shape of a wedge. Her sister's death once again became a mystery. She stepped back from the window, and decided to unravel it. She would find out why her sister hadn't come back, and who was responsible for it.

One rainy afternoon, Haeri picked out a dress from her sister's closet. The sky-blue dress with white polka dots looked old fashioned. The waist and shoulders fit Haeri like custom-made clothes, but the hips were tight and the sleeves short. But she didn't take off the old dress, because by wearing dead people's clothes, she could indulge in the illusion that she was wandering around without knowing she was dead.

Even though the rain had stopped, dark clouds remained, and a swollen, muddy stream surged past her feet. She headed for the toilet on the riverbank as if she had come to a decision. She locked the door and took the knife she used to sharpen pencils out from her bag. Sharp pain and dizziness followed one another.

A woman cleaning the toilet forced open the locked door and found her. A report was sent to the sergeant in charge of juvenile delinquents and domestic violence, stating that a female student had been found injured on the riverside. Nam Bora, who had worked in the transport division for five years after the Howard House scandal, had just returned from attending to a local case of domestic violence.

There, a woman had been squatting, holding a baby. The husband was not at home, and a boy who looked to be about five or six years old stared at Nam Bora with frightened eyes. The woman denied that her husband had assaulted her, even though her cheekbones were swollen and the bruises on her arms were clearly visible. When asked what had happened, she merely repeated, "It's nothing," and glossed over it. The language of women accustomed to violence was silence and lies. Nam Bora felt shame that she could neither punish the violent nor protect the victims.

When Nam Bora read the report about the student collapsed at the riverside, she hurried to the hospital. The girl was still asleep when she entered the hospital room. Her guardian had not arrived yet. The doctor was in his midthirties, in horn-rimmed glasses.

"It could have been dangerous if she had been found a bit later," he told Nam Bora. "She hurt herself in the thigh, but the wound was deep. It was a stroke of luck she didn't touch an artery. She'd been suffering from hypothermia and bleeding all afternoon. Fortunately, she's stable now. This kind of deep self-harming is rare, and it's not something she's only done once or twice. Negative emotions must have been accumulating in her for a long time."

The sleeping girl frowned and moistened her lips. Was she having a bad dream? Nam Bora opened the backpack on the bedside table to check her contact information. It contained a couple of reference books, a school exercise book, *The Brothers Karamazov* with corners folded down, and a colorful cloth pencil case.

Between the slightly worn pages of the novel, an old family photo was stuck. Nam Bora looked closely at the characters in the picture. They were people she knew: the Howard House family, murdered or dead, whom people had forgotten about. Nam Bora was not sure if it could still be called a family photo.

There was a creak from the mattress behind her. The girl must have woken up. Nam Bora looked round and said as softly as she could, "Hi, I'm Sergeant Nam Bora from the women and youth division at the Central Police Station."

Haeri did not answer and avoided Nam Bora's eyes. She wondered if Nam Bora would remember her, or what kind of person she would remember if she did.

"Do you recognize me? We met when you were very young."

The girl glanced at her, then lowered her gaze. Nam Bora vowed not to ask her why she cut herself or scare her by saying she might have died. She had probably heard that for too long, too many times.

"If you're a cop, is it OK for you to take someone's picture and not return it? You said you'd give it back when you took my sister's picture."

The child's eyes glistened with hostility. It was not vague hatred or anger but a hostility that felt like a plea for help. Nam Bora realized that she had completely forgotten to return Jisoo's photo, the one she'd taken for the flyers, after the case concluded and the investigation team disbanded. It must still be in a case-file box, in the police station's archives.

"I'm sorry. Come see me when you feel better. I'll find your sister's picture and give it back to you."

Nam Bora handed the girl a business card with her work address and contact number. The child lay back and turned her head away from Nam Bora.

"That day, too, you said you'd give it back right away. I heard it all from the top of the stairs."

The child, who remembered what had happened as vividly as if it were yesterday, seemed to be living in that moment, rather than forgetting her sister's death.

"I'm sorry. I was immature and clumsy at the time because it was my first case. But I know it's wrong, so I can fix it."

Nam Bora sat on a corner of the bed and laid a hand on Haeri's forehead, a smooth hand warm like gravel in sunlight, a hand that made her feel as if good things might happen.

"I still don't understand what happened to my sister," said Haeri. "I think there was something wrong about it all, but I don't know what it was."

Nam Bora was not confident she could explain the case to Haeri's satisfaction. All she had done as a new recruit was run minor errands. She spoke plainly, as if talking to herself. "I don't understand everything, but I think I can reconstruct the case when more time has passed and you're old enough to understand."

Nam Bora said this, but she was skeptical that she would be able to. No matter how much time went by, the child wouldn't understand. Even if she did, it wouldn't be the truth, just an explanation. Nevertheless, this girl needed the truth, a truth that had to be accepted even if it was too harsh to accept. Perhaps such a truth did not exist. The news was a mixture of truth and lies, or neither, and most of the gossip and rumors were false.

Haeri had scrutinized newspapers, weekly and monthly magazines, and popular tabloids plastered with scandals at the time of the incident in the periodical section on the third floor of the city library, and had even searched the microfilms. The origin and history of Howard House. The architectural aesthetics. The case data. The police investigation. The trial. All the related articles she could find. She also visited her neighbors, her sister's friends and teachers, and witnesses. Some of them were dead and some of them were alive. Some kept silent and some didn't even remember.

Haeri read between the lines of the old articles, met people, and struggled to recall the colors, smells, and sounds of that day. She read, wrote, and collected even seemingly irrelevant gossip that had nothing to do with the incident. It belonged to her, to no one else, and she had the right to own her share of the truth.

She would gather small fragments of memory that had not found a context and reconstruct facts that had not been considered meaningful. Even if the tangled truth revealed itself, it would not be possible to go back to before that day, but she would be able to correct her own life.

Haeri quit school when she was in her second year of high school. Just before she quit, she would often bunk classes to wander around the neglected gardens of Howard House, returning to her uncle's house late at night, like the last lord of an abandoned citadel, the last revolutionary confronting the enemy after the death of all her comrades, the survivor of a terrible battle.

There was a rumor among the children that someone had seen a ghost wandering around the overgrown garden and lights shining from the windows of Howard House at night. It was ridiculous, but it wasn't nonsense, because she herself was the ghost. She had died that summer, and never lived for a moment after that.

There was nothing illegal about the foundation's decision to name Hanjo as Howard House's manager. Haeri wasn't sure whether to be glad or angry to see Hanjo again. She ought to hate the murderer's son, but she couldn't.

Hanjo's coming meant that her memories of him would return. He was the only one who could talk about her sister's death. She wanted to reconstruct every moment of that summer by shaking off the dirt that was muddying her memory, and matching the scattered pieces. Even if Hanjo and she failed to do so, they could understand and heal each other's pain by just sharing memories.

The night Hanjo returned, Haeri looked at Malcolm House from the second-floor window of Howard House. She wanted him to know that Howard House was not a run-down ruin; it was not an empty house. There was still an owner: herself.

Hanjo, on his return, did not recognize her. She thought this was a good thing. If he recognized her, his memories would be damaged or distorted in some way. She would not tell him what she believed to be the truth.

One afternoon, they were side by side on the sofa, looking at the family picture on the piano. Smiling Heejae's black pants had sharp creases; the white lace on Seonwoo's dress was sparkling white. Jisoo's bobbed hair had comb marks in it, and a young mongrel dog was sitting next to Haeri, who was showing a gap where her front teeth were missing as she laughed.

Haeri crooned to herself upon seeing the dog. Hanjo said the dog had been mobilized in the search for the missing Jisoo. "November remembered the smell of Jisoo much better than the police dogs," he said.

Haeri didn't remember that, but her heart filled with joy when she heard the name November; she felt a sense of pride because it proved that her past was not a delusion and that her memory was not a lie. She and November had been comrades in pain, preserving the same memories. They had been like animals from the same litter, babies born of the same womb. They had grown up together, and she couldn't figure out why they had only now met again.

The family in the picture seemed to be convinced that their happy, firm smiles would never disappear. But Haeri felt that they were not really happy but only making happy faces.

The last time she'd seen her mom and dad, Haeri had just said *Hi*. She wanted to say too much, and so couldn't say anything. She didn't know what to hide and what to reveal when it came to her complex emotions, and she couldn't distinguish between contradictions and facts, or between deceit and misunderstanding.

As time passed and the floating particles sank, the lies and secrets became clear. Her sister hadn't kept her promise, and her mom had lied. And her dad had tricked everyone with his death.

Her parents had died after visiting Jisoo's grave at the memorial park, and the police concluded it was poor driving on a freezing road that had caused their car to fall off the bridge. But she knew that adults were good at lying, and that you couldn't believe what they said.

Her parents had no reason to go to visit her sister, because they thought she was still in Howard House. They were looking for an icy section of road, not her older sister.

One day, when the light was unusually strong, Hanjo told Haeri about his dream.

"I was painting a picture. No matter how much paint I applied, the brush remained dry, and no matter how much color I used, the canvas remained empty. I'm scared that I won't be able to paint again, like in my dream."

He was begging her for help, to get him out of his quandary. Regardless of whether she could or not, Haeri was thrilled by the fact that he had made such a mournful and sincere confession. She was the only person who knew what kind of a person he was, the only witness who could prove he was alive.

Haeri wanted Hanjo to love, hate, and fear her and to make him fret to her heart's content. She wanted to make him love her more deeply than he had loved her sister. If his talent was saved, she believed his life would be saved, and she would escape from her exitless darkness.

"It's not that I can't paint; it's just that I can't find something to paint. If I can only find that, it'll be a great work."

Haeri lay with her arms spread out on the canvas on the floor and looked at him as if asking, *What about painting this? Look at me with the eyes of a kite floating high in the sky. Look at me like a dragonfly with thousands of eyes, like a lion chasing its prey at night, like architects looking at blueprints and geographers looking at contours.*

Now he would find his own way of looking at a subject. He would draw her from a point of view that no one had ever seen. To do that, he wouldn't stop looking at her, and she could believe it would last forever.

It was never supposed to happen. Haeri hoped it would be forgotten in time, but it left a deep scar on her, becoming a stain between them and defining their relationship forever.

The part of her that had yearned for and loved Hanjo for years died that day; he killed it. In an instant, Hanjo robbed her of the relief and joy he had brought her.

She didn't want to have sex with Hanjo. At least not then, not there, not like that. It wasn't because she didn't love him. She loved him. Nevertheless, she could not readily accept him when he was so inflamed with desire. It was because of her mixed feelings of remorse at having survived, longing for her family, and anxiety that she loved a murderer's son.

After that day, Haeri kept asking herself the same question. Why hadn't he stopped?

Hanjo said it was because of love, and that he could not stop because he loved her. But how could love that ignored trust be called love? Love without perfect trust was no love at all. It was also true that even if his love was sincere, he had made an indelible mistake. Haeri thought it was because of an illusion or misunderstanding, and blamed herself for causing that illusion. But if it was an illusion, it was his fault—how could it be hers?

Suddenly, she remembered the group of nude sketches she had found in her sister's box. Rather than loving her sister, Hanjo had satisfied his physical desires. He had not understood her, only chased and fulfilled his artistic impulses. His self-interest in using someone he loved in his work in that way made her angry, and her love for him turned into disgust.

Nevertheless, Haeri could not blame Hanjo. If he had been a bad person, she could have hated him. But he loved her, and he was the man she loved. This fact made her suffer.

She even considered legal means. However, she knew from experience that the world did not mourn or protect victims. People had initially sympathized with her murdered sister and her parents, who had died in an accident, but they soon became annoyed with them and eventually forgot.

Neither the police nor the law nor the lawyers were on the victim's side. This was evidenced by trial records and rulings, sentencings that concluded there was insufficient evidence, settlements, suspended indictments, dropped charges, and perpetrators released without charges. While the victims were being whispered about and kicked out of their homes, workplaces, and schools, were suffering or killed themselves, the perpetrators agreed to settlements or petitioned for mercy.

If she accused Hanjo of assault, the questions would be directed at her, not him. *Why did the little girl go to the house where the man lived alone? Why did you take off your clothes when you were alone with the guy? Why didn't you scream?* Questions would become criticism and turn into contempt. Because she had no parents and had left school, she was a bad girl.

Disputes between prosecutors and lawyers inquisitive about every last detail would lead to the final question: *Did the plaintiff love the defendant?* She would have to say *Yes*. The judge would be annoyed and would ask, *Then why did you sue the accused?*

Nam Bora, who was working on a report for the women and youth division of the Central Police Station, recognized Haeri at once when the girl walked into her office. She closed the file she was working on and took out a brown envelope from her desk drawer.

They left the building and entered a small park next to the police station through a side door. In the sun, Nam Bora looked a little fatter than when they had met at the hospital. They sat on a bench under a zelkova tree on one side of the park.

Nam Bora held out the envelope. There was a faded picture in it. In the photo, whose edges had faded due to the corrosion of its chemicals, Jisoo seemed both angry and smiling. She also seemed to be watching Haeri's expression after asking questions that were difficult to answer.

"I want to hear about Howard House," Haeri said, still looking closely at the photo. "Or more precisely, not about Howard House as such, but about the murder of my sister, who lived in Howard House."

Nam Bora had heard this question dozens of times, and by now the situation was familiar: a victim's family suddenly coming in after the case was closed, criticizing the poor investigation results, and demanding the truth. She believed it was her fault that this girl had gone searching through the investigation reports and trial records. If Nam Bora had done it right then, it wouldn't have happened.

"It was the first and most memorable case for me. I was part of the investigation team, but I only made the coffee. *She's a woman, she's a newbie, she's not from the world of violence*—it's an excuse, right?"

Nam Bora raised her hand to her lips and tore off some dry, dead skin.

"I'm not trying to find out right and wrong now," Haeri said. "It won't change anything, and no one will be satisfied."

"Then why did you come to me?"

"I just . . . I just wanted to know. From what point did things go wrong?"

It took some time for Nam Bora to accept that she could no longer turn a blind eye to the case—and should not. On the surface, the investigation had been sufficiently successful. At the end of the investigation, praise had come from the top levels, and the team members were honored with special promotions. She was also promoted. Nevertheless, she could not shake off the idea that something had been wrong.

"I want to talk to you, but I don't know what to talk about. I'm not sure what you want to know or if I can give you the answers . . ."

"Tell me about Jinman," Haeri asked. "How did you know he was the culprit?"

Nam Bora briefly organized her thoughts. If Lee Jinman's guilt had been proven without a doubt, many people's lives would have been different from what they were now. It was an unproven truth, an unanswered question that had killed, driven away, and destroyed the families in Howard House and Malcolm House. She took a long breath like a diver about to dive, and said, "As we narrowed the investigation dragnet, the Malcolm House men remained. The two sons were close to Jisoo and had an alibi. Even if we couldn't believe them completely, the brothers were together at the time of the crime. On the other hand, Lee Jinman's alibi was incomplete, and he had a previous conviction in his youth. The focus of the investigation was on him. After newspaper clippings about the incident and photos of Jisoo were found in the studio, the charges became clearer . . . And, conclusively, we had a test of the fluid from the victim's body."

"Whose was it?"

Nam Bora shook her head slowly. "At that time, genetic-analysis techniques couldn't produce complete data. The sample was small, and the evidence insufficient . . . but it served to elicit a confession from the suspect. Lee Jinman confessed to everything even before it was discovered that he had the blood type identified in the body fluid. He told us that he had followed the victim to near the dam they used to go to, sexually assaulted her, killed her, and dumped the body in the reservoir. Yet I can't help feeling vaguely uncomfortable about something . . ."

"The criminal confessed, so what's making you uncomfortable?"

"Lee Jinman asked whether the investigation would be completely closed if he confessed. When the team leader confirmed that it would, he told us not to touch the children, because he would confess to everything. It's weird, isn't it? It's an out-of-the-way request that he didn't have to make if he really did it?"

Nam Bora could not rid herself of the habit of finishing sentences in a question. At that moment, Haeri realized that her life was built on a false foundation.

"Why was he put on trial when the only evidence was a confession?"

"It doesn't depend on how plausible a lie is; it depends on what people want to believe. At the time, the investigation team was under pressure from high up, as well as from the media, to find the criminal quickly. We had to get someone, even if we had to manufacture the criminal."

"It was not an investigation. You were putting together a plausible killer."

Nam Bora bowed her head. The wind that brushed her face stung like a needle.

"We're not gods. Are we going to save people from a killer and find out the truth about everything? We just think and think again about what we don't know based on what we *do* know. We guess, assume, infer, and get things wrong. That's the only thing you can do. The language of investigation is logic and evidence."

"Why didn't you do that back then?" Haeri argued.

Nam Bora was embarrassed. She made feeble excuses. "From logic and evidence, it was clear that Lee Jinman was the culprit. The blood type of the fluid in the victim's body matched his. Even if there was some doubt, it wasn't enough to overturn the confession. It was much more likely for him, an ex-convict, to be the criminal than his young sons . . . It may sound like an excuse, but back then the team head had three investigative principles. First, it should be a verifiable truth—at least close to the truth, if not the truth. The second was to consider the position of the perpetrator and the victim at the same time. Finally, society should have an acceptable basis to believe it. The case didn't go against the principles, but I couldn't help feeling heavy whenever I thought about it. The pieces of the puzzle fit, but the picture wasn't clear."

"Close to the truth is not the truth," Haeri said. "If you put in one drop of poison, the whole well becomes poisoned."

Haeri stood up and walked away. She did not believe the brothers' statement that they were together at the time of the incident. Why had they lied? It must have been to protect one of the two.

But which one?

Haeri's idle speculation that Uncle Malcolm might not be the culprit had changed over time into a conviction that he could not have possibly killed her sister. Uncle Malcolm was a man who could neither plan nor execute a murder, nor have the ability to live with himself. He might be blinded by anger and lose his reason for a moment, but he was neither emotional nor reckless enough to kill someone. He'd become a murderer not because he had committed a murder but because he had *admitted* to a murder. There was no doubt that he had confessed, but his confessions left many questions unanswered.

If he had killed Jisoo, would it have been a premeditated crime? Or an accident? Did he think he could kill someone, then go on living as if nothing had happened? If he hadn't been arrested, would he have killed someone else? But if he wasn't the culprit, why would he make such a ridiculous confession?

All these questions converged on one inevitable question: Who the hell had really killed her?

Haeri constantly talked to Hanjo about her sister's death. She questioned him directly as well as hinted at things after irrelevant conversations. When he talked about his father, the tendon in his neck bulged and he stuttered. He also seemed to feel remorse while discussing him.

One afternoon, they sat side by side on the bank overlooking the stream. It had rained a few days before, so the river was running full. At the far end of the path, the dam was visible, and the lights of a patrol car slowly traveling along the riverside road flashed.

Hanjo had sat there on the day Jisoo's body was found. The scene that day came alive: red letters on yellow tape—**No Access**—wet uniforms, the riverbank, the flashing lights, the loud sirens, the buzzing roar of a helicopter . . .

Hanjo wondered if he had cried in that moment, but he couldn't remember.

"The morning before my sister disappeared I made a promise with her," Haeri said. "Before I went to sleep, she would read me the last part of *The Hound of the Baskervilles*. But even though the sun set and it was dinnertime, my sister hadn't come back. I went outside and leaned against the wooden fence, waiting for my sister. Then I saw three people."

Hanjo had the impression that Haeri had constructed her story carefully, over a long period of time. He also had a feeling that it might be a story designed to protect herself.

"What kind of people?" he asked, doubtful.

"Uncle Malcolm and my sister, and one other," Haeri said quietly. "Uncle Malcolm was sitting on his chair on the porch at Malcolm House, drinking beer. Just then, my sister suddenly came running up the stairs from the basement of the annex. She went running straight up the hill without seeing me. I think she was crying; she was covering her face with her hands. I was glad and was about to call to her, but she disappeared on a bike over the hill. Then I saw someone follow her. That was the last I saw of my sister."

Hanjo stared at the firm bottom of the quietly flowing river. He recalled heavy gravel and water patterns that had sunk deep into his memory, fish swimming slowly in the wavering light and billowing water weeds. There was nothing he could do but imagine himself in the scene, because he felt so miserable. He squeezed the words out.

"Who was it?"

The sun hanging in the western sky was a yellowish color, like a festering wound. A wind carrying the scent of coniferous trees shook the bushes in the forest.

"I don't know," Haeri replied. "It was too dark to see his face clearly."

Hanjo didn't push her any more. Haeri was relieved. She was afraid that if he asked, the face would become clear and she would say the name. She longed for all her forgotten memories to be clearly recalled, but also hoped they would remain vague. Only then would it be possible to keep as much memory as everyone expected and needed from her without digging up her buried pain.

That day, when Haeri went down the hill crying, Uncle Malcolm was drinking beer on the porch. She vividly remembered the sound of the wooden planks creaking beneath his feet. His breath smelled sour from the beer, and the crushed grass smelled bitter. Haeri told him that her sister had ignored her and gone running over the hill, although she had promised to read her a story.

"Did your sister do something wrong to make her run away? Did someone go running after her?"

She couldn't say for sure whom she had seen. She thought nothing would happen to her sister if she didn't say the name.

"Some guy."

His thick eyebrows wiggled. After thinking for a moment, he took Haeri's hand and walked with her up the hill, as far as the front of her house. As he approached the gate, he stopped and said, "Wait at home. I'll look for her. Then I'm going to grab that fellow and scold him."

However, he could not find Jisoo, nor catch the man who'd followed her. And that night, her sister hadn't come back. Uncle Malcolm had told a lie. However, this did not justify saying he had committed the murder.

"Why did you keep quiet back then?" Hanjo asked. "If you had told people that, my father might not have become a murderer."

The lukewarm wind carried the smell of exhaust fumes from cars speeding along the riverside road. Haeri couldn't stand the headache and dizziness.

"No one asked me. At that time, I didn't know the meaning of what I had seen, didn't know whether I should speak about it or not. It was only after I became a middle school student that I vaguely realized it was an important clue. I suddenly remembered it one day, but what could I do then?"

"But now you're saying it was not my father?"

Hanjo twisted his lips. His distress pierced Haeri's heart as if it were her own. She was drawn toward him like a fallen leaf sucked into a drain, and she held him close to herself. Her face, as it touched the side of his neck, was as cold and hard as ice.

Hanjo asked, "Well, who was it?"

Haeri didn't answer. She couldn't answer, not because she didn't want to. It was an answer that might take her a few nights to say—or maybe the rest of her life might not be long enough. Gnats flew dizzily through the evening air. Birds quickly pecked with shiny beaks at the little bugs as they flew around.

Hanjo wondered whether she couldn't answer because she didn't know, or if she was avoiding answering although she knew.

That evening, Haeri had seen Hanjo. Her sister, after running out of the studio crying, rode her bicycle over the hill without noticing Haeri. Hanjo had followed her sister up the stairs and then run frantically over the hill where she had disappeared. The hill led to the Borim

Stream path, and farther upstream, it was connected to the reservoir and dam where her sister had died.

Haeri didn't know how the two facts were connected at that time, but when she saw Hanjo's *Ophelia: Summer*, she felt as if she vaguely understood her sister's death.

The woman in the painting was lying in the water, her face covered with a thin, translucent veil. A grassy hill rose beyond the black mud where brown reeds were growing, and Howard House was visible. The window on the right-hand side of the second floor was open. It was a desolate landscape, full of a vague anxiety.

The half-submerged woman wearing a flower crown looked vulnerable. The body, with scars here and there, was thin and pale. It could be said that Hanjo had expressed the mythological aspect of Ophelia using Haeri as his model. However, this was a delicate figure that he had never thought of as a real person. He was definitely looking at Haeri's face, but he kept thinking of someone else.

At one point, she was strongly convinced that the Ophelia in the painting was her sister, not herself. Why had he drawn her? Had he seen her sink into the water? As she sank into the water, did her sister smile like the woman in the painting? Whom did he think he was drawing, Haeri or her sister?

She was confused by the fact that her dead sister had a stronger grip on Hanjo than she did, she who was directly in front of him. The next moment, however, the facts that she had discovered in the meantime made sense, and the memories that had been scattered were back in place.

Hanjo had always drawn her sister, and his eyes had always followed her. Her sister secretly enjoyed his attentions without accepting his love. Her sister must have visited his studio without their parents knowing. The nude drawings in the sketchbook in her sister's secret box were evidence.

Hanjo's violent nature, which did not make exceptions even for people he loved, had been experienced directly by Haeri. Could it be that Jisoo came crying out of the studio because she was trying to escape Hanjo's coercion? If this was true, the fluid detected in her sister's body was also explained.

False confessions and wrong judgments had hidden the truth. Yet the Howard House family had all turned away from the truth anyway and fled reality. They couldn't confront their daughter's death face to face: they hid behind their sorrow, or fell into alcohol and depression before dying. Since the statute of limitations had passed, it was impossible to reinvestigate or hold a new trial for Jisoo's death, and there was no point now in revealing the true culprit.

Haeri was now responsible for the crime that the law and the system had failed to resolve.

The most classic way to punish someone for murder was to execute them, eye for eye, tooth for tooth! There were countless ways. Guns or knives, poison or electricity, cars and drugs . . . You could kill them yourself, or you could order other people to do it. But wasn't a quick death too lenient for a murderer? The murderer either would not realize his sin at the moment of death or, if he did, would be freed from remorse and suffering too soon.

Haeri wanted her sister's killer to suffer for longer and to lose more than Haeri had. She wanted him to receive colder looks than she had endured, swallow tears saltier than those she had tasted, and cry more loudly than she had cried. She wanted to inflict bigger and deeper wounds on his body than those she had inflicted on herself.

What was needed was a form of revenge involving great pain, although it would still be insufficient even if the murderer endured it for a whole lifetime. But the methods she came up with were too complex, or too direct, or otherwise too weak. Then an idea flashed through her mind. The structure of her idea, which seemed absurd at first, took on an increasingly concrete and distinct form over time.

The goal was to deprive the murderer of something extremely dear and precious. The problem was that Hanjo had nothing to take. All he had was discouragement regarding the future and despair regarding his life. For anyone who has lost their desire for life, death is neither punishment nor revenge, only an inappropriate kind of mercy.

To take something away from him required him to have it in the first place. Success, fame, wealth, and authority, a comfortable home, a beautiful wife and children, such as he had never dreamed of . . . It was at the moment when he was enjoying his achievements to the full, satisfied that he had everything and convinced it would never collapse, that all should be taken from him.

What would he most fear to lose, and what would be most painful were he deprived of it? The source of the most immediate and deadly pain would be love. Property, fame, and reputation would come next. Therefore, revenge had to begin with love and end with betrayal. It was a meticulous plan that required long hours of patience and sacrifice, subtle psychological manipulation, and a sophisticated imagination.

Now Haeri needed to confront two questions: Would she be able to continue to love the murderer as she had before? If she thought she could, could she maintain her hatred of him in love?

She left Isan in order to find the answer to those questions. So long as she loved Hanjo, she couldn't doubt him. She couldn't stand the contradiction of having to hate him as much as she loved him. It became clear that she had to leave him before she could ruin him.

She wanted Hanjo to understand that she had no other option but to leave, that she wasn't abandoning him but had to leave him in order to discover something—and that once she found it, she would immediately return. She had to leave him now in order to meet him again someday, and she would still love him when she met him again, but she would love him in a different way than before.

"Wait! Don't move! Stay still."

At those sharp voices, Haeri froze completely. The eight students surrounding her were immersed in sketching her body with serious expressions. The sound of 4B pencils and pieces of charcoal brushing over paper rose from all sides. She curled up with her hands around her knees and stared at Agrippa.

She remembered the night she'd left Isan for a future she couldn't imagine, without any preparation or fear. As the train bound for Seoul sped through the night, a shower of rain rattled the windows like a hail of arrows. It was a surreal feeling, as if she were moving from one viewpoint of memory to another, not just from one city to another.

She had been told that Seoul was a tough and dangerous place. Nonetheless, or perhaps because of this, Haeri admired Seoul. Before this, she had been unable to leave Isan. But now she had found a clear direction and a firm goal in life. There were countless things she had to do if she were to become indispensable to Hanjo. In order to destroy him, she had to carefully coordinate and control her life toward her treacherous goal of loving him without betraying herself.

The following year, Haeri passed the college entrance exam and entered the art history department of a university. The tuition for the first semester was settled with the money accumulated through her monthly trust payments, which her uncle managed. She felt sorry for her uncle, but she wasn't stealing it, because it belonged to her.

After she paid the university's registration fee and the deposit on a semibasement room, her small balance was exhausted. She worked part-time in galleries, studios, and shops selling art materials, both large and small. She carried things all day long at exhibition sites and did not hesitate to work as a salesperson in art stores.

When a friend mentioned a part-time job that didn't take up much time and paid well, Haeri asked no questions. It was only when she was about to go for the appointment that she realized she was to act as a nude model for art students. She was standing behind a thin curtain that served as a changing room.

"Are you still not ready?" a girl said urgently from beyond the curtain.

"Yes . . . I'm coming."

Haeri undressed as if she had made up her mind, took out the rolled-up bandages from her bag, and wrapped them around her arms and thighs. Over the years, she had started assembling emergency kits with bandages and disinfectants in preparation for impulsive acts of self-harm, although they had never actually happened.

The students who saw her for the first time looked upset, perhaps because of the cumbersome bandages. She sat huddled in front of the eyes watching her. Then all the students opened their sketchbooks together. They seemed to think that the texture of the bandages and the curve of the drooping line of her back would make a change from a conventional nude croquis.

Soft pencils grazed paper. Haeri changed her pose as she was told, sitting, standing, raising her arms, or lying on the floor. The chilly air created a bluish network all over her skin, which had lost its color.

Finally, when she went back behind the curtain and came out fully dressed, the girl who had been urging her to take off her clothes held out a white envelope. There were three ten-thousand-won bills in it. It was a considerable remuneration, considering the hours of work. Haeri also liked that it was paid on-site in cash, and she did not have to pay taxes. She felt both a slight sense of embarrassment and triumph that her wounds were worth money. The girl put her hands behind her back and untied her apron strings.

"Can you come again next week?"

The following Tuesday, Haeri went behind the curtain, undressed, and took up her pose on a white table surrounded by twelve students.

"Off you go."

The students looked serious as they moved their pencils. The sounds of pages being turned and of knives sharpening pencils were like scythes brushing through blades of grass. Her curved back muscles grew tight, her bloodless arms got cramps, and her buttocks lost all feeling under her weight.

She was called Mummy, Frankenstein, or Nefertiti—the students did not ask her name. They only looked at her as an object to be drawn. Hanjo had been different. Even when she stopped posing, he drew her minute movements, open wounds, memories that she herself had forgotten.

During the summer vacation, she was offered a job as a model for an individual exhibition by a veteran artist. The artist said he had heard about her from students at the university. She worked in his studio three days a week throughout the vacation. His portraits of her at the spring exhibition the following year were a huge sensation. Wounded, she was reminiscent of Joan of Arc, who did not surrender, and Marianne, who led the French Revolutionary Army.

Visitors wondered whether the woman in the painting was a real person or someone the artist had imagined. The artist's agent evaded these questions and encouraged their curiosity. Haeri was angry that the artist had sensationalized her body and that she had become an object bought and sold for money. Ironically, however, it brought her unexpected luck. The striking image in the paintings attracted the attention of advertising photographers.

She began as a model for a summer catalog of a large travel agency, after which several advertisers and studios contacted her, and before the year was over, Haeri had become a model for two fashion catalogs and ads for a franchise restaurant.

Now she had enough cash without doing simple part-time jobs carrying wares or selling art materials. But she didn't stop working part-time. She constantly called art publishers and magazines to gain the experience she needed, and so found work. Several artists and gallery owners recognized her writing skills and asked her to write copy for exhibition catalogs.

She managed to do any kind of work related to painting and maintained close relationships with the people she got to know through her jobs. Her work with artists who had multiple connections allowed her to grow familiar with the structures and details of the complex art world, which was like a spider's web.

Haeri almost burst into tears when she discovered Hanjo's name at the end of the art magazine *Kunst* in the fall of her sophomore year.

Lee Hanjo Individual Exhibition
Okin-dong Dangju Gallery October 16–October 29

A short article introducing four new artists' exhibition schedules included a painting the size of a business card. Haeri recognized the woman in the painting at once. The light flowed like a carpet over the woman's shoulders, and you could see the veins of her body, which was transparent like dragonfly wings.

On the last day of the exhibition, Haeri visited the Dangju Gallery. A pale light shone from the window, like an old motorboat moored on a dark night sea. The street was strewn with leaves, torn from the trees by a strong wind.

Hanjo walked back and forth slowly, like the owner of a noodle restaurant waiting for customers who didn't come. His tight lips were filled with despair. Haeri watched a man who seemed to be a gallery employee drag Hanjo outside, probably intending to help him unwind with a glass or two of soju over supper.

When Haeri opened the gallery door, a female employee at the entrance looked at the wall clock. In a cold voice, she snapped, "There are eighteen minutes left until closing time," implying that she could come in or not as she pleased. Haeri paid no attention and entered the empty exhibition room.

There was her past: *Ophelia: Summer*.

At that moment, all the sounds, smells, and colors around her disappeared as memories of their lovemaking and flirting returned, together with the sound and smell of rain that had been falling all day long, the resonant sound of rainwater pouring down drainpipes. It was a piercing, warm, lovely rain.

The techniques and elements found in *Summer* were shared by the other paintings in the series. Ophelia in *Spring* had crawled onto the bank, edging her way over the mud of the garden. A thin veil was wrapped around her face so that her features were barely visible. In *Autumn*, she lay straight in the middle of a flooded living room. Through an open window, a golden beam of sunlight poured over her scarred body. Behind her were an old piano and a bookcase.

In *Winter*, she was under a transparent sheet of ice, looking up at the surface with wide-open eyes. The white bandages floated in the current like water plants.

The paintings contained his vivid voice, which she longed to hear. *Look! This is you. You whom I worship, who looked at me with love. True, you left me. But this is you, the you that I've kept in time, the you that I love . . .*

Haeri looked at the bold yet delicate canvases full of light, a concentration of the joy Hanjo had achieved in his despair. They were so bright, she had to close her eyes. But the colors, composition, and shapes remained on the inside of her eyelids. How nice it would be to have Hanjo next to her. Then she would tell him . . . how amazing these paintings were, what wonderful work he had done, how much people would love them.

She wondered if Hanjo knew why she had left one day so suddenly. Perhaps he didn't know. The thought was hurtful. The employee spoke from behind her.

"You'll have to leave. It's time to close."

The next morning, Haeri called the gallery. There was no vitality in the gallery owner's voice over the phone. This was the best condition for bargaining. She offered to buy *Spring* from the four *Ophelia* paintings. There was silence. She had to wait a long time before the gallery owner groaned a reply in a voice as thin as a gambler holding the worst cards.

"It'll be hard to go below one hundred fifty."

"Let's make it one hundred," Haeri said calmly. "Instead, I'd like to buy all four paintings, *Spring*, *Summer*, *Autumn*, and *Winter*."

Over the phone, the owner's cough and speech merged together, as if a sudden intake of breath had stuck in her throat.

"Then let's make it one twenty!"

Two days later, when the four paintings arrived, Haeri was relieved. In reality, she was the one desperate to make the deal. Hanjo, whom she knew so well, was a painter who should not be allowed to disappear after idling on the edges of the art world without selling a single work at his first exhibition. His paintings had enough charm to catch the eye of the beholder, and were worth keeping. All he needed was a little bit of luck to attract a clear-sighted collector or meet a prominent sponsor.

Haeri was willing to become his luck.

In the autumn before she graduated, there was an ad at the back of *Kunst* for a position as an assistant editor of a book that was to be published as a supplement to the magazine. It was a temporary editing job that did not involve much work, but it was something Haeri had thought she wanted to do for a long time, and felt she ought to do. There was no real basis for it, but she felt convinced that *Kunst* was the path by which to approach Hanjo. And, although it had been an inconspicuous article, *Kunst* was also the only magazine to mention Hanjo's first exhibition.

The *Kunst* office building, which she visited for the interview, was in a residential area where old brick houses huddled together. She was unable to determine the age of the editor in chief and publisher, Choi Inyong, because of her short hair. Her narrow eyes without double eyelids and her firm mouth made a resolute impression.

"Why do you want to be an assistant editor?"

"Because I can do it well."

It was a straightforward answer, if not accurate. What Haeri wanted from *Kunst* was not money but influence, the overall task of observing the artist closely and interpreting the work in his own perspective and language to capture new trends, and the power to encourage change through this observation. It was an opportunity to detect the vast and delicate flow of the art world that never stopped, and to approach that world's most powerful members . . . Inyong was not more inquisitive.

Haeri's job was to be the editorial director of a column, Faces and Representations, a series of interviews in which a photographer and essayist, Kim Junman, explored the studios of twelve artists and their works. The interviews were to be serialized over one year in *Kunst* and published as a separate volume. Haeri recruited artists from a wide range of fields, from traditional painting to sculpture, handicrafts, installation, and performance art. She was in charge of the relevant research and toured the artists' studios.

Published in the autumn of the following year, *Faces and Representations* attained sales rarely seen in art books, and had to be reprinted. It was an unexpected achievement, proving that both laypeople and established artists shared a similar sort of anxiety and pressure, no matter how far apart their lives seemed.

After publication was complete, Haeri stayed in her office late one night, packing her things. She didn't want pitying looks from other employees. She was tying her hair up with a rubber band, preparing to clear her desk and empty the drawers, when Inyong came into the office.

"Are you packing up? Where are you going at this late hour?"

It didn't sound as if she were scolding her, but she did not sound natural either. Nevertheless, her words felt affectionate for some reason.

"My contract is over, so I have to find another job. It was fun, but it's over."

They went out together to the terrace. Inyong leaned against the railing and lit a cigarette. Inside her lips, the smooth, thick tongue glistened red. The smoke rose like a ribbon.

"The contract may be over," Inyong said, "but the work is not. Like children being born, like the earth revolving. Suppose I give you the job of working on a sequel to *Faces and Representations*? We'll bring together twelve artists from all over the world. We'll have to be prepared for huge production costs."

She rarely used conjunctions when speaking. She seemed like someone determined not to waste a second on unnecessary words, because there were so many precious things to get done. Therefore, she showed intense concentration in every task she undertook, and changed the ideas of the people around her.

Haeri believed Inyong was trying to change her life by offering better working conditions and more remuneration, maybe even a brighter future. But she didn't want her future changed by someone else.

"Well, it was a good opportunity, but once is enough."

"Then what do you want to do? Be a company receptionist answering the phone? Classify the stocks? Be a warehouse manager?"

Haeri stared at the shabby, helpless woman reflected in the glistening windowpane. She had lost six pounds in weight and a considerable amount of hair over *Faces and Representations*, and her face had lost a year of its youth. Nevertheless, the dim eyes glistened like scraps of iron heated with longing. The possibility of the life she so wanted was beginning to come alive. The person who suggested the game was Inyong, but now Haeri wanted to play the game with her life. She spoke proudly, like a gambler who was flipping over her cards.

"What are you going to do about *Kunst*? Are you going to keep it like it is?"

"*Kunst*? What's wrong with *Kunst*?"

Inyong seemed to be sounding her out. There was the Inyong who enjoyed wearing bright, candy-colored T-shirts in summer, and then there was the Inyong who liked wearing striped suits at events. Each Inyong seemed a different age, like mother or daughter, depending on what clothes she wore. It was an impressive, chameleonlike ability to look different depending on the situation or person confronting her.

"*Kunst* is like the dinosaurs; it's not adapting to a changing environment. Not right now, perhaps, but it'll die slowly. It's going to be a world of sleek, fast mammals."

"So how are you going to save *Kunst*?" Inyong had taken firm control of the conversation.

"*Kunst* should sell pride," Haeri said. "Becoming a reader of *Kunst* should give people the impression of being a successful person, as well as someone who loves art. Instead of complicated and tortuous art theories, you should use language and images that make people feel like they are the very center of society. For example, slick, chic, and sophisticated photographs that make artists look like competent IT company CEOs."

Haeri said it all, even though she knew she could come across as patronizing or rude. Inyong surveyed her like a merchant looking to close a deal.

"Then why don't you test your luck with me at *Kunst*?"

Haeri felt dazed, as if a bomb had exploded near her ears. This felt as unrealistic as a dust storm on a distant planet. Inyong said a few more words, but she couldn't understand them. Editor? Senior editor? This was what she seemed to be saying. What did this reckless woman think she was doing, handing over *Kunst* to a newbie part-timer?

"But you don't even know me very well, surely?"

"I've been watching you work. I don't want to let you go. Of course it's sudden. You'll need to prepare. Take your time and think about it."

Haeri simply could not believe that Inyong had taken her seriously. She still had a lot of questions, but she thought it was polite not to ask more, so she said, "I'm ready. I don't need more time. It's what I wanted. I want it so badly, I get cramps all over."

Inyong's eyes were fixed on Haeri. They conveyed a sense of obligation and expectation, a readiness to grant whatever Haeri demanded. What Inyong needed was a daredevil who would penetrate into the very heart of the art industry rather than an expert who based her approach on traditional methods of success. Someone with the determination to simply ignore rules and conventional wisdom, an intuition capable of reaching the core without avoiding or skirting scenarios, a vital force capable of surviving anywhere. There was no need for age or experience.

Inyong had not been born the daughter of a wealthy president of a media group. *Kunst* was one of six magazines published by the media group Seoul Magazines, which also published *Women's Garden*. The president, Nam Jewon, had made various magazines successful and poured a fortune into establishing a daily newspaper.

When the financial crisis forced banks to call in debts, Nam Jewon had frantically rushed around to pay his loans and had a heart attack. As he lay in an intensive-care unit, he signed a memorandum of understanding unconditionally transferring all rights in *Kunst* to Inyong, its editor in chief and most capable employee.

At that time, *Kunst's* monthly deficit was more than twenty million won. She was in a position to refuse, and of course she should have refused, but instead, overnight, she became the publisher of a deficit-ridden magazine. She played the role of advertising manager, editor, and reporter, as well as photographer, accountant, and secretary when necessary. Because of her tall height and short hair, she gave the impression of a boy out on the streets to support his family.

People endured the financial crisis with despair, pessimism, fear, and faint hope, just like the crew of the *Santa María* in their quest for the New World. The continent they landed on was a new world where new technology was unrestrained. The new IT wave brought wealth and prosperity that overflowed into all sections of society, and design and art were the talk of the new era.

Art was the ultimate investment for the rich. People who made money bought luxury clothes and luxury cars, bought houses and real estate, and, finally, bought paintings. *Kunst* survived by fulfilling their ostentatious desire to present themselves as sophisticated, cultured intellectuals.

Six months after Haeri joined the planning team with Inyong's unprecedented support, *Kunst* had turned into an art-management guidebook, not an art or design magazine. This was the result of expanding its scope by integrating art and industry and merging art activities with management principles. At a joint meeting between the editors and the planning and sales departments, Haeri said, "Art is no longer the lofty discourse of the cultured. Art should have the power to move and change the world. Capital is the force making the great waterwheel spin. Capital must flow into the art world."

An associate editor in his late forties, who had been listening silently, asked, "How can art with capital on its back still be called art?"

"Does art necessarily have to be called art?" Haeri replied. "If we have to, we can give up on art, surely?"

Haeri elicited comments from the artists she interviewed that might usually be found in speeches by business leaders trying to encourage their employees, statements such as *A passion to create a work of art is not limited to artists. We can be passionate in the office, in our presentations, as if we were making a work of art. You, too, are an artist, so work like an artist and live like an artist.*

The strategy of incorporating art into corporate management was successful, and *Kunst* gained an ally in capitalism. Naturally, there was criticism concerning the degradation of art, and some employees who disagreed with the editorial policy resigned. Haeri didn't care. Like

Manet and Duchamp, Inyong and Haeri expanded the domain of *Kunst* with the nourishment of envy and insult.

The murmuring behind her back categorized her as a mysterious creature. She was immoral but strong and successful, if cunning. Inyong sometimes wondered whether her ability to create opportunities after reading the demands of the times was innate or learned.

The editorial office was always feverish with excitement, and it seemed no one wanted to leave even for a second, in case they missed what was going on. At meetings, Haeri waved her long finger like a baton. This added conviction to her words, and Inyong couldn't help nodding. It was not because Haeri was autocratic or coercive, but because she was irrefutable.

Their discussions continued after the meetings. At a small snack bar on their way home from work, they shared ramen and gimbap and continued to talk. On the streets, in restaurants, in supermarkets, in cars, with their ingenious world-changing imaginations, they shared endless talk that would amaze people.

Haeri returned to Hanjo when she felt a balance of power had been established. She was no longer a child who lived in his neighborhood, nor a child who longed for his love. Now she would be the guide leading him up from the depths of wretchedness to a new life, an advisor who would give direction to his work, an agent who would present his talent as that of a genius, and she would not refuse to be a dealer selling his works at an enormous price. For this moment, she had honed herself as a tool of revenge.

She wrote an article about his talent and the limitations that Hanjo didn't realize. Whether the article was true or not, it would be true if he believed it and tried to be like that. That was the image of the artist she wanted him to be.

One autumn evening, as the rain fell, they walked carefully through the wet streets and arrived at her house. She laughed as she jingled the keys she took out of her bag. When the front door clicked open, Hanjo asked himself if he deserved to step inside, like a priest standing at the entrance to a sanctuary, and felt sure that he did.

The house was not heated, but it did not feel cold. It looked rather like a refugee camp that would have to be left soon. There was no TV, and the only furniture was a sofa strewn with cushions and a bookcase. The floor, covered with rough brown rugs, was stained with water. She went to the kitchen, where there was no complete set of dishes, and boiled water in a coffeepot.

As he wiped his wet hair, he looked around the house. Here and there, on the empty walls, parts of his own missing past were hanging—the four seasons of *Ophelia*. The women, like secret symbols who had closed their eyes, looked away, or stopped breathing, reminded him of bleeding saints. The rich light, gold like honey and infusing the paintings, was full of abundance, making them almost overpowering.

The cheerful sound of the coffeepot bell rang behind his back. With a look of surprise and anger, he asked, "Why are these paintings hanging here?"

Haeri smiled, handing him a cup of coffee.

"Because I bought them."

Hanjo could not understand how it had turned out like this. The four-piece series was the first and last work he had ever sold. It had been his only asset, and there was a possibility that he would never sell anything again. Even when he raised a bottle to his lips because he couldn't produce any paintings, he would return to the canvas the next day because of his belief in the anonymous buyer. But it had been her. Fate seemed determined to hurl him down, trample on him, and tear him apart.

"Why did you deceive me?" he shouted, with a strange look of sorrow and anger.

She shrugged. "I just didn't tell you."

"If I had known it was you, I wouldn't have sold them."

"At that time, you were an unknown painter who was prepared to sell his soul to the devil. I just invested in works that other people hadn't recognized."

"I was filled with wild hopes with the pennies you threw me."

"That's good. What's wrong with having hope?"

"It wasn't hope; it was just my stupid imagination. Since four pictures had been sold at my first exhibition, I had vain expectations that forty would be sold the next time. But it was you . . ."

Hanjo wept because of his own wretchedness, and because he now knew that she was the source of that wretchedness. The wind shook the window. The air was chilly and the short autumn day felt threatening. She let her gaze rest on *Ophelia: Summer* hanging on the wall.

"What about me? Even though you painted it, that's a portrait of me, so I have the right to own it. The important thing is not who bought them, but the fact that the paintings were sold."

He raised his face from his pudgy hands—it seemed impossible these hands could have painted such delicate paintings. Only now did he understand that the paintings had always belonged to her and no one else. He felt suddenly relieved that she had bought them.

He was poor and miserable, but she could be his savior. If she didn't love him, she couldn't save him, but she did love him. He knew it. This fact was so clear that his eyes were blinded.

Hanjo hesitated when Haeri said she wanted to return to Howard House after the wedding. Living in the house was a different matter from missing it. Howard House was even more lovely from afar. Remorse that his father had destroyed Howard House made him more hesitant to return. Haeri did not back down, and explained her plans for renovation by drawing sketches with a pen.

"I'm going to remove the walls of the annex, reinforce the beams, and decorate it with self-portraits. If we remove part of the ground floor and combine it with the basement, the ceiling will be over four yards high, so you can draw masterpieces. Some of the cellar rooms that still have ceilings can serve as storerooms for paintings and archives . . ."

Throughout the construction on the annex, they stayed at the main house, contemplating the size and function of the studio and determining the size and location of the windows by measuring the angle of the light. Instead of using workers, they painted the walls themselves and put new cloth on the old sofa. Haeri splashed cement and paint on her eyebrows, hair, and cheeks like snowflakes.

However, life is not a fireworks display: the fireworks that light up the night sky disappear in the blink of an eye. Hanjo went to the studio every day and held a brush, but he could not paint. The ability to try new techniques and concentrate was gone. One color was painted on top of another, then yet another color was added on top of that. The impeccable new studio seemed to have taken away his imagination and left no trace.

One evening, Haeri went to the studio. It was late and everything was all over the place. Hanjo's breath smelled sour. He must have hidden a bottle somewhere in the studio, like his mother, who had hidden bottles of soju in the kitchen of Howard House.

"What? Are you here to check on my homework? Feel free to watch. That's all I've done for the past week . . . I've painted and painted, but I can't produce a painting."

Hanjo, who was pointing at the dark canvas, was on the verge of tears. Because of the repeated applications, a thick layer of paint had formed on the canvas, and after six or seven layers of achromatic colors, the surface was close to black. The colors, which seemed to be painted with a fierce sense of purpose and amazing concentration, looked crude together, like mosaics that did not fit.

"This work . . . it's not bad," Haeri said. "There's something there. I can see you in the picture, your solitude, your past, your joys, your pains."

Haeri's expression was ambivalent, but Hanjo couldn't shake off his frustration. He took a bottle of whiskey from under the workbench and swigged from it.

"If I'm in there at all," Hanjo replied weakly, "it's only my incompetence, my pretense, and my shame."

These were facts he had never spoken aloud, the truths he never faced out of fear. He looked as if he were determined to destroy himself.

Haeri didn't say anything obvious, like *You'll be able to paint if you get some rest* or *Everyone goes through a slump*. Instead, with the sharp look of an inspector picking out the 0.1 percent of defective products from a manufacturing line, she said, "Customers are like impatient kids; they're always asking to be shown something new. I'm tired of telling you what I told you before. While you're deepening the techniques of the *Ophelia* paintings, you have to come up with new techniques and themes that will go beyond them."

Haeri looked at Hanjo like a young mother soothing her spoiled son. Hanjo couldn't stand the fact that she was the only one who knew all his flaws, and that she always remembered each and every one of them. Even her encouragement and comforting revealed his weaknesses and inferiority.

"Don't tell me that—it's none of your business. A businesswoman like you pretending to know about my paintings . . . I'm sick of it."

If he hadn't loved her, he might have used more euphemistic and less crude expressions. But Hanjo loved her. Should Haeri feel humiliated? She wasn't. But that didn't mean she wasn't hurt.

Haeri jumped up and strode across the studio. Hanjo watched for her next move, feeling helpless. She stopped in front of the easel and picked up a half-empty bottle and poured it over the canvas. The sharp smell of alcohol spread.

He couldn't decide whether he should be angry or try to stop her. He wanted to beg her not to do that, but gave up. For him, resignation was always easier than any other choice.

"Yes, it's not a painting. It's trash, so just put it somewhere out of sight," he giggled, drunk. Haeri didn't listen. He wouldn't remember what he'd said when he woke up the next morning, anyway. Hanjo always berated his talent; it was his habit. Haeri had never agreed with his foolish whining. He had talent. This was so clear that she was convinced wasting it was a crime. She had to rebuild his confidence. His incompetence was equal to her frustration, and his fall would be her failure.

Haeri swallowed the dregs of whiskey in the bottle. The hot liquid burned her throat and warmed her body. She looked at the canvas and picked up a cutter from the workbench. The sharp blade flashed. *What is she going to do?* he wondered as he lay down on the sofa. His curled back seemed small, the bones of his spine protruding.

Haeri picked up the canvas and slammed it down on the workbench. The impact broke one side of the frame. She drew the blade across the canvas. The thick layers of paint accepted the sharp knife. A cross section of turquoise and white paint was revealed under the layer of red paint scratched away by the blade.

She felt the sharp addictive pain of the blades she had dug into herself as a child. She kept slashing at the canvas that Hanjo hated, desperately, as if wanting to tear it to shreds. The blade cut, slashed, and scratched the paint at a faster and faster pace.

Haeri didn't realize how late it was getting. She was lost between what was revealed and what was concealed, what was seen and what was hidden, what was said and what was unsaid.

The next morning, Hanjo woke up after ten thirty. He felt as though thorn bushes had been growing in his head all night long. He looked around the messy studio, his hair disheveled and twisted.

His errors, incompetence, and shame lay scattered like so many painting rags. Canvases lay torn or cut, showing sharp slices and scratches everywhere. Someone seemed to have been determined to ruin his paintings. Stupefied, he looked at the wreckage.

Depending on the movement and direction of the blade, various primary colors were revealed below the canvas's solid achromatic surface. Bright colors and complicated knife marks collided, creating an unexpected dynamic. The colors cut out in the shape of wedges had a particularly strong presence.

What had happened that night? He recalled a bitter quarrel with his wife but couldn't remember anything else.

The morning sun poured through the windows. Haeri entered the studio with a glass of cold orange juice, wearing a loose, stretched T-shirt.

"What's been going on here?" she asked, looking at the tattered pictures with round eyes. "Those pictures . . . Did you do that?"

It was same thing Hanjo wanted to ask her. He looked at her blankly, still hungover.

"Me?"

He had no memory at all.

Haeri asked again. "Did you pass out? How far do you remember? Drinking whiskey? Fighting with me? Yelling at me to throw the paintings away?"

He remembered that far. Then what had happened?

"Did you pour whiskey on the painting? Or did I? How did this happen?" he asked with a suspicious look.

"Whatever was going to happen happened. I thought you were drunk, and I was trying to get you to sleep before I went back into the house, but then you went crazy."

"Crazy? What do you mean?"

"You were lying on the sofa, and I was about to put a blanket over you when you suddenly jumped up and ran at the canvas as if you were going to destroy everything."

A vague memory flashed across his mind. The silver blade of a cutter picked up from the workstation. The surface of the canvas gleaming. The snap of the cutter blade, the feeling of it digging into paint, and brilliant colors emerging through the cracks.

"You brought out the essence of the painting by cutting, scratching, and destroying it with a knife. Anyone could see that you were ashamed of the painting and, at the same time, loved it."

He looked at the disorderly, dazzling wreckage spread before him. The primary colors revealed by splitting open the achromatic surface evoked the abyss hidden at the bottom of peaceful, daily life. Memories that suddenly tear through the shell of consciousness and come to mind like a clap of thunder. The truths in life that cannot be seen without the courage to let oneself be hurt, like colors that are revealed when torn, cut, scraped, or scratched.

A new world had awakened before him. Now he knew what to paint and how to paint it. Instead of paintings on canvas, he would cut, scratch, dig, and grind wood panels to reveal colors. And it would give meaning to the memories shining between the layers of time accumulated within him.

He could now believe that such brilliant colors existed in him. He even regretted all the time he had wasted not knowing it.

When I realized that it wasn't that I didn't love him
but that I loved others more, I decided to leave him.

On the day she began her novel, Haeri wrote this sentence and then set aside her pen. She didn't know how to write the next one. She didn't want to think about who he was or who she was. Only after she stopped thinking about him, about death, about love, about violence, about destruction, could she write about him.

Suddenly, she thought she wanted to have a child. Maybe two. She had the qualities of a good mother and wanted to be a good mother. In the end, this was why she didn't have children. She was afraid she would love her child, fret if he was sick, spend more time with him. She was even afraid of being loved and respected by him. It wasn't because of the trauma caused by her parents' demise and death. Her parents' lives had been disappointing, but good memories also remained. They were respected and generous and cultured.

Nevertheless, Hanjo was enough for her. She took care of him like a son. She made him do what he had to do and made sure what he wanted happened. She saved him from depression, turned him into a painter and a rich man. He was the brilliant result of her hard work and dedication.

If she had had children, they would have influenced all her decisions. Her determination to reach her goal would have turned into indecision, and she would not have been able to crush or ruin Hanjo.

So what about their only child, the one Haeri had lost and the one Hanjo had missed his whole life?

Haeri had never lost her child, because she had never been pregnant. Her fake pregnancy was so thorough as to be heartless, even to her. Even while she felt pity for Hanjo, who was plunged into anguish by the loss of a child that had never existed, she was intoxicated by her secret victory, at having punished him without anyone knowing. She thought of Medea, who had stabbed the two sons of Jason that she had given birth to. Killing their children, the proof of their love, was how she punished her immoral husband, a deadly revenge that could be realized only by then destroying herself.

Haeri felt her thighs with her writing hand. She could feel the jagged textures of the big and small scars beneath her fingers. Sharp, vivid memories of pain came back, clearly telling her that her past was not a dream.

The white collar of her sister's water-soaked school uniform, her father's bloodshot eyes, the people who stopped talking and clacked their tongues on seeing her, the nights when she fell asleep alone, the day she was kicked out of school, the laughter she heard from behind her as she went plodding across the endless school playground, the afternoon she took a train to Seoul after packing just a few clothes, the unfamiliar streets of the unfamiliar city, the lights and the voices . . . Haeri drew on the grief, sorrow, anger, and hostility in each scar and turned them into writing. It wasn't a memoir that presented the past in a plausible way or looked at the past calmly. It was a documentary that dug up the buried truth and reconstructed a lost past—an accusation denouncing a hidden criminal.

Her writing would become a bomb. Buried in the very heart of Howard House, the bomb would tick on silently, poised to shatter the life of the man she had loved forever.

Then one day, when the time was right, she would press the detonator. The bomb would come alive, the clock ticking down, the furious beep of an alarm, then—

Boom.

Yun San

The garden's lilac tree cast a shadow over them as they sat side by side on the bench. A plane was drawing a silvery trail across the sky. A sharp feeling of grief pierced Hanjo's breast like a blade.

"Your . . . your writing is full of lies. You've turned me into a shameless villain who seduced a minor. You were already a college student when you met me. How could you have been only eighteen?"

"I never lied to you," Haeri replied coldly. "I just said I was not a high school student, but I never said I was a college student. It was you who mistook an eighteen-year-old high school dropout for a college student."

Wearing dark sunglasses, Haeri reminded him of the main character in a movie they'd watched together in the past. Hanjo shook his head, stuttering, "The . . . the person I know is not like this."

"Then what kind of person do you think I am?"

Hanjo wondered how to answer. What kind of person was she? He couldn't think of an answer. Once he had thought he knew her better than anyone else, but now he seemed to have no idea.

"I . . . I don't know. I used to think I knew everything about you, but now I don't know anything. The you I know can hide something as if it had never happened but can't boldly fabricate things that never happened."

Haeri didn't answer immediately. It wasn't because she had nothing to say but because she was unsure of where to start.

"I didn't fabricate anything," she said. "I wrote what I saw and heard. It's a story about things that you saw and heard. But even if we saw and heard the same things, can we say it's the same story? Just as you have your story, I have my story."

"Tell me what my story is and what your story is, how the two stories differ."

"Your story is always bright—amazing talent, brilliant success, noble character, and people's praise . . . That's not our story, and it's not mine. My story is dark and painful. It started and ended with making one person into an artist. I had to pour everything into loving you to achieve that."

"You think I don't know that? Without you, I would be nothing, a complete failure. Yes, we've done a great job so far. I was able to achieve what I wanted . . ."

"You wanted it, not me."

"It's the same no matter who wanted it, surely? You did everything you wanted, so what the hell is this?"

Haeri, after looking at Hanjo for a while, answered briefly and calmly.

"I'm trying to destroy you."

Hanjo could not understand Haeri's words. All he could do was stare blankly at her and keep talking—anything to stave off the reality of what she had just said. "No, please don't say that. I really don't know why you're saying that."

"I wanted to destroy your talent, your wealth, your reputation, and your love. But you didn't have any of these things. There was a high possibility that even the only talent you had would never see the light. So if I wanted to take something away from you, I was obliged to make sure you had it first."

Hanjo shuddered at the thought that his only talent had become a deadly weapon to destroy him. Fury made his body heat up with a whine, like an old refrigerator. He forced his stiff lips to make a noise.

"To destroy me is to destroy my paintings. Is that what you want?"

"How are they your paintings? Can't your eyes see the scars in the pictures? Those scars—cut, sanded, and chiseled—are my life that I painted in my dark room, in the bathroom beside the river on rainy days. They might not be beautiful or great, but I didn't throw them away. They might be ugly and painful, but I dragged them all the way here. Because they were my life. They are all I have, and if I threw them away, I'd be throwing everything away. So how can you say that they are yours?"

"You're right. My achievement was your creation from beginning to end. All I did was paint you, and steal part of your talent."

"But you said the paintings were yours, because you thought you owned me, and you mistook my life for your own. You took me for granted, like everybody else. But you don't have the right to own someone. No one does."

"But we're a couple. I'm your husband and you're my wife . . ."

"Yes, you can look at me. You can listen to me, or you can tell me things. You can touch me, love me, or draw me. But you can't own me. You cannot make my life your own. Do you understand now? Why the paintings are mine, not yours?"

Haeri's voice roared in Hanjo's ears as if coming from deep underwater. Every hair on his body stood on end like a thorn.

"You loved me, didn't you?" he asked, imploring, pleading. "Why are you doing this to me?"

"You ruined my life and that of my family."

Her expression was so blank that Hanjo felt guilty, as if he were abusing her or abandoning her. But it wasn't her—it was he who was being abandoned. Hanjo was defenseless against this woman who was determined to destroy him, and was seized with fear that there was a reason for her revenge. He struggled not to stutter.

"You . . . you have some kind of misunderstanding about your sister's death. It's not that there isn't something suspicious . . ."

She lowered her head for a moment and organized her thoughts before speaking.

"When I asked about my sister's death as a child, my uncle avoided answering, saying that not knowing was OK, that it was better for me not to know. Only later did I realize that the incompetent police, the flatulent media, and the impatient public had joined together to make a false conviction. Everyone deceived everyone, and everyone was fooled by everyone."

Haeri pushed her hair back, using her sunglasses like a headband. Her body smelled of dry dust.

"Ah . . . if it's not my father . . . do you think it's my brother?"

Hanjo recalled his brother's radiant, clean-cut face. He was surprised at himself for asking the question. The sun hung low in the western sky, preparing an orange-gray sunset. From the playground, they could hear girls laughing and boys shouting as they played baseball. She answered.

"Your brother is too smart to kill someone. He was the opposite of your loving, naive father. I read the records and met the witnesses. Finally, I figured out your lie."

"Lie? Me?"

"You weren't with your brother at the time Jisoo was dying. You perjured yourself. Whether they were being stupid or crafty, the police took your word for it."

Hanjo opened his mouth wide. He grabbed her by the shoulder and spoke as if begging her.

"I was terrified. I couldn't refuse to provide that alibi, even if my brother had a different purpose. I had to protect him if he was involved in the case in any way. Just like he did me . . ."

"A lot would have been different if you hadn't said that then. The conclusion of the investigation and our lives would be different from what they are now. But you said it. That lie."

A chill was spreading from Haeri's icy body. Hanjo pulled his words together with all his might. "Do . . . do you think it was me? That . . . that I killed Jisoo?"

It was in this moment that everything changed. Every minute spent with her, every conversation, every action took on a new meaning.

"During the summer vacation that year," Haeri said quietly, "my sister posed as your nude model in the annex studio. It may have been voluntary or forced, but that night you tried to do something terrible to her. Just as you did to me."

She looked at him calmly, as if she were staring at the murderer hidden inside him. A shudder swept through his body. Hanjo felt dizzy. "It's a misunderstanding. Jisoo never undressed. What you are thinking never happened."

"Another lie! I saw your sketchbook, and your nude drawings of my sister."

She was agitated now. At her raised voice, Rothko woke up from his nap and looked around.

"Yes, it's true I drew nude pictures of Jisoo," Hanjo said. "But the pictures were just my imagination. I know it wasn't right. But my love for Jisoo was unrequited, and I couldn't help longing for her like that."

A tremor spread from the tips of Haeri's fingers all through her body. There was no knowing whether she believed what he said or rejected it. Struggling to maintain her calm, she said, "That night, I saw you chasing my sister over the hill. She was crying and running away from you. After you came back to Howard House, you assaulted me against my will and didn't even feel guilty. No matter how much I love you, my hatred is firmly lodged in my heart and won't go away."

Hanjo didn't believe that she had loved him—the years of loving and helping each other, gazes directed at each other, the sweet words whispered to her, her touch on his face, the hours of laughter they shared . . .

This was not fate. It was retribution and punishment. Hanjo's whole body hardened with guilt: he had instilled a lifelong hatred in the person he loved so much; the more she loved him, the more she suffered; and he had not even imagined his error, let alone realized it. Now he understood why she had married him.

He sprang to his feet. He didn't mean to go anywhere. He just wanted to get out of there. He ran across the garden. His wide back, arms swinging like the scrawny wings of a thin bird, the hair on his neck, his shoulders slightly tilted to the right moved away from her, mingled with the words they had shared, the secret sounds of their love, the amazed laughter in the morning when they discovered they'd each dreamed the same dream . . . Rothko stared with dejected eyes in the direction Hanjo had disappeared.

Hanjo crouched in the studio like a soldier who had jumped into a trench to avoid artillery fire. His breath was short, and there was a buzzing in his ears. After a while, there came the sound of her car starting, followed by the crunch of tires crushing gravel and the sharp noise of wheels skidding, sounds that faded away one after the other.

Hanjo visited Yun San at a 160-bed nursing home in the suburbs, which was about thirty minutes from downtown. Yun San worked as a security guard there. He did not go into any details, but said he had retired from the police nine years before. Afterward, he spent some time as an interim manager of a security company, ran a garden-produce wholesale business, served as a manager for an apartment complex, and finally lost his life savings due to a series of investment failures.

He had been fired from the security company three years before, and spent time drinking until he had a stroke. He nearly died, his right side was completely paralyzed, and he was admitted to the nursing home to undergo two years of rehabilitation. When he had recovered to some extent, the director, who noticed his perseverance and willpower, offered him a job as a security guard.

"If only your father were still alive. How happy he would have been to see you become a great artist . . ." Yun San, wearing an old shirt and a fluffy jacket, stayed seated as he held out a hand. He was no longer the tenacious detective Hanjo had known, but instead gave the impression of being a good-natured local restaurant owner. His short hair was white, as if it had been frosted, and surgical scars were visible on his scalp through his short hair. The wrinkles around his mouth had deepened. Even though his stomach bulged, overall he looked smaller than before.

"My father was prouder of my brother than of me."

"I know. That's why he would have been happy to see you succeed."

Yun San took Hanjo to the visitors' room on the first floor, where there was a café. He sat curled in his seat, his strong back bent. He talked about the fall of a retired detective, the comforts of old age, and approaching death. Then he asked, "You must have come looking for me on account of what happened back then, right? There would be no other reason for you to visit me."

He added that whenever he saw Hanjo on TV, he wondered whether this day would ever come. It was as if he knew what Hanjo wanted to ask him more clearly than Hanjo himself did.

"Do you remember it?"

"I still feel frustrated when I think about it. The investigation was at a standstill, and we were under pressure from higher up . . . There was no result from extensive searches and inquiries. Nothing unusual came up when we interrogated ex-convicts and criminals, and the investigation of the election candidates was futile."

Yun San could see that year as vividly as if it were projected on a screen.

At their seventh assessment meeting, Kang Ilho, the team leader, hypothesized that the murderer might be an acquaintance, since there were no signs of physical violence on Jisoo's body.

"There was no bullying, no commotion, no injuries from beatings. There's no sign of her being killed and transferred from elsewhere. The victim went to the scene voluntarily. We need to find someone she was close enough to to meet alone and trust. Can you think of anyone who is close to the victim?"

Choi Daegon spoke up first. "The Malcolm House men were close to the victim. They were the closest in distance. There were also testimonies that the eldest son often went walking toward the dam."

The members of the team shook their heads.

"The brothers were together in the studio in the annex on the evening of the incident," Yun San said. "It doesn't seem to be a lie, seeing as the details match."

Choi Daegon stared at Yun San. "That man called Lee Jinman," he said, "he has a previous conviction for violence. If you look closely, there are gaps in his alibi. It's incomplete rather than a complete blank." He smiled slyly. "Lee Jinman, who finished working on the pipes around six p.m. on the day of the incident, stopped by a building-supplies merchant about ten minutes' walk away. The alibi is good up to that point. There's a problem from six forty to ten p.m. He says he walked straight home from the building-supplies store, but there's no one able to confirm it. His wife stated she saw her husband leaving the bathroom around ten o'clock when she returned from work at Howard House. Does it make sense that someone who came back home dusty and sweating early in the evening would wash up at ten o'clock? In the scorching summer weather? If you believe him, it means he was home alone until his wife came back, right?"

Yun San checked Lee Jinman's alibi by consulting his notebook. "He remembered the nine o'clock evening news, about the restructuring of the Peace Bank, and also mentioned interviews with the families of laid-off workers."

"The financial crisis, restructuring, mass layoffs are always on the news these days," Choi Daegon refuted. "Dismissed bankers, suicides of pessimistic recruits, joint suicide of families in extreme poverty . . ."

Yun San raised his voice. "Look at the people, not the alibi. Let's look at the moon instead of the finger pointing at it. A gap in an alibi doesn't mean he's a killer. He's weak. There's no indication he would kill someone."

"There's no knowing who might kill someone."

Kang Ilho knocked on the table to bring the meeting to order.

"Despite the credibility of his statement and the integrity of the person making the statement, a gap is a gap. That's when the girl died. That's the estimated time of the victim's death."

Yun San swept a hand over his graying hair. He looked older because of the wrinkles around his eyes, but he had a gentleness common to old men. His face gave the impression that he reckoned all human beings were generous, honest, and trustworthy.

"The investigation team persistently questioned Lee Jinman on his whereabouts from six forty to ten. He repeated that he was at home . . . That's when conclusive evidence was secured. It was the test of the fluid from Jisoo's body. It was a very small amount and it was impossible to analyze it accurately after such a long time, but the blood-type marker was consistent with Lee Jinman. Then he confessed to the crime, even though we didn't get results significant enough to be considered legal evidence."

"Have you ever doubted the truth of his confession?" Hanjo asked.

"There was no evidence that his confession was false. There was no evidence to refute his claim that he was alone at home, and the suspicion he committed the crime was supported by a photograph of Jisoo he'd taken at the dam. The investigation team had enough evidence to support his confession."

"Do you still believe my father killed Jisoo?"

Yun San thought of Kang, who was in a nursing home with Alzheimer's disease, and Choi Daegon, who'd died of cancer six years before. He longed for one of them to come forward and answer for him.

"The key was not the alibi itself, but whether we believed it or not. His confession sounded mostly true, and there was plenty of circumstantial evidence to support the suspicion he'd committed the murder. But I was hesitant."

"Was there any chance it wasn't Father?"

"It's possible. He wasn't meticulous, he wasn't brave, he wasn't deliberate. In other words, he wasn't up to killing someone."

"Who did it, then? Who killed Jisoo?"

"Is there any point in trying to find out now?"

"Yes, I need to know, even now."

Yun San frowned, trying to recall the investigation as accurately as possible. Although he couldn't pinpoint a plausible culprit, he told Hanjo what he could remember of the evidence and testimony they had obtained during the investigation. Among the suspects, Suin had often been seen around the dam at the time of the incident.

"What do you mean, bringing my brother into it?" Hanjo burst out in a rage.

Yun San nodded, as if asking for forgiveness. "Don't get me wrong. I only said it because I thought you needed to know all the details. In fact, I couldn't give up my belief that Jisoo's death was a suicide. But the possibility of suicide was ignored or rejected. There was excessive media coverage, pressure from higher-ups, and other kinds of pressure."

"Such as?"

"The family of the victim . . . More exactly, the father of the victim. Jang Heejae not only refused to accept his daughter's suicide but also insisted that the investigation team should *say* she had not committed suicide. It's not that I can't understand parents refusing to accept their daughter's tragic death, but it wasn't just because of that. He was the victim's family, but he was also the candidate hoping to win the local elections the following year. If his daughter's death was ruled a suicide, it would count against him in the election. You know what people are like, don't you? *This person wants to hold public office, but how does he control his family? And if he can't even control his daughter, then what kind of leader is he?* And so on . . . Then your father confessed when the investigation was faltering."

"It was a lie that everyone could agree on."

"That's not the point of my story."

"Then what is?"

"About ten years after that . . . I heard from Sergeant Nam Bora about Howard House's youngest daughter. She came to the police station to ask about her sister's case, so Nam Bora explained it to her and sent her away, but Nam Bora said something still bothered her. It wasn't because of what she'd said or heard but because of something she couldn't do. She hadn't been able to tell the girl that her sister's death could have been a suicide."

"It must have been because she didn't want to cause her more confusion, and increase her burden."

Yun San's voice trembled. "She couldn't bear to tell her that her dead father had dismissed the possibility of his daughter's suicide. How could she tell her that her father had hidden the cause of her death and made the wrong person into a murderer?"

Darkness came crawling from behind red clouds. The thin black line of the low wooden fence stretched beyond the workroom window. Maple branches flashed white, like the bones of night. Entering the studio, Suin shouted as he switched on the lights, "Let's order pizza. I'm hungry."

Hanjo lay almost buried on the sofa. He looked like a drunkard suffering a hangover. His hair, which hadn't been washed for days, was tangled, and his lips were dry. He staggered to the refrigerator and ordered pizza from a restaurant whose number was fixed to a fridge magnet. Then he took out a six-pack of beer and handed it to Suin.

"You're already drunk, aren't you?" Suin asked.

"I just had a drink waiting for you to come."

Suin drank some beer and wiped his lips with a sleeve. Hanjo's eyes were bloodshot. Had he been crying alone before Suin arrived? Hanjo, who had once waited more than an hour for him and had not cried, even after getting lost in the middle of the city. From outside the window came a gentle breeze with a sweet scent of flowers.

"What will happen to us now?" Hanjo asked.

Suin still couldn't answer that question, even though he was now an adult. Hanjo drank the remaining beer, crumpled the empty can, and threw it toward the trash can. The can bounced off the wall.

"Let's just drink."

This was what Suin had said on the night their father was arrested, forcing Hanjo to drink soju. He had wanted to reassure his brother. There was nothing else he could do. But now, seeing his younger brother drunk, he felt guilty for having made him drink that night. If they hadn't drunk soju then, perhaps his brother might have lived without knowing anything about alcohol.

He could never forget his brother's expression at the table that night, his small body curled up on the hard chair, the worn-out collar of his old shirt, his fragile collarbone. His brother was already the taller of the two at that time, yet he seemed never to have grown up.

Hanjo rambled as if drunk. "You told me one day, didn't you? That I was going to ruin my life with alcohol. Yes, I guess I ended up being like our mom. But even if it wasn't alcohol, my life would be ruined. Don't you think so?"

"Wake up—your life hasn't been ruined yet."

"Have you ever wondered why Father confessed to the murder? When I was young, I thought it was for us, but from that point on I've grown really curious, whether he did it for me or for you. But I didn't really want to know. I was afraid it would confirm that I was the unloved son."

Suin looked pityingly at his bulky brother in his thick shirt. "Father talked once about Haeri," he said. "Haeri mentioned she saw something near the annex studio that night. Jisoo came running out of the studio, crying, and someone followed her over the hill. She didn't see his face."

Hanjo realized what Suin was thinking. It was a thought he had never entertained before.

"You think it was me?"

"I don't know," Suin said, unusually evasive. "I don't want to know. I just wonder why Jisoo was crying as she ran out of the studio that day. What did you do to Jisoo?"

"I said something to her."

"What did you say?"

"I confessed that I liked her. When she accepted my request to be a model, I thought that Jisoo liked me. But I soon realized that she only thought of me as a stepping-stone, a way of approaching you. But it didn't matter. It was just nice to be able to look at Jisoo every day."

"Jisoo agreed to be your model, you were drawing her, and you were both spending time together each day. Why did you tell her you liked her when things were already going so well?"

"Remember? We went on a picnic together. You, me, Jisoo, Haeri . . . I think Jisoo's attitude changed little by little after that. By the end of the summer vacation, she lost interest in my paintings and modeling. She had already crossed over to you; she didn't need a stepping-stone."

"Tell me about that day. What happened?"

"That day, Jisoo said she would no longer be coming to the studio. She said that the person she'd loved from the beginning was not me but my brother, and that he loved her, too. I was so angry that I didn't know what to do. I said something stupid that I shouldn't have said, because I wanted to hold on to her. I wanted to hurt Jisoo the same way she had hurt me. I just wanted to let her know she was wrong . . ."

"What did you say?"

"That you loved another woman and were suffering because of her. That you were only pretending to like Jisoo. I thought Jisoo would give up on you. But Jisoo couldn't believe it. No, she refused to believe it. I told her to go to the villa right away, that you would be there with that woman."

"Were you crazy?" Suin shouted, his eyes widening. "Who were you to tell Jisoo that?"

Hanjo continued quietly. "Yes, I did something stupid. I woke up when I saw Jisoo running away, crying. I followed and saw her cycling over the hill. I followed Jisoo along the riverside trail. It was dark; there was nobody in sight. I didn't know what to do. I sat by the river, waiting for Jisoo, regretting the crazy words I had said. When I met her, I would apologize, say it had been lies, and that I wanted to go home with her. Jisoo never came back. It wasn't until late at night that I went home alone."

Suin realized the story wasn't finished yet, and that he would need to hear its end. His next question was both accusatory and an excuse.

"Why did you think I liked another woman?"

Suin's question revealed an eerie truth. He should have asked, *Why did you lie about that?* Hanjo stroked the rim of his beer can with his finger. He answered slowly, like a prisoner under interrogation.

"I happened to see your diary. No, it was not an accident. I'd often peeped at it before. I know. It was stupid. It was a bad thing, too. But I've always been stupid. I just wanted to know about you, see that you, too, had weaknesses and shameful thoughts. No, that's not it. It was not you I wanted to know about—it was Jisoo."

"Did you find what you wanted?"

"Your diary back then was plastered with expressions of longing, longing for a woman who didn't accept your love. It wasn't Jisoo."

"Is that all?"

"By the end of the summer, you were feeling better. The diary was filled with excitement that you were going to meet her in two days' time. You didn't mention the time and place, but I could guess from what was written that it was the villa at sunset."

"But how were you so sure that you told Jisoo this?"

"I checked the living room cabinet—the drawer where they kept the spare keys for Howard House, the annex, and the villa for Father to use when he needed them. But there was no key to the villa. Yet Father had been busy with the school drains all day."

That summer remained an indelible stain on Hanjo's life. The realization that his love for Jisoo had been the catalyst for her death broke his heart. Hanjo asked, in a toneless voice, "Did you kill Jisoo?"

"Surely you know I didn't."

"That's not an answer. Did you kill Jisoo?"

Suin's gaze, as he sat there, bolt upright, was looking into the distant past. Hanjo waited patiently, like a priest waiting for a confession. He was afraid to face the truth he wanted so much to know. Suin crumpled the beer can with his hands as if he had made up his mind.

"I wasn't in the villa then. I wasn't with Jisoo . . . I left before she came."

The lilac leaves in the front yard shone brightly in the lamplight. Hanjo asked Suin a question that he couldn't postpone any longer. "Then where were you?"

"I was in the car."

"What car?"

"Jisoo's parents' car."

"Where was the car?"

"Farther down the river, from where you can see old barns and private houses. We stopped by the side of the road and looked at the flowing river. We didn't say anything; we just looked at the river."

"Did you say 'we'? And you weren't with Jisoo?"

"No, it wasn't Jisoo."

"Then who were you with?"

"Jisoo's mom."

Suin seemed about to burst into tears, like a child slapped on the cheek—not because of regret and guilt, but because of longing and love.

Suin

Suin was there that night, staring at the flowing river that glistened like metal, not saying a word, with her. The current moved quietly past them and along the gently curving river.

She was wearing a blue dress printed with large bracken leaves. Colorful reflections from the river played over her face. A faint vaccination scar could be seen on her right shoulder, which was deeply tanned. Suin imagined her around the time of the injection. She would have been a bobbed-haired little girl with a front tooth missing. Would he have loved her if he had met her then?

Last week, his mother had mentioned that the floor of Howard House needed repairing. It was rotting thanks to water leakage from the plastic drain of the old sink. But there was no one to do it. His father was busy finishing the pipes before school started, and Hanjo was locked away in the studio and never showed his face.

The next morning, Suin headed for Howard House, carrying a replacement floorboard and his toolbox. Jisoo's mother opened the front door. Suin, who naturally expected his own mother to open the door, was embarrassed.

"Your mother went to the market," she said, wiping her dripping hands. "I've invited guests to dinner."

The house was hushed and smelled sweet. There was a loud sound as a flying bug hit the glass, maybe a dragonfly or a cicada.

Suin examined the floorboard, which had cracked from constantly soaking up leaking water and then drying again. He had watched his father at work, so he knew how to replace it. She watched Suin as he tore out the cracked plank, sanded the ends of the hole with sandpaper, accurately cut the board to replace it, put it in place, and applied varnish to the surface. She handed Suin a Coke and removed a splinter from his thumb, disinfected it, and put a Band-Aid on it.

While waiting for the varnish to dry, Suin sat at the table and read a paperback edition of *The Sun Also Rises*. She said she had also read it in her school days, but only vaguely remembered it.

"I don't remember the name, but the bullfighting festival was amazing. It's still fresh in my mind, as if I had seen it myself."

"The Fiesta de San Fermín," Suin said, handing her the book. "Read it again. I'll read it later."

She accepted the book, even though she shook her head and said it was OK. There were so many pages with the corners folded down that the top bulged. It was not a book that Suin gave her but a chronicle of his longing and pain that he couldn't say aloud, conveyed now by the words he underlined, the pages he desperately sympathized with and turned down, and the notes he wrote in the margins when unable to restrain his rising emotions.

She had an eye for pain and knew how to read love. She could also sense the meaning of unbearable silences, and notice eyes that were glancing at her while avoiding being caught. Suin was sure she would recognize his desires, both beautiful and bad.

But what would change if she understood his futile confession? She was still a wife and a mother of two, and he was the son of a housekeeper. Maybe she could feel pity for him. Or she might consider it a joke. But suppose she accepted his heart . . .

There had been no news from her for days. Suin was afraid to go to Howard House. He didn't feel confident enough to meet her gaze and talk to her. She might have told the whole truth to her condescending and authoritative husband. Suin blamed himself for handing her the book, unable to overcome a momentary impulse. He was dismayed that he might lose her by his carelessness.

In the first semester, Suin had taught math to Hanjo and Jisoo in the Howard House parlor, but once the summer vacation began, he moved their place of study to the studio, because of Heejae's offer to cover their college-tuition fees if they all clearly raised their grades during the vacation. However, Hanjo said that he preferred to concentrate on painting rather than studying, using a separate room. One day Jisoo said that she did not want to disturb Hanjo's work, and insisted on moving the place where the two of them studied to the villa. She had previously promised Hanjo, who was bitter, to model for him in the studio during the vacation.

"Instead, we must keep it a secret that only the three of us know. If Mom and Dad know, we'll be locked up in the parlor and monitored. Then it's goodbye to studying and painting and everything."

Suin and Jisoo, who went to the villa alone, opened their books on their desks and were as silent as old lovers. Then they could not stand the silence surrounding them and drew closer, as if to soothe each other's anxiety with one another's breath, then closer . . .

"My mom wants me to return this book. You left it behind on the day you repaired the kitchen floor . . ."

Jisoo had been about to leave when she took out a small paperback from her bag and handed it to him. *The Sun Also Rises*.

On the way home, the August evening sky shone like blue velvet. Suin gently pedaled as if he were gliding across clouds. He stopped his bike along the trail, sat on a bench, and opened the book.

The bottom corner of page 116 was folded into a triangle. It wasn't a mark he had made: he habitually folded the top edge to mark passages while reading a book. If he folded the bottom corner, it would be uncomfortable to flip through the book.

On the page, some words were underlined with blue ink, not his black pen. It was a scene where the main character goes to the Île Saint-Louis on the Seine River in Paris with a friend who had returned from a trip.

> *"Where shall we go?"*
> *"How about going to the island?"*
> *"That's good."*

The next page folded at the bottom was page 182. The blue ink underlined:

> *I could see a white house under some trees growing around the mountainside.*

A white house under trees on an island across a river? It was the riverside villa, for sure. When the dam was full, the forest with the villa became an island surrounded by water. Suin turned urgently to the next folded page: page 195, with blue underlining:

> *"What day is it?" I asked Harris.*
> *"I think it's Wednesday. Yes, yes. Wednesday."*

And the next folded page was 198:

> *"Let's go fishing together again sometime. Don't forget this promise. Harris."*

The last page folded was 355. There was no need to look for the blue underline. The words leaped off the page.

It was not until the sun was setting that I walked along the path after passing the harbor and eventually went back to the hotel for dinner.

This was what the blue underlines meant: at the riverside villa, Wednesday, at dusk, don't forget the rendezvous.

Even though it was something he had dreamed of, he was so afraid he felt he might choke. He wondered why she wanted to meet him. There were two possibilities: either she had accepted his confession and love, or she would rebuke him for his immaturity. There was a ninety-nine percent chance it was the latter.

Of course she wouldn't browbeat or scold him. Instead, she would calmly and carefully try to discourage his delusions, or desires. No one else would know what had happened between the two of them, but Suin would never be able to face her after that. Yet even though he knew this, he was looking forward to the day.

Suin thought about what day it was today: Monday. He had to get through Tuesday to reach Wednesday. If only today were Tuesday. If only it were Wednesday evening. How good would that be?

No, if only today were Thursday . . .

Suin left home at three o'clock on Wednesday and pedaled along the riverside path. It was close to four when he emerged from the forest and arrived at the villa. He decided to sit on the porch's wooden chair and wait, even though he had the spare key. Jisoo would be with Hanjo in the annex studio, so no one would be coming here.

All through the afternoon, he watched the sunlight shining through the forest like golden columns and the twilight approaching like a feral cat. Vastly inflated expectations pushed everything else out of his head. He wondered what he was so desperate for. He didn't know. He reckoned he might be all the more eager because he did not know.

As sunset began to color the clouds, the quiet sound of an engine could be heard approaching through the forest. A white car left the forest road and turned into the driveway of the villa. Suin got up slowly and walked down the steps. The car stopped after quietly sweeping across the gravel of the front yard. The car window slid down, and white fingers fluttered like a lace handkerchief inside the dark car.

"Shall we go inside and talk?" she said.

She smiled an almost invisible smile, got out of the car, took a key out of her handbag, and opened the front door. Suin felt an eerie dread of what would happen next and a sharp feeling of pleasure pass through him.

They sat opposite one another on the sofa occupying the middle of the hall. A smell of old furniture filled the house, which was like a small spaceship floating in the dark. This was always what Suin imagined in his fantasies: a sense of comfortable isolation, the two of them alone in a vast space with no water or air.

Suin's fantasies about her were filled with pure, extremely metaphorical imagery. He dreamed of his soul streaming into her body like smoke, or climbing up the branches of a beautiful tree rooted on her white feet, while vivid images of him being her son, lying in her arms or holding her in his arms and both of them turning into hard stones, captivated him.

She looked out the window, deep in thought. She seemed to be wondering what to say. But no matter what she said, Suin didn't want to hear it. It was only important that he had become so important to her.

She finally spoke. "When I was young, I never thought about what kind of person I would be. I just wanted to be a teacher, a poet, and a painter. It didn't work out in the end. I've never been disappointed or regretted not being the person I dreamed of. But I think I had to dream of a concrete and clear future at least once. An ambiguous and vague future is no future."

Air bubbles burst at the surface of the cold Coke in the glasses on the table. She was trying to use the future to destroy his present. Suin didn't want to be persuaded.

"Why are you talking about the future? I want to talk about the present. What I think of you and what you think of me. It's neither ambiguous nor vague; it's concrete and clear."

Water dripped into the drainpipe of the sink. A faint smell of perfume wafted from her as she sat back.

"Do you know how much potential you have? I didn't have that. I wasn't smart and I wasn't good at anything; I was just lucky. But you're an outstanding child. You can and must become whatever you dream of—so you have to think about the future, not now."

Suin didn't believe what she said was sincere. She couldn't have called him here just to say this. He didn't want to think about whose wife she was or whose mother. He didn't even want to know why he was here now. His heart was torn by a longing for time to stop.

"I don't want to be a president or a judge. I don't want to be anything. If I have a future, you are it, only you."

She sighed deeply. At this moment, it became clear to Suin why she was here: she was trying to dissuade him. As a responsible adult, she wanted to appease the immature boy's poor curiosity.

It was impossible for Suin to persuade her in this short meeting. The best thing he could expect now was to return to their previous relationship, an ordinary situation in which she had not recognized the meaning of his underlined lines, folded pages, and notes, and they had not met at this remote villa.

Even if she didn't accept his love, she might not let their friendship break down. It was his last chance, if he was not to lose everything. If he could seize this opportunity, he could continue to love her in his own way, hiding his swelling desire by peeping at her white ankles from a distance alone, envying or hating her husband and waiting for him to die in an accident. The rest would be settled in time.

Suin hastened to say more. He continued to speak as if he were being pursued by something, words that could restore their previous relationship, words easily shared between a next-door neighbor and a boy, everyday, ordinary stories, silly jokes . . .

Meanwhile, she was seized with anxiety that she might ruin this boy's future. A clever boy caught up in a senseless passion had to be brought to his senses. As if nothing had happened, she had to go back to her daily life and do right by this boy. They were like accomplices desperately digging a hole to bury the body of someone they had killed.

Darkness approached the house like an unfamiliar animal and peeped inside. An open window let in a scent of pine needles and moss. She reached out and caressed Suin's cheek lightly. Her hands were surprisingly cool.

"Suin, you don't know how precious and dear you are. You shine. You'll be loved by everyone, and you'll be everyone's light."

Suin stared at her lips. Her fingers on his cheek were as painful as fire.

"Just then, I thought I heard something."

Suin picked up his lukewarm can of beer and took a sip.

"What do you mean?" Hanjo asked, with an odd, remote look.

"Something shaking outside the dark window," Suin said, picking up a fresh can of beer. "There was no one visible beyond the window. But I still thought someone was watching us in the dark. It was scary to be in a remote villa by night, and I was worried that other people might find me alone with her. Or maybe I was reacting to her quiet persuasion . . ."

Suin remained silent for a long time, hesitating about whether to continue or not. Maybe he shouldn't have started talking. He wanted the silence to go on forever. Finally, Hanjo screamed a single word—

"Brother!"

It was a question, an entreaty, an accusation.

"We drove down along the river in her car," Suin said quietly. "If I wanted to go home, I had to turn left and cross the bridge, but I said I wanted her to drive a bit further. She didn't answer. We left the town and continued downstream. She parked the car on the riverbank, from where we had a view of the old barns and private houses in the distance. We didn't say anything, just looked out through the car window at the black river. We stayed like that for about thirty minutes; then she started the car, drove back along the river, and dropped me off at the bridge. The phone rang soon after I got home. Father put the phone down and said we should go to Howard House. Jisoo hadn't come back . . ."

Hanjo was incredulous. There was no reason to believe him: someone who tells a lie once can do it twice.

"There's no one left to prove what you're saying is true. They're all people no longer in this world."

"The truth doesn't disappear because there's no one to prove it."

Hanjo kept wishing he had not listened. He went out to the terrace and leaned his head against the railings. Weeds had sprung up in the lawn, where only weeks before he had enjoyed a birthday party with his wife. Suddenly, the house looked enormous. This lovely meadow and well-kept garden, his recent paintings, all were like mirages.

"What I think is that we were surrounded by lies and told the truth," Hanjo said.

"No matter what we said back then, nothing changes."

"Was there really nothing outside the window then?"

Hanjo's voice was icy. Suin did not answer. Hanjo spoke again. "Perhaps the person you thought you saw in the dark wasn't Jisoo? Perhaps it was someone else?"

Suin couldn't understand why they, as brothers, had never spoken about that night, why he had not confided in Hanjo what had happened. It wasn't that he hadn't thought about it. The idea had occurred to him every moment of his life, but he'd always turned a blind eye to it or shook it off with all his might. Hanjo must have done the same. Perhaps they'd never confided in each other because they hadn't wanted to hurt each other. But now lies had grown up from within their long-held silences and threatened to destroy them.

"Then I killed Jisoo," Hanjo said. "Is that true?"

Hanjo's eyes were bloodshot. The sparse streetlights and glowing signboards at the bottom of the hill permeated the soft night air.

"Don't blame yourself," Suin said.

"If I hadn't said that in a fit of anger, Jisoo wouldn't have gone to the villa and wouldn't have seen her mother with you. Then Father wouldn't have felt obliged to confess to a murder he didn't commit; then Jisoo's parents would not have died."

Inside Hanjo, something exploded with a roar. Like a circuit board when a short circuit occurs, there was a crackling in his ears and a smell of smoke. No matter how hard he struggled to escape from his terrible fate, he was still an eighteen-year-old boy, lonely, vulnerable, and in need of protection and love . . .

"Maybe so," Suin said. "If you hadn't told Jisoo that, if I hadn't been there at that time, if Jisoo hadn't read my underlined book, if we hadn't done everything we did, if we had done everything we didn't do . . . then none of this would have happened."

"But we did. I told Jisoo, and you were there at that time, and she read the things you had underlined. And so it happened."

Suin remembered the night his father was taken away, when Hanjo and he drank soju at the kitchen table. Many questions plagued him: Did his father know Suin had been in the villa? Was that why he'd made such a plausible confession? But then a voice in his head told him to stop thinking. At that moment, he sealed his memory, and he never opened that door again. He believed that if he didn't think about it, he could live as if it hadn't happened.

Hanjo leaned back on the sofa and sighed deeply.

"Are you asleep?" Suin asked.

Hanjo did not answer; his eyes were closed. Once, when Suin was nine years old, Hanjo fell out of the bed. Awakened by a whimper from the dark floor, Suin got out of bed, lay down next to Hanjo, and told him stories until he fell asleep. Suddenly, little Hanjo flinched and frowned. He seemed to be having a bad dream. The next morning, Suin asked his brother what he had dreamed. But Hanjo couldn't remember. He hoped his little brother had dreamed a good dream.

"I'm not going to sleep," Hanjo murmured, opening his drunken eyes. "So don't go. Don't go anywhere. Stay here."

But Suin couldn't stay. He had a family waiting for him. He stretched his little brother out on the sofa and covered him with a blanket.

"Right, get some sleep. You'll feel better tomorrow morning after a good night's sleep."

Eighteen-year-old Jisoo's face looms in the dark water. She hasn't aged since that day. He can still smell the scent of her hair and the fresh starch of her white school uniform. He also vividly recalls seeing her back as she pedaled unsteadily over the hill. If he had grabbed her wrist as she ran out of the studio . . .

Jisoo pedals as if she is rowing a boat. The bicycle follows a dark trail into the wind. A heart torn with pain flutters like an old flag. Her back is sweating; her underarms are slippery with sweat. Her face is ablaze. Who is it? Who is the woman Suin loves?

The bicycle crosses the embankment and enters the narrow forest path. The forest is still, as if it is asleep and as cozy as a dream. The drooping branches of tall conifers on both sides of the road form a dark tunnel. When the wind passes through, the trees shudder and shake. The darkness thickens, and the air in the forest is fresh.

In an instant, her sweat cools and goose bumps form on her back. She doesn't know whether the coolness is fear or dread. Suddenly, she feels an urge to go back home. It's not too late now. Go back home and read a book to Haeri!

At that moment, she glimpses the white eaves of the dark villa between the branches. She gets off her bike and hides it in the bushes by the road. The bulb hanging from one corner of the front porch creates a round pool of light, and more light leaks out from the living room window. The lights are yellow and warm and seem to be calling to her.

She leaves her bike lying there and makes her way through the darkness. The moonlight is too dim and the forest dark. Branches strike her face like whips. Sharp conifer needles prick her calves. Her forearms are scratched by brambles, and her neck is tingling from the thorns of wild roses.

She takes a step toward the light. The sound of branches bending, the rustling of her dress, the noise of a rotten branch snapping . . . She is startled. She is like a moth flying into a flame.

The windows of the villa are half-open. She sees two people in the light . . .

Shadows waver on the water over her face. If you look closely, she is not looking down at the surface; the surface is above her. She purses her lips, her eyes wide open like a curious child's. The moon, bent like a sickle, paints the ripples on the surface.

She sinks slowly. The moonlight drifts away and the darkness hides her. Her fragile back touches the soft mud with a soft sound, like the gentle roar of the world collapsing.

Hanjo opened his eyes wide. He didn't know what time it was. He didn't keep his watch in the studio, because it interfered with his concentration. He looked around in case his wife was beside him. There was no sign of her. He didn't understand why she wasn't there.

There were empty whiskey bottles, soju bottles, and crumpled beer cans. He wanted to cry as if he had lost his parents. He wanted to cry, tearing his hair out. He thought all this had been destined from a long time ago.

Was his wife asleep now? When she was asleep, she made a panting sound. Sometimes she dreamed alone in the middle of the night and sobbed. She rarely cried during the day, but in her dreams, she cried more vividly than when awake. Then she fell back asleep. If he watched quietly, he could see the dreams nudge her eyelids, like a fetus kicking.

He rubbed his dry mouth with his hands. The beard that had grown while he was asleep rustled. He poured the leftover whiskey into his glass. The whiskey was as sticky as honey. The alcohol burned as it went down his throat, as if starting a fire. He wondered whether his depression and drinking habit were inherited from his mother or caused by what had happened that summer.

There were many ways to forget pain. You could listen to Bach's *Well-Tempered Clavier* repeatedly or run along the river until you were exhausted. You could eat sweet food until you tired of it, or you could find a new love. His mother, however, had chosen alcohol and sleeping pills instead, so that was what Hanjo did.

It was still dark outside the window. Hanjo swallowed the leftover whiskey as if drinking poison. He eagerly waited to hear the door open behind him and for someone to approach him nimbly. He missed the moist, cool lips and the smooth, quick tongue. But his wife would not come back. He was devastated by the fear that everything had collapsed. Things crumpling one by one was not collapse—true downfall came in an instant.

He could still tell his wife and the world the truth, even now. His father hadn't killed Jisoo; nor had his brother; nor had he. The murder had been just a stupid lie. That was the truth, but what was the point of a truth that caused everyone to suffer?

Hanjo looked back on the results of his malicious revelation intended to hurt Jisoo. But it was Haeri's face that came to mind before Jisoo's. Her life, in which she had to deal with the pain brought about by his words, passed before him like a picture. To destroy his life, she had to give up her own life completely.

He knew that his wife had chosen the wrong target for her revenge. And yet he did not deserve to escape her revenge. He had triggered Jisoo's death with his anger and distorted her death with his false testimony. And in so doing he had ruined many people's lives, Haeri's more than anyone else's. There were plenty of reasons for her to punish him.

Hanjo now understood the extent of Haeri's love and her revenge, and he knew that she had achieved her goal. She had so captivated him in his love and need for her that, even at the moment she'd destroyed his dream life, he could think only of her. T hinking about her journey of revenge, which must have been exhausting, his heart filled with belated sympathy for his wife.

He would accept his punishment; he would make no excuses. He would erase all trace of himself from every part of Howard House and restore it to its state before it had been contaminated by his ambition and desire. By executing his wife's revenge on himself, he would wash away his mistakes and prove his love for her.

Hanjo slowly approached the paintings piled up in layers, like a weary, weak prisoner of war tied to a rope. He could smell dry paint. *Ophelia.* She had been thinner then than she was now. The collarbone, shoulder bone, and anklebone looked sharp enough to penetrate her skin, long, blunt scars scattered all over her body like constellations.

The moonlight shining through a gap in the curtains made the paint gleam faintly. Hanjo stroked the rough surface of the canvas. He sensed the bumpy gray scars like twisted ropes under his fingertips. It was hard to face her wounds head-on, but he didn't look away. He felt that he shouldn't.

There was almost no light inside the room. Suddenly, the woman in the picture looked unfamiliar. He couldn't tell who it was he'd painted. Like a bright dawn, a slow but irresistible realization approached. It reminded him of a long-forgotten face.

Only then did a sharp awareness penetrate his body. From the first moment she'd seen the painting, she must have known that the Ophelia he'd painted was Jisoo. He wept, embracing Ophelia, his wife, and Jisoo. Time flew backward, and the room was empty.

He pulled canvas and panels down from the rails and stacked them on the floor, the colors seething under the achromatic surfaces that were like winter fields, memories swirling under quiet time, gold hues and red flesh glistening under surfaces dim as if coated with ash.

The pile of canvases was like a great grave. The paintings lay still, like black corpses. He took a lighter out of his pocket and lit a corner. The canvas bearing the flame soon had a round hole in it; the flame spread along an edge, dark red. He lit the opposite corner as well. The walls and ceiling glowed red. Smelling the fire, Rothko ran from the darkness of the garden, scratching the glass with his claws and whining.

Hanjo leaned over the stairs and looked at the flames. His life, love, and memories lit up the darkness. The garden glowing green in spring rain, the crisp touch of grass on the soles of feet, the smell of soil and grass in the late afternoon, Rothko jumping and running around, the face of his wife sunburned a rosy pink, the moistness of her lips touching his cheeks. The small, quiet, old intimacy and affection that made up their lives . . .

Jisoo's black eyes stared at him from the pictures. Sounds became a great roar as they mingled. The sound of fireworks flying, of trees crackling as they burned, of paint sizzling, of canvases hissing.

Flames licked Jisoo's cheeks, neck, and shoulders. Fluttering flames wavered red. Smoke wound up to the ceiling and heat filled the room. His ears were buzzing; he felt nauseous and dizzy. Soon the flames would fall, the paintings would become ash, and the memories would disappear.

He closed his eyes. Flames glowed inside his eyelids. They reminded him of a scene from a long time ago. A white car rattling up over the hill, swaying gently like a beetle. A family of white birds, a dark river at night, moonlight glistening on the water . . .

ABOUT THE AUTHOR

J. M. Lee's books have sold millions of copies in his native Korea. He is the author of *Painter of the Wind*, the historical mystery that launched his career and was adapted into a popular and award-winning television series in Korea; *The Boy Who Escaped Paradise*; *The Investigation*, nominated for the Independent Foreign Fiction Prize and among the final six books selected for the Italian literary prize Premio Bancarella; and *Broken Summer*, an instant bestseller in Korea and currently in production as a television series.

ABOUT THE TRANSLATOR

An Seon Jae is an award-winning translator who was born in England in 1942. He has lived in Korea since 1980 and took Korean nationality in 1994. He has published fifty collections of translated modern Korean poetry under the name Brother Anthony and currently translates contemporary Korean fiction under his Korean name. He is a professor emeritus at Sogang University and a chair professor at Dankook University in Seoul, and he has been a member of the Community of Taizé in France since 1969.